W9-BWR-048

Abou and the Angel Cohen

Abou and the Angel Cohen

a novel

CLAUDE CAMPBELL

BRIDGE WORKS PUBLISHING COMPANY

Bridgehampton, New York

Copyright © 2002 by Claude Campbell

All rights reserved under International and Pan-American Copyright Conventions. No part of this book may be reproduced in any form or by any electronic or mechanical means, including information storage and retrieval systems, without written permission from the publisher, except by a reviewer who may quote brief passages in a review.

Published by Bridge Works Publishing Company, Bridgehampton, New York, a member of the Rowman & Littlefield Publishing Group.

Distributed in the United States by National Book Network, Lanham, Maryland. For descriptions of this and other Bridge Works books, visit the National Book Network website at www.nbnbooks.com.

First Edition

The characters and events in this book are fictitious. Any similarity to actual persons, living or dead, is coincidental and not intended by the author.

Library of Congress Cataloging-in-Publication Data

Campbell, Claude, 1929–
    Abou and the angel Cohen : a novel / Claude Campbell.—1st ed.
    p. cm.
    ISBN 1-882593-51-0 (alk. paper)
    1. Conduct of life—Fiction. 2. Middle East—Fiction. 3. Angels—Fiction. I. Title.

PS3603.A47 A64   2002
813'.54—dc21   2001037995

10 9 8 7 6 5 4 3 2 1

∞ ™ The paper used in this publication meets the minimum requirements of American National Standard for Information Sciences—Permanence of Paper for Printed Library Materials, ANSI/NISO Z39.48–1992.
Manufactured in the United States of America.

To

Audrey

Abou Ben Adhem

Abou Ben Adhem (may his tribe increase!)
Awoke one night from a deep dream of peace,
And saw, within the moonlight in his room,
Making it rich, and like a lily in bloom,
An Angel writing in a book of gold:

Exceeding peace had made Ben Adhem bold,
And to the Presence in the room he said,
"What writest thou?" The Vision raised its head,
And with a look made of all sweet accord
Answered, "The names of those who love the Lord."

"And is mine one?" said Abou. "Nay, not so,"
Replied the Angel. Abou spoke more low,
But cheerly still; and said, "I pray thee, then,
Write me as one that loves his fellow-man."

The Angel wrote, and vanished. The next night
It came again with a great wakening light,
And showed the names whom love of God had blessed,
And, lo! Ben Adhem's name led all the rest.

—Leigh Hunt

Abou and the Angel Cohen

The First Darkfall

ALTHOUGH ABOU BEN ADHEM dreamed often, only once, more than twenty years before, had an angel appeared—an astounding vision named Yousef, who wore the most beautiful white, flowing gown and glimmering, golden feathers.

The apparition who appeared to Abou on the seventh day of *Shawwal,* in the Christian year 2001, was rather short, in an ill-fitting white linen suit that had seen better days and was in desperate need of cleaning. His head was enormous with wild, black hair and he had a somber, leathery face. To top it off, his nails were bitten to the quick. But even in the dim light, Abou could see that this angel's eyes were bright and alert. He introduced himself:

"My name is Cohen."

Abou was horrified. "I don't want a Jewish angel," he complained, really a bit awed by the presence, but adamant. Abou knew his own name was rather odd, almost Jewish sounding, but he was Muslim through and through. His father thought it would be a nice touch to name his son in recognition of the debt the Muslim faith owed to the Old Testament.

"Where is Yousef?" Abou asked.

Carefully picking his teeth as if he'd recently left a wonderful dinner, the angel named Cohen studied Abou from across the room.

The whole experience was so real that Abou found himself wondering if his tent had been invaded by some malcontent from the neighborhood. But no, that wasn't possible, for surely the miscreant wouldn't refer to himself as Cohen in that part of the world, even in jest. But this specter was like no other Abou had ever seen or read about, and he was an avid reader, so he knew what angels were supposed to look like. Angels were supposed to look like Yousef. Now that was an angel— manicured nails, nice wings that fluffed up in a breeze, and a melodious voice that Abou could still hear. Yousef had been a real angel, not like this one, and certainly not a Bouguereau, those ghastly, plump depictions that Abou had seen in many American stationery stores during his stay in that country.

Finally the scruffy apparition stopped picking his teeth and shrugged. "Old Yousef is taking some R and R. He's really had it. He's worn out keeping his gowns clean, as well as his underwear. We told him time and again that he doesn't have to worry about dirty underwear, being an angel and all, because he wasn't going to be in an accident, but you know what a worrywart he is. Scrub. Scrub. Scrub. And those wings! I mean, he must have spent three hours a day grooming them. No wonder he's burnt out."

Abou took umbrage at this. Sitting up, he adjusted his *aba*. He was quite tall and thin, a testimony to more than seventy years of abstinence from alcohol and tobacco, as well as to hard work. Secretly he was rather proud of his appearance, even though his nicely trimmed beard had turned quite gray. "I don't wish to offend you," Abou replied, "but I would really be more comfortable with someone of my own faith."

"Sorry." Cohen shook his head. "No can do. No more denominational or ethnic matches. We have strict rotation now. And that's from on high." He looked up and Abou followed his eyes to the smoke hole in the tent, but there was nothing there but the night sky. "Besides, all humans are really pretty much the same, you know. All this nonsense about race, religion, and whatever else you can think of to set you apart is really foolishness. I mean, your name means Abou, the son of Adam. Probably would have been better to have named you Abou Ben Eve, but who knew humans were basically female? Anyway, you think of yourself as a Muslim, but you have a Hebrew name, and all Hebrews and Muslims are the sons and daughters of Eve, who mated with Adam, so you all should be buddies. All Muslims, Jews, and Christians should be really close, or, at least, that's the way we see it. Besides, the next angel on the roster is Diem Ng, so that wouldn't satisfy you either."

Abou simply didn't know what to say.

Cohen grinned a thin, humorless smile. "Let me be frank, Abou. We could afford mix and match for a while. I mean, we knew it made you humans more comfortable to think you had an angel of your religious preference, so we went along with that little charade, but face the facts, old bean, you humans create new religions every day. I mean, it's mind-boggling. We would need an angel for every splinter group. That's just far beyond our budget. So we went to rotation."

"You have a budget?" Abou questioned.

"Everything in the universe is on a budget. Can you imagine the cost overruns if we just did everything we felt like?"

3

"You seem to be a nice enough fellow, but I don't think this will work out." Abou spoke slowly, choosing his words so as not to offend. "I don't see how you can help me."

Cohen stared at him, his face impassive.

Abou became a bit annoyed. "It is more likely you would help those with their eternal building of apartment houses and the desecrations of our holy sites."

"You mean the tunnel?"

"Yes, the tunnel, among other things!"

Cohen nodded. "I got to admit it was a dumb move, but you need a little understanding. First of all, this Ariel—wasn't it nice they elected a prime minister named after one of us?—and his bunch have this cinder block and mortar compulsion, and secondly, they dote on tourists. Tourists mean money. Big bucks. I don't think they gave one thought to the sanctity of the tunnel. As for their building of endless apartments, it's an ethnic thing, I think. Build. Build. Build. They had this guy Robert Moses in New York who poured concrete on everything. And remember, Abou, your people aren't helping matters with your bombs blowing up innocents all over Israel."

Abou looked down at his hands. He too dearly wished the violence would end, but he also ardently wished the Israelis would leave his homeland. Still, he was forced to admit, "It is not good to see children killed."

Cohen smiled and pulled a small pad from his shirt pocket. "You wanted an update."

"Ah . . ." Abou sighed, pleased that his wish had been heard. Alone in his tent, away from the ritual of public devotion, he had asked in prayer if he were still held in high esteem for his love of his fellow man, except, that is, for the Jews who annoyed him no end with their land-grabbing, pushy ways. "Would you care for some Japanese tea? The urn is still warm."

"Thank you," Cohen replied. "That would really hit the spot." Abou took a small cup and filled it, and then he filled one for himself. They both sipped the sweet, rich tea with pleasure.

"You wished to know if you still top the list of those who love their fellow man," Cohen said, after he had set his cup aside and raised his hand when Abou motioned to refill it. "I am afraid, Abou Ben Adhem, you no longer head the list."

"How can that be!" Abou scratched his head. "I am pious. I have multiplied. I am kind to those less fortunate. I give alms. I pray religiously. In my business dealings I never . . ." he hesitated. "Well, almost never cheated. Early on, when I tended my father's goats, they were always healthy and well treated. What else could I have done?"

"I don't think you understand," Cohen replied. "It isn't a matter so much of past deeds. It's about staying current. Doing good deeds here and now. And, well, you are getting on in years, you know. You're just not keeping up." The affront was painful. Cohen added hastily, "It isn't your fault. It is just the way things are, and we're aware that living with your son-in-law is difficult. Perhaps you've been preoccupied."

"Who is first now?" Abou asked, his voice quavering.

Cohen quickly flipped the pages of his notebook. "Jimmy Carter."

"The American?"

"Yep, Jimmy's *numero uno*."

Abou pulled his shawl around him. It was almost as if he were shrinking before the angel's eyes.

"Look, it wasn't a lifetime award. Mortal life is transition. You pass things on to the next generation." When Abou avoided his eyes, Cohen added, "Hey, the competition has become really stiff over the years. Gandhi, Mother Teresa, Bill Clinton. You know what's going on in the world."

A crafty expression crossed Abou's face. "I don't even know you are really an angel. You have no wings."

"Corrective surgery," Cohen replied easily. "Wings make tailoring a suit very difficult."

"And what was the name of my mother's grandfather?"

"Abu Zent," Cohen replied with a sigh. "Look, I'm really sorry you lost your place, but it happens. You just have to look at the big picture."

Abou drew himself up, sitting erect, a bit piqued. "I am not an educated man, Mr. Cohen. I read my own language and also some English. Now that I no longer trade in goats or drive taxicabs, I spend my day reading books and magazines that my daughter and son-in-law are good enough to supply from his small business, which is, unfortunately, not doing too well, so they have many back issues that haven't sold. Is it not enough that you inform me that I am no longer in favor, but you must belittle me, too?"

Cohen spread his hands. "It wasn't a put-down, Abou. What I meant was the really big picture. How you got here. How the world began. That sort of stuff."

Abou's interest was ensnared. "Like my grandfather, his father, so on?"

"Well," Cohen replied cautiously, "I just had the passing thought that you didn't clearly understand how these awards were made. You people are evolving. I mean, in his own day Genghis Khan wasn't such a bad sort, but today people think of him as some sort of monster." He looked at Abou carefully. "I was thinking more in the line of giving you an overview, like years before there were people living around here or, for that matter, before there were people at all."

"How many years are you talking about?" Abou asked, wondering if this angel was really all there.

Cohen pursed his lips and looked up at the smoke hole. "Oh, maybe 19, 20 million years. Of course, if you're thinking about more humanlike creatures, then we're talking only 6, maybe 7 million."

Abou laughed aloud. "Are you serious? The world couldn't be that old."

"Sorry about that, old fellow," Cohen replied casually, "but it is far older than that."

"Are you quite sure?" Abou asked in a small voice. He really had difficulty believing this fellow, but he somehow couldn't bring himself to dismiss him as completely mad.

Cohen smiled openly for the first time. He had absolutely beautiful teeth and his smile lighted his face as if a spotlight had suddenly settled on it. All of a sudden the somber look was gone. "Sure? Oh, yeah. We're omnipresent and omniscient, you know, which means we're spread a little thin, but we've seen the whole megillah from the beginning."

"The whole megillah . . ." Abou repeated. He had lately taken to repeating the last three or four words someone said to him, as if he had trouble assimilating everything and wanted to make sure he had heard it correctly. Actually his hearing was beginning to go, but he wasn't ready to admit that to himself.

Very slowly, as if picking through a plate of dates, Abou chose his words. "Just what were we like 20 million years ago?"

Cohen settled himself on Abou's clothing chest, pulling a small rug over his lap to lessen the chill of the night air. He was obviously pleased with Abou's question. "How do you think you got here?"

"We were made in the image of our Maker," Abou replied with certainty. Allah's image was never portrayed in the Moslem world, but Abou believed this privately.

"I see," Cohen replied, thinking a bit. "Look, if I explain what I know, will your feelings be hurt? I mean, I don't want to step on your toes or anything."

Abou pursed his lips, trying to divine exactly what Cohen was saying. "I don't fear truth," he said. He had read that somewhere and it had struck him as very apt.

Cohen spread his hands. "Look at it this way. The Americans have an expression, 'Shit happens', which may easily be the most profound thought mankind ever had. And angels do not interfere in human development. We advise. Sometimes we cajole. You might say we're guidance counselors." Cohen giggled at this, but immediately forced himself to be serious. "But we never interfere in the sense of curtailing your choices. If you really want to do something, we keep hands off. Before intelligent life developed, there was no problem. We just watched with fascination. We would sit around and try to figure how things might work out, and we were often wrong. I really lost a pile on that mammal vs. reptile thing."

"You gambled on our development?" Abou couldn't believe he was hearing correctly.

"Well, yeah, we did. I mean, this was a real boring period before you kids got up and running."

"I thought you said you were omniscient and omnipresent," Abou responded, really doubting that Cohen was an angel. He was again beginning to think his tent had been invaded, not by a miscreant, but by a full-blown maniac.

"Only the past, and we don't know what you humans think."

"Then you don't know our future?"

"Why would we bet if we knew your future?" Cohen asked, perplexed.

"And you don't know what we think?"

Cohen grinned. "Absolutely clueless. Thinking came pretty late in your development and we weren't empowered. We operate with the powers we were given. We aren't retrofitted when you develop new skills. Makes it kind of difficult at times. You really need state-of-the-art angels, but hey, you take what you can get. Right?"

Abou shook his head, not believing what he was hearing. "Then events just happen?"

"As far as we can tell," Cohen admitted.

"No order? No higher power?" Abou questioned.

"None we can see," Cohen agreed. "Of course, you humans have attempted to impose order in your world, but it hasn't been very successful. We just watch the process and try to help out any way we can."

Abou found he had mixed feelings about this. The heresy was very hard to stomach, but the apparition's casual explanation was intriguing. "But years ago, wasn't it Allah who favored me above all others?"

Cohen flushed. "Look, don't take this the wrong way, but we angels got together and voted you into that position. I mean Yousef was really upset that you were being passed over."

"And President Carter?"

"Yeah, we voted him in this year," Cohen admitted.

"And Allah had no say in all this?" Abou asked in a whisper.

"I wouldn't go that far," Cohen protested, but he didn't deny the suggestion either.

Abou was stunned. "Why would you do such a thing? All these years I thought I was His chosen."

Cohen sighed. "Look, I can't tell you how tiresome it was ministering to dinosaurs with their endless chomp, chomp, chomp. Nothing really developed that was interesting, so we kind of liked giving you kids a leg up when we could. Of course, Gabe cautioned us rather severely that the point of human development wasn't just for our amusement."

"Gabe?"

"Gabriel. The big enchilada."

Abou paled at the comment and Cohen suddenly looked concerned.

"Look, you need some sleep," Cohen said.

"I am asleep," Abou reminded him.

"Point taken," Cohen replied crisply. "So you want to know how you really got started?"

Abou nodded and Cohen leaned back. "You ever see popcorn popping in a hot pan? That's what creation was like. Stars bursting all over the place. Galaxies formed. Really a great show. This galaxy," he said, pointing at the floor, "was formed rather late. The Americans named a candy bar after it. Milky Way. Very toothsome. Ever had one?"

"No, I don't believe so. I drove a taxicab in New York when I was younger, but I don't think I ever had a Milky Way."

"Anyway," Cohen went on, "once most of the popping stopped, all this junk began pulling together and life started here on earth. First, little creatures began wiggling in the ooze, then reptiles and mammals. Did I mention how much I lost on that reptilian sting?"

"You said you lost a lot," Abou reminded him.

"Taken to the cleaners," Cohen admitted. "I'm still paying it off. I could get a new suit if I could just get ahead on my payments."

Abou looked at the seedy suit with some sympathy. "Have you no other clothes?"

"I have a go-to-meeting suit, but it isn't much better than this one," Cohen admitted.

"Perhaps," Abou suggested, gesturing toward his clothing chest, "I have an extra *aba* . . ."

"That's damn decent of you, Abou," Cohen gushed. "Nobody has ever offered me a change of clothes before. It wouldn't stand up to the traveling I do, but thanks anyway."

Abou acknowledged this with a nod of his head. "Once life began?" he prompted. For some inexplicable reason, Abou wanted to hear what Cohen had to say. He was certain he was wrong, but still, he said he was an angel. . . .

"Oh, sure. Creatures popped up all over the place, but most of them couldn't hack it and died out, and you did have those slammers."

"Slammers?" Abou asked.

"Yeah, when asteroids hit head on. Two really big ones. Let's see . . . 65 million years ago and the other one was over 300 million. That last one knocked the dinosaurs on their asses." Cohen shook his head sadly. "Big loss."

"Wiped out all life?"

"No, I'm talking about the money I dropped," Cohen replied, drew a deep breath, and continued. "Put your money on cockroaches, Abou. They're indestructible."

"But humans?"

"Oh, yeah, well your forebears prospered after the lizards stopped eating them. First they stopped using their front paws for walking, although they knuckle-walked for eons, but they finally learned to sit and eat a banana with dignity, peeling it and everything. Then they came down from the trees out on the savannah and a really great thing happened. Humans learned to stand on their hind legs."

"My mother used to tell me to stand on my *hind* legs," Abou mused, easing his aching back.

"Cohen nodded. "A very, very old expression. Very old. Of course, it didn't help the lower back problem, but I don't have to tell you that, do I?"

"My back? What has my back to do with your story?"

Cohen shrugged. "I'm no doctor, but humans weren't meant to be on two legs. I mean, who ever heard of an animal complaining about an aching back?"

"I've never heard an animal complain about anything," Abou observed dryly, then added, "Well, donkeys, maybe."

"Very good," Cohen said with a smile, "but you look pooped. I'd better shove off."

"Aren't you sleepy?" Abou asked.

"We don't sleep," Cohen replied. "We mostly work the swing shift."

"You don't work at all during the day?"

Cohen shook his head. "Almost never. Well, there was that famous visit Gabriel made to Mary. That was day work."

Abou remembered vaguely, but he couldn't think about it just then. He was too tired.

"Thanks for offering your robe. That was really nice," Cohen said and disappeared.

The Second Day

When Abou awoke, he was very excited. He wanted to tell Sophia, his daughter, of the visitation, although he thought it might be better to leave out Cohen's name. His visitation from Yousef many years before had been received with some skepticism, especially by the clerics. He washed quickly in the pail outside his tent, relieved himself, and, gathering his robes, rushed to the house to tell his news.

Abou's usual custom was to arise and perform his morning prayer outside his tent, and when this was done, he would wash himself with great energy, coughing and sneezing, clearing his head of the night's accumulation, and then he would walk, in a stately fashion, to the house, where he waited outside the privy until it was free. His grandson, Akbar, had to be in school and Yasser, his daughter's husband, was rather short-tempered when he was forced to wait, so Abou deferred to Yasser's younger, albeit intemperate, bowels. Today, in his excitement, this was forgotten, so he was underneath the kitchen window, hurrying to the door, when he heard Yasser's voice.

"The tent is an eyesore and it shames our family."

"It is harmless, and when he first suggested it, you thought it a good idea. He would be no longer underfoot in the house," Sophia replied.

"That is true," Abou's son-in-law replied, "but that was before I knew they were laughing at us in the medina. Everyone thinks it's absurd that this old goat herder is living in a tent in our orchard. I think it is time we find him a pension."

"His heart will be broken, husband," Sophia whined.

"They are also laughing at Akbar's school," Yasser replied, knowing how she cherished her child's position in school.

Abou heard no response. Dejected, he turned away and returned to his tent, looking at his belongings, wondering what would become of him. He had known for a long time that his son-in-law held him in the contempt the young sometimes feel for the elderly, but Yasser was usually civil and did provide ample reading material from his small store, old newspapers and outdated magazines that couldn't be returned for whatever reason. For this Abou was grateful. The old man dearly loved to read and learn, as did his daughter, who also read many of the periodicals, although women reading, for leisure at least, was generally frowned upon. Now, Abou heard he was going to be cast out. He sighed, returned to his tent, and curled up on his rug.

At ten, Sophia came down with a tea urn and some sweet cakes. "Father, you aren't feeling well?"

"I slept badly, daughter," he replied, sitting up. "I had a dream of an angel."

"Again?" She had heard about Yousef's first visit when she was a little girl.

"It was a different angel," he replied. He thought she would be off on her daily duties of shopping, cooking, and cleaning the house, but instead she sat next to him and looked into his face.

"Are you happy here in this tent, Father? It seems so old-fashioned."

Abou answered, "The house is too crowded. Akbar needs a place to study at night and Yasser should have peace when he comes home. And, as a boy and young man, I spent many wonderful hours in my father's tent as we tended the goats. This suits me just fine."

Sophia was an uncommonly pretty woman. Abou had insisted on naming her after the remarkable edifice in Istanbul that he had visited as a young man. When he had entered the mosque and removed his sandals, he had simply stopped and looked up at the dome—a kilometer high, he thought—as others, accustomed to the sight, tried to get around him to begin their worship. There were other wonders in the city, the ancient Roman aqueducts, still standing after almost two thousand years, and the great market, unbelievable with beautiful rugs, pottery, great mounds of food, and clothing galore, but it was the Hagia Sophia that remained strongest in his mind. It had seemed only fitting to name the small infant, who was born just after his return from America, for one of the many marvels he had seen throughout the world, and there was no question in his mind about which one. His wife had objected at first, of course, but that was her way.

Sophia touched his arm, something she seldom did. "Yasser thinks you would be happier in a small pension."

Abou looked at her brown eyes, so soft, so warm, the soul of womanhood.

She rushed on, unnerved by his silence. "My husband thinks you should find a place where there are men of your age who will keep you company."

"There are few men of my age left," Abou reminded her. "They have all died, along with your mother, who was my best friend, leaving only me." He was feeling very sorry for himself.

"You visit in the market with your friends."

"They are children compared to me," Abou replied. "The newest one is sixty. That surprised me when I learned his age the other day. Only sixty, and he no longer works, but Absollah and Ammon are still very much employed."

She made one last attempt. "We could find you a place near here and you could visit us each day and see the children."

Abou didn't reply. There really was nothing *to* say. He was a burden, unproductive, was raising no children for Allah, and had little or nothing to offer. When he was a boy, the elders recounted stories, the history of the people, and some could even read. Now, many people read books and this usefulness of storytellers was over. He nodded at his daughter in understanding.

Her eyes moistened and she turned her face away, rose, and hurriedly left the tent. Abou stared at her retreating figure. When you are young, he thought, you have some control over your life. Not much, but some. When you are older, you are the pawns of the young. At the same time, Abou felt sorry for his daughter, for he was sure she didn't want to do what Yasser had asked. *His* parents had the good grace to die early and spare him the terrible responsibility of disposing of them while they still lived. Abou sincerely hoped he would have been kinder than Yasser had he faced the same situation.

He dressed carefully, determined to visit his friends in the marketplace, join them in coffee and American cigarettes. He wanted most to tell them of his dream, but he also wanted to say that he might soon be moving away, too far to visit. In spite of what Sophia had said about living nearby,

Abou felt that Yasser wanted him far away. His friends should remember him with kindness.

Abou met Hamid coming out of the post office, his hands filled with literature from various groups and companies. Hamid loved mail, so he wrote to everyone he read about, and when the idea of mailing lists caught hold in the Middle East, as it had a few years earlier, he was suddenly inundated with mail from all over the world, even Japan. With glee, he would take his daily cache, stuffed in his burnoose, and make his way to the Camel's Hump, a tawdry coffeehouse on the edge of the market, unremarkable in every way, except for its prices, which were uncommonly low, and the coffee, which Abou felt was the best south of Damascus.

Once there, Hamid would sort his mail and examine the envelopes carefully, saving the openings until the group had gathered. Hamid received a small pension from a Cairo firm where he had been in charge of the receipt and distribution of mail. From what he said, the job wasn't very demanding, but he had been dedicated, never missing a day in thirty years, so when a Saudi conglomerate purchased the firm, his employer pensioned Hamid off. He had wandered north to Gaza, and finally to Abou's village, a small hamlet in west Gaza named Helar, where he settled in. He lived a frugal life in a small room at the edge of the town.

Abou walked with Hamid, telling him of his dream, but Hamid couldn't concentrate on his friend's words, so excited was he over the huge delivery he had just received. Seated in the Camel's Hump, Abou smoked his one Marlboro for the day and drank thick coffee as Hamid cooed and caressed each envelope. Abou knew better than to interrupt, for when you live alone, as did Hamid, small things become terribly important, and mail had become the most important event in

Hamid's life. Instead, Abou examined his rangy friend's gaunt face and great black eyes.

Hamid saved three of his letters to be opened later. He read with difficulty, so it took him a long time to digest a letter, and since he read only his own language, those in other languages were set aside for translation by his more literate friends. Abou, who spoke and read English quite well, and Ammon, the barber, who could read some French as well as Farsi, a gift handed down from a grandparent, often complied. Absollah, the banker, read Spanish and German, but only words that related to banking, which severely limited his usefulness to Hamid.

"It is good to be in communication with the world," Hamid observed.

"It makes one feel alive," Abou agreed, knowing he was not being honest with his friend. Letters for him seemed to bear only ill tidings. He dreaded them. But, because of Hamid's pleasure in his mail, he had never said how he really felt.

"You said something about a dream?" Hamid asked, stroking the open letters on the table.

Abou told him of Cohen, although he omitted his name. When he concluded, his friend looked at him critically.

"Have you been enjoying too much of the poppy, old friend?"

Abou was indignant. "I dreamt it! The description of the beginning of the world was most convincing."

Hamid ran his hand over his letter, enjoying the texture. "You have no control over your dreams, Abou, but dreams like that should be put out of your mind. If our mullah were to hear you, things would become very difficult for you. Even now, if someone were to overhear, we would both have to answer for this heresy."

Abou realized suddenly his friend wanted to hear no more of his dream, of Cohen's theory of evolution, that it frightened Hamid, and that it might end their friendship if he persisted. "Well, it was only a stupid dream unworthy of discussion." "That is true," Hamid replied with a grateful smile. "Let us examine my mail. It will afford us both pleasure." And that's what they did until Ammon, the barber, joined them. Then they discussed politics and the latest Israeli atrocities. Actually the conversation lacked verve, as the Israelis had done little that was really monstrous in the past days, but reviewing their past sins back to 1948 was always enjoyable, although Abou almost ruined the discussion with the passing observation that it was a shame that Jewish children were being killed by their gallant fighters.

"Unfortunate, yes, but these things happen," Hamid observed as he gleefully folded his letters and put them away. "Israel's children only grow up to be warriors who hate us and will destroy us." His was a rote response dictated by those around him. Actually, Hamid cared nothing for politics or the Jews. When alone with Abou, away from the crowds and close tables, he often said how much he yearned for peace.

Ammon was a different matter, with definite ideas about the problems facing the Palestinians and what should be done about them. He was particularly adamant about the Americans, who seemed to support the Israelis in everything. "Without oil, the Americans just don't listen to you," he complained, apparently unaware that Israel had no oil. "And without the Americans, the Israelis would be much more reasonable."

Abou nodded sadly, aware that what Ammon said was partially true, but still he thought there should be a better way to settle these disputes than bombing innocents. He looked at his barber friend with his barrel chest and honest eyes. "I had hopes for Oslo," he murmured and Ammon nodded agreement.

"We all did. It looked like it might be settled after all these years, but the Likud wouldn't have it." Ammon sipped his coffee. "These are a stubborn, hateful people who really don't want peace."

Abou couldn't dispute this, but somehow he felt Ammon was more zealous than most in his hatred of the Jews.

The conversation drifted to other topics, and finally Hamid asked, "Is Absollah not joining us today?"

"He must be busy at the bank," Ammon replied with a laugh. "It is difficult to get away when you are making as much money as our friend."

"He works very hard," Hamid said defensively.

"I agree," Ammon replied. "Very, very hard."

After Ammon had left for his barbershop, Abou spent several hours with Hamid going over two English documents, one about the care of poultry, and the other a mailing from America about the opening of a branch of some obscure brokerage firm in Beirut.

"Things must be calm there now," Hamid observed as he handled the letter lovingly. "I have read they are rebuilding the city."

"I hope so," Abou replied and rose. "I must be off."

"You are lucky to have Sophia to cook for you, Abou. It is a blessing to have children who care for you."

SUPPER THAT EVENING was strained, although the couscous was superb and the lamb tender to the tooth. Yasser kept glancing at Sophia, and little Akbar, not yet seven years old, sensed something was wrong and managed to upset everybody by spilling tea across the whole table. Fortunately, the baby only sat and gurgled. Abou tried not to pay any attention, eating slowly, for his teeth were old and good only for delicate use. Abou delighted in the delicious tastes of food and dreaded the day he wouldn't be able to eat some of his favorites.

"Did my wife speak to you today, *abooya*?" Yasser asked, after the meal was finished. To bring up anything so unpleasant during the meal would be unheard of in polite society.

Abou hated to hear his son-in-law's use of the familiar word for "my father". "Yes, we spoke before I went to meet my friends at the market."

"And you understand what an embarrassment your tent has become?"

"No, I don't understand."

Yasser glared at him. He was swarthy, with unkempt hair, intense black eyes, and ugly, bulbous lips. Abou often wondered what Sophia saw in him, but he had long since decided that the attraction between people was unanswerable. When Abou had been approached by Yasser's relatives, Sophia was open to the match.

"People wonder why you live in a tent in my orchard. Are we too churlish to allow you in the house?" Yasser explained. "And if the house is too small, can we not afford to add a room? Well, we know the answers to these questions, don't we, *aboo el madam*?" Abou noted it was now "father of the wife", not "my father". Yasser continued, "I am not a rich man. I cannot add a room. What can we do?"

Abou considered his answer. "My happiest days were when I tended goats, *ibnee.*" Abou threw in "my son" just for spite. "I loved living in my tent. I was never really happy in the cities, in foreign lands, in strange places. The solitude pleases me. Would not our friends understand that? Being an old man, I find solace in the night sky and the silence of the orchard.

I am very happy there." Abou knew he wasn't being entirely candid. He did love the tent, especially as he grew older and he thought more often of his youth, but he had been enthralled by the bustle and life in Istanbul and although he had never admitted it to anyone since his return, he had found New York exhilarating with its splendor and variety, although there were certainly some frightening aspects.

"All very good," Yasser replied, smoking his pipe furiously. "But we are being criticized. A person of my standing cannot afford to be laughed at."

"Please, my husband . . . ," Sophia began, but Yasser cut her off with, "Silence woman, men are speaking!" She fell silent, her eyes downcast, as she had been taught.

Abou looked at his daughter in despair. Her pain was his. Hastily he responded, "I do not wish to cause a problem. You are like a son to me, and you are the father of my beloved grandchildren. I would do nothing to cause dissension in your household," he finished and with these words sealed his fate.

Yasser beamed. "You are an understanding man!"

Abou left the house shortly after supper and crossed the darkened yard to the orchard. Generally optimistic, he was dejected by his son-in-law's request that he strike his tent and move to some ghetto for the ancients. He liked the coolness of his tent, the solitude, the freedom to come and go as he chose, the dignity of his isolation. Now he would be penned in by walls and noise, ever fearful of offending his neighbors.

He sat in his tent, unable to sleep. His daughter had thoughtfully provided him with hot tea as he left the house. He was sure she was distraught about this turn, but what could she do? Yasser's father was dead, killed in a bombing by the Israelis that Yasser lamented constantly, often shaking his fist at the blue sky. Yasser adopted a suitably doleful expression when

Sophia's dead mother was mentioned, but apparently he found breathing parents a distasteful encumbrance, for he seldom spoke or visited his own mother, who lived on the other side of the village.

Abou tossed and turned, thinking of his plight, unable to sleep. He even prayed on his knees, but he didn't know what to pray for, because he somehow understood that Yasser had right on his side, that he *was* a bother, all old people were, and they prevented the young from forging ahead with their lives. He had heard that the Chinese revered their elderly, but then he read of their cultural revolution, which seemed to sweep young and old alike into oblivion. And there was talk of the elderly Eskimos who just went out and sat on an ice floe in the evening when they felt they were no longer contributing members of society. Certainly Abou was forced to admit he no longer worked and he no longer fathered children, so there was no reason for his existence, if that was all existence was about.

The Second Darkfall

WHEN ABOU FINALLY FELL ASLEEP, Cohen was there, sitting on his clothing chest, cleaning his nails with a small pocketknife. If anything, the angel appeared scruffier than the previous night, his tie askew and his coat buttoned in the wrong hole.

"Thank goodness! You've certainly kept me waiting a long time."

"I'm sorry," Abou responded, rubbing his eyes. He felt as if he'd hardly slept at all. "I didn't know you were waiting for me."

Cohen shrugged and put away his pocketknife. "Apologies accepted. You've had a difficult day."

"You heard?"

Cohen nodded. "And saw. It's most disheartening. You really have worked very hard being a good person, Abou. That is not to say you couldn't have been better, but considering everything, you've been okay."

"Okay," Abou repeated, mouthing the word to himself. "When one looks back on his life, it's just *okay?*"

"You'd be surprised how many lives aren't okay. I would say 80 to 90 percent never meet that standard. Okay is very good."

"Is there anything better? I had always thought of myself as a good man who did what was expected of me as long as I could."

"Meaning?"

Abou shrugged. "Old men have little value, and a man as old as I—more than three score and ten—has no value at all. As young men we have children, we work and do things, but when we get old, we are purposeless."

"Utter nonsense," Cohen replied. "If age were the criterion, then I'm sure you could hold up your part. You're still virile, aren't you?"

Abou flushed and nodded modestly.

"Yes, you could have more children. And you can be certain there is some foolhardy female out there who would bear them for you, so you see, you still have a wonderful reason for living, at least by your standards."

"You make it sound so foolish."

"Well, it is, in a way. I mean, all species are here to multiply. But to make having children a basis for human evaluation is like saying that what he eats is how we judge a person's worth. Foolishness. I don't understand why humans put so much store in having children. Granted it's a biological imperative, but give me a break. Your earth is already filled with people eating every blade of grass in sight and every animal except insects, which will probably be next. It's procreation that needs curbing, not cultivating." Cohen hesitated and then added in a low voice, "Of course, we dearly love every last one of you."

"Was I considered okay because I had only one child?"

"No, no, no," Cohen answered. "Perhaps we should consider sexual prudence in our guidelines, but no, you are okay because you hurt almost nobody, you helped many, and you were generally kind and civil to people."

"But you think I could have done better?"

Cohen sighed and shifted himself for a better position on the clothes chest. "That's a judgment call, Abou. We don't make judgment calls. You did well. Perhaps you could have done better. Who knows? All we do is tally points and come up with the best each year."

"Some do better?" Abou found himself annoyed, again.

"Well, yes. Some do a really decent job. St. Augustine was working at it. He had a rocky start, but he did well toward the end. Do you know of Augustine's teaching?"

"No, I'm afraid I don't."

"Shame. Bright fellow. Wasted a lot of his time on theology, but he really tried to understand the world around him, and that means a great deal. Trying to understand and living right. That makes for a decent person. How about Darwin? Know him?"

"Evolution?" Abou asked, tentatively. "I read an article about him years ago. I . . ."

"Right!" Cohen interrupted. "It really delights us when one of you humans sees something and understands it. It isn't easy for you, but it's quite a thrill when you do it. Of course, it can wreak havoc in a person's life. That's what happened to Darwin. Really a decent sort. Scared to death by his own insights. Shame. Left him anxious all the time and constipated."

"And the Jew Einstein? Was he a decent person?" Secretly Abou had always admired Einstein, although he never spoke of his thoughts in public.

"Oh, now you're talking, little buddy, although you like to get your digs in, don't you? Well, he was close. Boy, was he close. Got hung up on order and chaos, but he was this close."

Cohen held up his fingers and showed a small gap between his index finger and thumb. "He really tried. Not always the best person personally, but generally a good sort."

"I am sorry." Abou was contrite. "You are right. His religion should mean nothing. He made a wonderful contribution, although I don't really understand it."

"Take my word for it," Cohen replied. "He was good. Very, very good. If he could have kept his view of his god out of it, he would have been absolutely remarkable. Remarkable!"

"His god?" Abou said, really annoyed by the angel's words. "His is not the true God?"

Cohen threw up his hands and laughed. "You are a sly one, my friend. How do I answer you with delicacy? Nobody's god is the true one, or, if you prefer, every god is the true one."

Abou was adamant. "Allah is . . ."

"No, Allah isn't," Cohen corrected him. "Allah, as you call the moving force, is not as humans think. First off, he is not a *he*, or a *she* as some seem to think. I mean the idea is preposterous. The ancient Greeks used to think their Zeus would drop down and knock up this gal or that, but as far as we have seen, the force is everything, knows everything, and is responsible for everything, but certainly has no interest in sex, other than as a means of procreation, of moving things along, so to speak. And this force certainly doesn't favor one group over another, be it Muslim, Christian, Hindu, or whatever. We've seen nothing like that over the past ten thousand years, since your religions got a little organization."

Abou was profoundly offended. Not only was he depressed by the day's happening, but now he was confronted with a heretic angel who defamed almighty Allah. Abou could hardly contain himself. But he realized there was no way of ridding himself of Cohen immediately, other than waking, and he was simply too tired for that, so he pressed on.

"And what's your role, may I ask?" Abou snapped, with all the hostility he could muster.

Cohen seemed indifferent. "*Moi?* Let me see. I guess you would call us facilitators or, better, guidance counselors. That's what I said last night. We aren't sent here to change anything, but we try to show the way, so to speak, drawing on people's innate goodness and common sense. The big problem is that sex sets up conflicts which make for very peculiar situations which often bring out the worst in people." He thought about this, then added, "It also brings out the best in people at times. Anyway, sometimes we fail. Actually, we fail quite often, but when we can help, it is a wonderful feeling."

"Did you visit Hitler?" Abou asked, interested again. Hitler had baffled Abou. It wasn't just the Jews; it was the man's over-whelming destructiveness that had confused Abou his whole adult life.

"Two of us were assigned to him day and night, but he was beyond help. That happens sometimes. And he wouldn't ac-cept any counseling."

"The devil prevailed," Abou replied.

"Well, now that's another problem," Cohen answered care-fully. "I know this is going to confound you, but there is no devil as such. I mean, if you understood the big picture, you'd see what evil is. Hitler, for instance, was a jerk personally and he did terrible things, but he wasn't evil in the sense that some sort of devil controlled his actions. He was simply a monster, a human aberration who gained power and used it dreadfully." When Cohen saw the expression on Abou's face, he nodded and continued, "Let me explain it this way. Generally, humans consider death evil, but of course it isn't. It isn't evil when an elderly person dies, but humans think it is an iniquity when someone is murdered. But that murder is the act of a person, not a devil or any such spirit."

"I will think about what you have said," Abou replied. He was still upset about Cohen's dismissal of Allah, but in spite of this, he found talking to the angel illuminating. Many of Cohen's thoughts were new.

"Your bewilderment will lessen if we continue our talk about early man," Cohen said in a conciliatory tone. "I must admit my colleagues are fascinated with this chat you and I are having. We all got together and talked about you today. It occurred to us that perhaps our approach might have been wrong all these years. I mean, we appear in a vision and people stagger off in awe, making up all sorts of silly things, when our whole purpose is to get people back on track. What occurred to us this morning was that if we were more candid, spelling out the universal picture to individuals, it might be a better way to help mankind with some direction. Of course, this could be damaging, so we want to assess the impact. However, my associates endorsed these discussions with you a hundred percent. We may be onto a good thing here, Abou."

Abou nodded, scratching his head. "You seem to think walking on two legs a remarkable first step. Do you think chatting with me is as important?"

"That's a good one!" Cohen exclaimed, clapping his thighs in delight.

Abou smiled thinly, and Cohen sobered, spreading his arms in a grand gesture. "Chatting you up could be very important. We don't know yet. But walking, we know about. The first step was undoubtedly the greatest step taken by mankind. Man would never have become what he is today without learning to walk on two legs. It was really remarkable!" He hesitated, then continued, somewhat abashed. "I'm a little flip at times. You'll have to excuse me. When I joke about early man's aching back, I am making light of a very important event. Once man's forebears walked on legs, food gathering became easier. Hands developed dexterity! Thumbs! There was one cunning creature who developed hands and fingers for plucking fruit but kept these strange feet, which were splayed like a bird's to give it great stability. Died out after a while, but it was really cute. Called *Oreopithecus bambolii* by your scientists, and by the way, someone should do something about these preposterous scientific names you think up."

"Human!" Abou was genuinely startled to think an early human could have bird feet.

"Oh, no, no," Cohen replied. "Not in your family tree. Just a cute little ape who had strange feet. Your forebears were more like you. Those old fellows could hold things, carry things, and finally make things—stone tools, and then, as they progressed, pots for transporting water, cooking equipment, and all sorts of neat stuff. Weaving is very old. Came from putting together sleeping mats in trees. It was safer sleeping in trees if you didn't have a handy cave to plop in."

"Is that really true?" Abou asked. "Walking upright is what separates us from the chimpanzee?"

Cohen smiled. "Well, not the only thing, but very important. Just think about it. These little fellows that you came from could gather food to feed their kids. When I say just think about it, I mean think about the chimp knuckle-walking home with dinner, one arm loaded with food and the other on the ground. Not very efficient is it? And these early folks had to take care of their young until they could feed themselves, and that made it necessary to increase the food supply over an extended period. And today, look how long it takes to get kids out of your house. Have you noticed that?"

Abou nodded. "I have read that in Europe and America, children spend years wandering in markets looking for goods to buy but still living at home. Is this part of the development you mentioned?"

"In a way it is. Shopping is much the same as hunting. All that mall walking is really training to acquire what you need." Cohen pursed his lips and thought about that. "But not quite the same. I mean, a bear knows when its cub is ready to care for itself. Then the cub is pushed out of the family and expected to hunt for food. For humans, it's a bit more complicated. Nobody seems really sure when the child knows enough. Some are still dependent at thirty; others, their entire lives. Apparently humans have a hard time determining a cutoff date."

Abou nodded sagely. He had often thought about this problem. "A boy child should work when he wishes to lie with a woman. It is time. He must accept responsibility."

Cohen shook his head back and forth like a rug merchant trying to decide how much a customer will pay for his rug. "Oh, I don't know about that. Humans are able to copulate very young. It is one of the bitterest ironies of human existence that humans seem to master living skills later and later but are sexually active earlier and earlier." He hesitated and then added, "Perhaps it isn't so odd after all. Maybe you have to have babies earlier so you have the additional time to raise them, or you'll be dead before the little rascals reach maturity."

Abou scowled. He didn't care for Cohen's breeziness. "Being human is very difficult," Abou added pompously.

"Amen to that," Cohen replied with a giggle.

Abou pulled his robe about him. "I think I need to sleep."

"Oh, come on," Cohen replied, still trying to restrain his merriment. "Don't be a spoilsport. I was telling my associates at the morning briefing about our talk last night and they all wished everyone would ask questions like yours."

Abou studied Cohen. This was certainly an unusual angel, if, in fact, he really was one. Abou still had lingering doubts. "Tell me more about the creation of the universe," he asked, wondering if he could somehow test Cohen's bona fides.

"A wonderful thing to behold," Cohen replied, suddenly serious. "Can you imagine billions of suns being born, giant explosions which seem to stretch forever, and gigantic mountains of clouds with galaxies forming within them. So much life! So much energy! As humans view spectacular sunsets, we, when we have a moment, sit in awe and watch the wonders of the unfolding universe."

"Is it still going on?" Abou asked, momentarily forgetting his pique.

"Oh, yes," Cohen replied, his eyes shut, a beatific expression on his face. "Oh, yes. It has lost some of the initial intensity, but wonderful events are still happening . . . beautiful displays that almost defy description. Galaxies appearing and imploding, monstrous fireworks in proportions unimaginable! I must tell you, Abou, you are lucky to live in such a place and to have self-awareness, however limited."

The comment confused Abou, but he didn't ask for clarification. He thought he would mull over Cohen's words and ask later, if the angel deigned to visit again. Frankly, he decided he didn't much care for Cohen with his flip comments and breezy attitude, but still . . .

"I wish I could see what you see," Abou said.

Cohen opened his eyes and looked at Abou searchingly. "Yes, I wish you could too. It is wondrous to behold."

"Will I ever see it?" Abou asked, almost afraid of the answer.

Cohen looked down and bit his lip. "I'm afraid not, dear fellow. It isn't part of the scheme."

"Not even after my death?"

"I'm sorry."

Abou took a deep breath. "Then it is truly generous that you have shared your knowledge with me."

Cohen smiled broadly. "You are a good person, Abou. I must say, you are really a fine person!"

Abou was flattered. "I would hear more, if you will tell me. It conflicts with much of what I've been taught, but I must admit I am enthralled."

"Yes, well," Cohen replied, pointlessly flicking a spot of dust from his suit. "But let me ask you. Have you any idea how much time I'm talking about here? I mean from the beginning of early humans, or maybe I should call them prehumans."

"Not really," Abou replied. "Great lapses of time, I suspect."

Cohen smiled softly. "I have a bit of trouble with your time-keeping. Each group seems to use a different system. That before and after Christ system the Christians use is particularly difficult, but anyway, the walking upright thing was about 20 million years ago."

"Twenty million! Is that possible? Could it be?"

Cohen shrugged. "Give or take a million. I really wish I had one of those little calculators you humans use. They are so cunning, and I could keep better track of all this if they were issued to us."

Abou raised his hand. "No, no. It doesn't matter. It's such a long time. I had no idea."

"Well, things progressed very slowly in the beginning, you understand," Cohen explained. "There were good and bad times. The little fellows, your forebears, prospered during the abundance, but when there were shortages, they suffered terribly. They really didn't have much going for them. They lacked the tiger's speed, strength, claws, and fangs. Wild boars made hash of them. The only thing in their favor was that they were just a little smarter than other animals, but not by much. You do know that certain species have been extinguished over the years because they couldn't hack it, don't you?"

"Hack? Oh, yes, I remember that expression from New York. I drove a hack, and yes, I've read about some species disappearing from the face of the earth," Abou admitted, then asked, "You're sure these ape creatures were our forebears?"

"Not *ours*, bubba," Cohen assured him. "Yours. I was created in an entirely different fashion."

"You weren't human once?"

"Good gracious, no!"

"But your name? Are you a Jew?"

"I'm not anything. I'm an angel. The name was given to me so that people could feel comfortable with me. I explained this to you."

"I'm glad you're not Jewish," Abou said. "I distrust the Jews."

"Yousef wasn't a Muslim, you know," Cohen countered.

Abou nodded his head. "Somehow I was more comfortable with him. I, at least, thought he was like me."

Cohen shook his head. "Frankly, Abou, this hatred thing baffles us. You're all so . . . so tribal."

Abou shrugged. "I suppose so."

"You just have to be identified with some group, don't you?" Cohen asked.

Abou didn't want to talk about that. "You said things weren't going too well for some of these early creatures. What happened?"

"Very simple," Cohen replied. "More were dying than were being born. With that happening, it doesn't take long to see the last of any group. Your ancestors were dying out at a dreadful rate during a terribly bad time."

"Did we die out?" Abou seldom made jokes, but he couldn't pass up the opportunity.

Cohen grinned. "Wise guy. No, something momentous happened."

Abou found this pronouncement most annoying. Finally he was forced to ask, "What?"

Cohen rose and dusted off his clothes. "Not tonight. You would have to stay asleep well into tomorrow to hear it all. I'm going to skedaddle."

"Skedaddle?" Abou questioned, but Cohen had disappeared.

The Third Day

IT WAS LATE in the morning when Abou awoke. He had the beginning of a headache, and his nose was stuffed. Blowing hard into a rag, he relieved the pressure somewhat.

"Are you awake, Father?" Sophia came into the tent carrying a copper pot of steaming coffee and other accouterments on a hammered tray. She wore a *chador* with her *hijabs* drawn over her face as was befitting a good wife crossing in public view from her house to her father's abode. Abou looked into the liquid depths of his daughter's eyes, the beauty of her brow, and suddenly he realized how clever Arab garb was. If she showed her face, a male would want to see her neck, and if she exposed her neck, he would want to see her breasts, and if these were exposed . . . well, it just went on and on until everything was bare, when the eyes alone were enough to incite and intrigue.

"Are you ill, my father?" She let the veil fall. He saw the loveliness of her face, her great oval liquid eyes, the unblemished skin of her beloved mother.

"No, no," he replied, raising himself. "I didn't sleep well. I had a dream which was very disturbing."

"Father," she began, her voice stronger as if she were prepared to make an important statement. "I know my duty to my family" (Abou noted to himself that she said *family*, not *husband*, as most wives would), "but I do not approve of this plan to send you to a small room in the city. You are harming no one here, and it doesn't matter if the other students laugh at Akbar in school." Having said this, she seemed suddenly to deflate like a balloon.

Abou took her hand in his. "There is nothing for you to do, my daughter. I know you would do me no harm, and I am thankful for that, but Yasser wants me out of his house, and we must respect his wishes."

Sophia sighed. "You have been most generous with money for food and presents for the children. I do not think he understands how hard it will be to manage without your contribution."

He patted her hand. "I can still give you money. I would not have you want for anything, if I can help it."

It was legend in the marketplace how Abou had gone off to America and worked for years as a taxi driver in the land of the infidels, that he had sent money to his wife, and that, after only forty quarters (those who discussed his business were not quite sure what this time frame was), he had qualified for a pension from the devil's government, and this money was sent each month to the local bank and deposited in his account. Rumors raged as to the amount that was sent, from twenty American dollars a month to thousands. Nobody knew, and certainly Abou never spoke of it to anyone, even to Hamid or Ammon, his closest friends, who were collared periodically and questioned by the busybodies in the marketplace. It was well-known that Yasser desperately wanted to know how much money his father-in-law had in the bank and how much money the Americans sent him. Even the wealthier, more respected men in the town wondered, and Absollah, the banker, was often asked about Abou's account over dinner or coffee, but he only smiled and asked, "Would you want me to tell your account balance to a stranger?" and this always put the questions to rest.

It was this rumor about money that had caused the open derision about Abou's tent. Many of the townspeople thought it was absurd for a wealthy ancient to be living in a tent in his son-in-law's orchard. But instead of asking why Abou didn't simply build an addition onto Yasser's house, they began joking about the matter, sometimes in front of Yasser, whom many didn't care for anyway, and he seethed with resentment, often letting others see his foul temper when he should have been more circumspect, if for no other reason than good business. When he couldn't find out Abou's worth, he decided the old man simply had to go. It wasn't a clever decision, not even a wise one from a business standpoint, but it satisfied his need. He resented Abou's solvency and his seeming indifference to Yasser's daily struggle for food and housing.

Sophia poured her father a cup of coffee.

"Are you going to join me?" he asked. It was seldom seen—a woman enjoying coffee with a man, chatting, even laughing. Sophia hesitated for a moment, then poured herself a cup. She had sugar, which she dearly loved, but her father drank his black with no sugar, a habit he had picked up in America, which he had found to be a strangely disciplined country in a haphazard way.

"Were you lonely all those years in America?" she asked as she sipped her drink.

He nodded. "Oh, yes. I have told you I lived in a section called Cobble Hill off Atlantic Avenue in a place called Brooklyn, which is part of the city of New York. Many of our people are there. That was good. When I finished driving for the day, I could sit and drink coffee . . . as we are doing . . . and talk about the day's events. It was pleasant. But I missed your mother very much."

"But you always provided for her, and you did visit when you could," Sophia replied softly. "When you first left, she must have been terribly lonely, although Istanbul was not so far away. But then . . . America. She must have thought she would never see you again."

Abou laughed. "Oh, she knew I was coming back. I sent her money and she banked a portion of it for years. I had to leave. There was no work here after the great war that followed the British betrayal. I didn't want my children to be raised on the largesse of the Saudis. It wasn't fitting. And when I came back, we had you and that was a great boon."

"Don't you miss her?"

"Oh, so much. It is a hard way to live. I'm only sorry your mother didn't live to see you grown and married. That would have pleased her, as your children would have made her life a wonderment."

Sophia thought about this. "Yasser is wrong."

"You shouldn't talk that way, my daughter. He is your husband. He does what he thinks is best for you and the children."

She flared up, something she seldom did. "He is jealous of you."

Abou waved his hand, dismissing the suggestion, but he knew it was true. "I have missed my first prayer."

"You are elderly. Allah understands."

Abou finished his coffee, gathered his robe, and stood. "I am not too sure of that, my daughter. As long as one is able, one should do his devotions. Age is not an excuse."

Sophia rose and gathered up her coffee paraphernalia. "I shall talk to Yasser again this evening."

"Do not cause dissension. You must live out your life with this man, while I shall be sleeping comfortably somewhere on a green hill overlooking a great body of water."

"Do not speak like that! I don't like the thought."

"When I was your age," he replied with a smile, "I feared it too, but now, somehow, I've become accustomed to the idea." Then, seeing her concern, he patted her hand. "Well, it will be many years. I am as strong as a donkey."

As he watched her return to the house, he wished he could tell her everything he did while in America, but it wasn't wise or safe to discuss the particulars of his stay there, especially his being granted citizenship, even with his daughter.

Abou washed himself in the bucket near the well and then carefully watered the flowers in his small garden with the dirty fluid. He dressed with great care, even snipping a few stray hairs from his beard. It would never do to appear slovenly and dejected because of small reversals in his life, but he certainly had to tell his friends what was being planned for him, so it was better if he appeared at his best or they would feel sorry for him. Sympathy was something Abou absolutely abhorred.

He had obviously missed morning prayer, but he planned to be in the square before the mosque for his noonday devotions. It was there, after the orison, that he met Hamid, with his homemade mailbag, and Ammon, the barber who had so much leisure time. With them was Absollah, the banker, who thought constantly of interest rates and such. They walked to the Camel's Hump for coffee, although Absollah offered to treat them at a slightly more upscale place. Being proud men, they declined. They were comfortable in their shabby café, in spite of the rumor that the barber could well afford better restaurants, that his wife had an income of some sort.

The usual amenities were exchanged and Hamid produced his mail. He had one flyer from Germany that Absollah was considerate enough to translate with his limited German.

"I may be moving away, my friends," Abou finally said in a soft voice after they had ordered coffee. He had rehearsed his explanation. "Yasser fears I may become ill in my tent, and there is no room for me in the house."

"Nonsense!" Ammon exclaimed without hesitation. "You have lived in your tent for years and you love it. Why would he worry now?"

"He is concerned now because of my age," Abou replied, unable to think of any better excuse.

"Perhaps he has heard the talk in the marketplace about how shameful it is that he doesn't provide you with adequate housing. I, for one, have always explained how you loved tent living with your father when you were a boy herding goats," Absollah offered.

"And I," Hamid interjected.

"People laugh at Yasser because he is so self-important," Absollah said. "When they say things about you and your tent, they are really trying to insult him. Everyone understands how much you love living as you do."

"I worry," Abou admitted. "I have been having the most interesting dreams of late, and I fear they won't continue if I move. They seem somehow suited to my tent."

Ammon said, "I would refuse. You gave a rich dower. You pay your way. I'm sure your daughter and the children don't want you to leave."

Abou smiled at his friends' loyalty. "You are kind. But I would not want to cause dissension in their household."

"I'm sure," Absollah replied, "but let us think about this overnight and decide what we might do. You *do* want to stay, don't you?"

"Certainly," Abou replied with a great smile. "I have the best of all worlds in this village of ours—a wonderful place to live, good friends, my family, and delightful food. No man could ask for more."

Before late afternoon prayer, they separated and Abou wended his way through the bazaar and alleys on his way home. He could not avoid seeing the young men clustered in small groups, sharing rare cigarettes, some without shoes or proper shirts, all angry. They had no work. If they could get permission to enter the Israeli sector, they might find work, but most were denied. Either their families were linked to Hamas, or they had distant cousins in Hizbullah. Israel considered both organizations terrorist. Yet, Israel had its own problems, Abou admitted. If Sharon were to become reasonable, which admittedly wasn't likely, the conservatives in his government would bring him down. And fanatics continued to enter Israel and blow themselves up in crowded streets. And while Arafat did little or nothing, deploring the violence when talking to the West, quietly encouraging it at home, nobody really listened. He was surrounded by corruption. Hamas ignored him. Abou shook his head in despair, for his daughter had been raised in the midst of this horror, and it looked as if his grandchildren faced the same future.

When he arrived home, the family was already sitting in a circle around a great pot of wonderful-smelling lamb stew. Abou could feel his juices flowing. "A thousand pardons," he said as he washed quickly and took his seat next to the baby, who looked up at him and smiled.

"I have found you a place to live, Abou," Yasser stated without even looking at his father-in-law. "Unfortunately it is not close by, but I think you will like it. It is on the road to Khan Yunis where there are some Israeli settlements, so travel may be restricted at times, but it was the best I could do. I would like you to move from your tent within a day or so."

"It is Allah's will," Abou replied and smiled at the baby, Leila. Not for a moment did he think it Allah's will. He accepted a slip of paper with an address on it that Yasser handed across the pot. Glancing at it, Abou saw it was in a village thirty kilometers away, past an Israeli checkpoint, which would make visiting very difficult indeed.

Sophia was crying. She had pulled her veil across her face, but her eyes were moist.

"It is but a small room, so you will have to decide what you wish to take. We can sell the rest for you," Yasser continued.

"You are too kind," Abou replied, waiting for Yasser to dip into the pot with his bread and take the tenderest piece of meat for himself, signaling that the rest could then eat. But Yasser seemed bent on making them starve.

"I heard more words of derision again today," Yasser continued, looking pointedly at Sophia.

Abou was rapidly losing his patience as well as his appetite. "I will take the bus and go to see the room tomorrow," he replied abruptly.

Yasser dipped his bread into the bowl and came up with a large chunk of spiced lamb. Abou dipped next, then Akbar, and finally Sophia, who fed some of hers to the baby. They ate in silence.

The Third Darkfall

ABOU RETIRED right after dinner. He had trouble falling asleep and it was long past midnight when Cohen finally appeared.

"Tough day?"

Abou smiled. He had come to enjoy the angel's casual language as well as his concern. "Very. My friends are trying to think of some solution for me, but Yasser has asked me to move as soon as tomorrow."

"Too bad," the angel replied, looking about him. "Not many of these old herder tents around anymore. You'd think the government would want to put them in a museum or something, just to show how you herdsmen lived years ago."

"It was my father's tent."

"Yes, I know. It's beautiful. Who did the wonderful embroidery?"

"My mother and my grandmother. And that chest you are sitting on belonged to my grandfather and perhaps to his father. It is very old."

Cohen looked at the delicate, worn inlay. "A wonderful piece. Things decay or are destroyed so rapidly in this world of yours, it's just great seeing something like this."

Abou thought for a moment. "Last night you said something momentous happened, but then you disappeared. I had a dreadful time staying asleep. I wish you wouldn't do that."

"Yes, well," Cohen replied with some hesitation, licking his lips nervously. "It is somewhat indelicate. I'm not comfortable discussing this with a man your age."

"My age?"

"Well, you know. Old-fashioned."

"I am not old-fashioned." Abou was indignant. "I stay abreast."

Cohen settled himself on the chest, crossed his legs, and said, "Okay, it was covert estrus."

"What?"

"Simply, women stopped going into heat."

"Gracious!" Abou exclaimed.

"Most animals have a cycle. The female signals when she is interested. The male doesn't bother her when she's not. She has plenty of time to have her kid, nurse it, and get it up and running. But that cycle was a disaster for humans. It was taking too long to reproduce, and they were dropping like flies from disease, lousy hunting, predators, and natural disasters. That's what did in your cousins the Neanderthals. If they had adjusted, you would probably be sharing this world with those huge brutes today. Of course they had other problems. Couldn't hold an ax very well. Goofed-up thumbs or something. Did you know they played wind instruments through their noses?"

"I didn't know that," Abou replied, still pondering Cohen's revelation. "Stopped going into heat? That hardly seems earthshaking?"

Cohen smiled. "Yeah, for sure, but it got things rolling. Overlapping kids galore! No longer was there that long wait while the little tyke got old enough to take care of himself. You understand, Abou, you people were on a very slippery slope. With that low birthrate, you were doomed. As you got smarter, your brains grew, which meant women had to have the babies earlier. I mean, a woman couldn't carry a kid around for five or six years, could she? So, as a trade-off, you needed this longer period for infant care. It was sometimes eight, nine, ten years between kids, and even then, a bunch of them got gobbled up or died of something else. And remember, life was hard, so people lived a shorter span. Some couples had only one child under the old system. So you made this slight adjustment and everything was solved. Well, it did cause a few problems, but what adjustment doesn't?"

"Problems?" Abou's mind was racing.

"You know," Cohen answered. "Usual stuff. The oldest kid had to help care for the younger kids. Caused a lot of problems. Girls got the worst of that deal, so they were always running away to get out of it. Lots of turmoil."

"That was the only problem?"

"Oh, no. *Mucho* others. It left a lot of guys feeling a little insecure. I mean, you aren't long for this world so you want kids you know are yours, but all of a sudden, your old lady can be screwing around when you're out on a hunt. Boy, if there's anything that ruins a fellow's aim, it's thinking about what the missus might be doing back in the old cave."

Cohen seemed animated by the topic. "And that led to infidelity, paternity suits, coveting, flirting, marriage, envy, modesty. Hey, you got the clothing industry out of it! And then prenuptials, palimony, wills, surrogate courts, cosmetics. Oh, I could just go on and on, but if those little fellows hadn't been so adaptable, you'd be history."

"My Salah was always faithful," Abou replied.

Cohen face clouded. "Yes, well . . ."

"She was, wasn't she?"

"Please, don't upset yourself," Cohen pleaded. "I should have never brought the subject up. It was thoughtless of me."

"Then she was unfaithful to me?" Abou concluded, his voice flat with pain.

"Come on, Abou. How long were you gone? Ten years? More? Humans are human, you know." Cohen coughed apologetically.

Abou buried his face in his cloak. The thought of his dear, gentle Salah with another man was just too much to comprehend. "It is not possible."

"My dear Abou, I don't want to shock you or destroy any cherished memories, but your race has been programmed to have sex. I mean, it's what you do! The whole point of your existence is replication as far as we can figure out. Why would your Salah be any different? And you full well know you weren't always a good boy, were you? There was that woman in Bensonhurst."

"Enough!" Abou replied, holding up his hand to deflect the angel's words. "Enough. I came home to visit as often as I could, but I . . . I . . . ," he admitted to his rue.

"There are many aspects of human relationships," Cohen said, "and separation is not good for them. Boredom is very bad, as is temptation. Most modern people don't like to admit it, but it just isn't good to leave your mate in the company of a dozen members of the opposite sex for any extended period. I mean, the strain is often too much. And then there are little things. Just think of clothes."

"Clothes?"

"Sure. I mean, until women began covering up, you guys didn't have too much to dream about, but once all the ladies wore clothes, you began to imagine all sorts of things underneath."

"And that's why we wear clothes?" Abou asked.

"That, and it got awfully cold when some of you wandered north. I mean, you needed something to keep you warm in Germany, and northern Russia was just awful. It still gives me the chills. Nobody wants to be topless on a tundra." Cohen enjoyed a good laugh.

"Is modesty wrong?" Abou asked, thinking suddenly of his daughter sitting next to him that morning.

"Wrong? Right? Who knows? It's part of the same process. If you're female and know some parts of you stimulate, you're reticent to show them to every Tom, Dick, or Hamid. Same's true of men. They aren't willing to show their privates. Invites comparisons. Bad for the old ego. That's one of the problems that developed when you lost a lot of your fur. Everything was just hanging out there for anybody to look at."

"Fur? We had fur?"

"Some of you still do," Cohen replied cheerfully. "Running did it. You just can't be a runner in a shaggy coat. You needed a better way to perspire. So you dropped your fur and gave up panting, although if you watch some of those guys who run long distances, they end up with their mouths open anyway, even if they are sweating like pigs." Cohen flushed. "An unfortunate expression."

Abou ignored him. "Why then would women appear as they do in Western magazines, half-dressed, provocative?"

Cohen grinned. "Woman are strange creatures, Abou my friend."

"In our world, we wouldn't tolerate such wantonness," Abou assured the angel.

"Granted. And I'm not sure if that's because you guys are so sophisticated that just an arched brow suffices, or so randy you can't stand seeing an ankle without pouncing on some girl's bones. Anyway, it's true; you people certainly like your women covered from head to tippy toe."

"It is only proper," Abou replied with a degree of severity.

Cohen sat looking at him, picking his teeth with that worn toothpick, saying nothing. The silence was unnerving.

"You mentioned other results which I failed to understand," Abou continued. "Wills, heirs, surrogate court? How are those influenced by sexuality?"

"Ah, yes," Cohen replied with a smile. "When you humans developed awareness, you projected your need to survive into a primitive concept of immortality. If you have to die, you could live on in your children. That sort of balderdash. So humans began passing wealth on to their children, as well as their names, either to the male or female heirs, but mostly the male. I'm not really sure why that is. Possibly it's the sheer weight of numbers. The male can impregnate twenty thousand females in his lifetime, while the female can have only twenty-five or so children if she's unlucky."

"Twenty thousand!" Abou exclaimed.

"In theory. You know the old saying, that man thinks with his prick. Males are here to impregnate. Females have to worry about caring for the little tykes." Cohen stopped and thought for a moment before continuing. "Although in some cultures, men now are giving a little more thought to the problem."

Abou pondered all this. He felt he could no longer question whether Cohen was an angel, but he did have serious doubts about some of Cohen's theories. So much of the angel's explanation of the human situation flew in the face of what Abou had believed for so long. Yet, he did know of men who had several wives and far too many children. This was a pastime of the very rich, but it did take place. Abou remembered his father telling him of an Indian ruler named Jahangir who had five thousand women in his harem. With glee, Abou's father likened this Indian to the goats they were tending.

"All this is to insure your genes are distributed to future generations," Cohen continued, "and somehow genes and wealth became confused in the human mind, although it isn't too much of a stretch. I mean, if human males want their genes distributed to as many females as possible, it makes sense that the guys would want to protect the gals with the assurance of food and whatever after death. *Voila!* You have accumulated wealth, wills, trusts, and all that foolishness."

"I have been thinking of creating a will," Abou admitted, "but I know little of trusts."

Cohen shrugged. "No matter. Just another device to pass wealth along."

Abou beamed. "Ah, but you have as much as admitted that we males care nothing about the survival of our children. Didn't you say that was the women's job? Why then would we think of leaving money to future generations?"

Cohen looked puzzled for a moment. "Good point. Look, all we have is a vantage point in this process. You people developed in your own nutty fashion. We can just look at the process and guess what's going on in your minds and with your emotions. You ain't dandelions, you know."

"Dandelions?" Abou questioned. Now what was Cohen talking about?

"Yeah, you know. They're apomictic. They reproduce without any outside help. Boy, are they boring."

"Apomictic?" Abou put up his hand in protest. "Please. This is too much for me tonight."

Cohen gave a huge belly laugh and disappeared with, "See you tomorrow night, old buddy. Talking to you is really fun, and the rest of us are listening in. And we're all sorry about the trouble you're having with Yasser. I guess I shouldn't say things like this about one of our potential clients, but he's really a pain in the ass."

The Fourth Day

As USUAL, Abou met his friends the next afternoon at the Camel's Hump. Hamid had his mail in a stack, but it remained unopened. As Abou approached, he saw all in deep conversation, and Ammon, who seemed never to barber these days, greeted him with a smile. Even Absollah was there, taking time from his bank.

"Ah, Abou, come sit and have coffee," Ammon insisted, raising his hand slightly to alert a waiter. He preferred the more delicate French moue to attract the waiter's attention, but as crowds grew in the cafés, waiters seemed less able to keep up with these subtleties.

"We have interesting news," Hamid said, fingering his letters and leaflets. "Just yesterday, Yasser had a dispute with Hafez, the tax collector, about taxes Yasser owes on the house. He said he could not even afford to house you, that you had to live in a tent in the back. Hafez was heard to say that it was well-known you were a man of wealth and could afford an addition to the house. According to those present, Yasser was dumbfounded. He yelled at Hafez that it was not true, that you were a poor man who depended on him for food and clothes, as well as magazines and newspapers. Yasser is most certainly having trouble paying his taxes."

Abou was puzzled. "Then why would he want me to leave? I mean, it is true about the magazines and newspapers. He brings home what he doesn't sell. The rest is nonsense. I give money to the household."

Nobody spoke for a moment, looking at one another with inquiring eyes, wondering who would volunteer to explain the situation to Abou.

"We hear he owes a great deal of money in back taxes, as well as other debts," Absollah finally said. "It is rumored that he cannot keep up the house. I suspect he wants you to move away to avoid the shame of your witnessing him and his family thrown into the streets."

The waiter brought Abou his coffee. Slowly he stirred the syrupy brew, reflecting on what he'd heard. "Then what would happen to my daughter and the children?"

"It is rumored that he plans to divorce her. He will probably cast her out with the children," Ammon suggested.

"She has done nothing but obey him and care for him and his children," Abou murmured, almost as if talking to himself.

Absollah replied, "I took the liberty of stopping by Hafez's office this morning and talking to him. Whoever pays the taxes will own the house. It is not a great amount. Buying the house for back taxes would be good business. That is certain."

"I see," Abou replied, sipping his coffee.

Hamid finally spoke. "Abou, good friend, I do not know if you have money enough to pay these taxes, but don't do it while Yasser is there. It is one thing to secure a place for your daughter and your grandchildren, but do not pay this man's taxes. He will only evict you anyway. I know . . . I know it is impolite to be so direct, but I worry about you. You are known to be too generous."

Abou put his hand on Hamid's. "Giving good advice to a friend is never impolite, Hamid. Your thoughts are welcome. But still . . . I had the passing thought that Yasser is not the type to lose his temper in public, as he did with Hafez, unless he wants rumors to circulate. Do you think that is possible?"

Absollah smiled. "You are a clever man, Abou. Dealing with you is like dealing with the Jews. I had not thought of that but, of course, you are right. He wanted you to hear his complaints. He thinks you will pay his taxes, and he will still be rid of you. You will be living far away, he will have his house secured, and nobody will be the wiser. Yes, that is Yasser's plan."

All those at the table smiled in appreciation of the complexity of Yasser's duplicity. And even better was that Abou understood Yasser's plan and could now counter it. This appealed to the trader's spirit that lay deep within all of them.

"What you say about living far away rings true. I told Yasser that I would take the bus to Shomi and look at this room he has procured for me," he told them, naming the distant village.

"I will drive you," Absollah offered. "I have my car just off the street in the rear."

"I can't impose," Abou replied, raising his hand.

"It will give us an opportunity to talk," Absollah replied.

They were on the road within minutes and Abou asked, "Do I have enough money in the bank to pay the taxes?"

"I will speak to Hafez," Absollah replied, driving carefully through the crowded, narrow streets. "I am sure he doesn't want to seize the property. Something can be worked out. Perhaps he will settle for less than what is owed. It is never wise to give tax collectors what they ask. It makes them only want more. But the answer is yes, you have more than enough."

"I will not pay it until Yasser has set Sophia aside. I paid a handsome dowry to him and he should have cared for her and the children. Or perhaps I will pay the taxes and put the house in her name. No! He will control it still if he doesn't divorce her. Perhaps I shall retain the title myself. I must think this through."

Absollah nodded. "Abou, if you do not wish to pay the taxes, I will do so. It is a good investment."

"Another friend of mine," Abou continued, ignoring Absollah's suggestion, "said that it was a shame that Yasser wanted to move me from my tent. He thought it was a tent of historical significance and should stand as a display showing how our forefathers lived. He thinks I should stay there."

Absollah looked at him briefly. "An interesting idea."

Abou said little else until they found the address of Abou's new home. The room was in a complex of whitewashed buildings, up a narrow outside staircase, a dark room with slits for windows, and a water tap and an outhouse in the back.

"Not where I would have my father-in-law reside," Absollah remarked as they descended the stairs. "Seen enough?"

On the way home, Absollah suggested, "How would you like to move your tent to the lot behind the bank? You could use the bank's facilities, at least during the day, where it is but a short walk to the Camel's Hump. You could do this until Yasser is, shall we say, *in extremis* financially."

Abou smiled.

"And," Absollah continued, "it would show your tent to the world and display what a herdsman's tent was like fifty years ago, while at the same time you will annoy Yasser. We will tell people it is a cultural event sponsored by the bank.

Perhaps you could show it to the schoolchildren as they come home from school."

"I would enjoy that."

"Good. Forget that dreadful hovel. Tell Yasser you are making other arrangements. I will have the bank's truck at your door at nine tomorrow."

That evening over dinner, Yasser's first question was, "What have you heard in the marketplace today?"

"Nothing really. I went and visited the room you found for me."

Seemingly satisfied by his answer, Yasser offered one of his rare smiles. "Is it not a princely room that I found for you, father-in-law?"

"It is very far away," Abou replied, prepared to enjoy the game.

"Yes, but you can visit us now and then. And Sophia can visit you on occasion."

"I will miss the grandchildren," Abou replied evenly, smiling at the serious Akbar and the gurgling baby girl. The little boy knew something was amiss and watched his elders with suspicion.

Yasser nodded, dipping into the pot early this evening, as he was very hungry from walking about town trying to borrow money. His business had become almost nonexistent, although he would never admit that in his home. "That is true, old one, but we all must make sacrifices. Think what I sacrifice for my family."

"It is truly wonderful," Abou replied, his face showing nothing.

Sophia was watching him, wondering at her father's sanguine composure. He was an old man being dispossessed, but he seemed strangely at ease, even content. Abou smiled at her and then winked, something he had learned watching American films.

"I dislike the Israeli checkpoint," he continued, watching Yasser slurp his food. Making noise while eating was a sign of appreciation and enjoyment, but his son-in-law managed to make it revolting.

"We all face problems, my father-in-law. We must accept adversity to better appreciate the blessings of Allah."

"Yes, that is true. Very true. But I think I would rather make other arrangements."

"Other arrangements? What other arrangements?" Yasser was suddenly alert.

Abou shrugged. "Nothing is settled as yet, but do not worry, son-in-law. I shall be out of your orchard tomorrow or the day after. I will find a place to live."

"The place I found for you is better," Yasser insisted.

"I am too old to go down a flight of stairs for a pail of water," Abou told him. "I am looking for a place with water and lavatory indoors."

"Indoors! Are you mad? That would cost a fortune." Yasser exploded, and then a crafty expression crossed his face. "Have you that kind of money?"

Abou smiled. "There were some things I didn't care for in America, but water and lavatories inside the house were a blessing. Nobody I met there had to wash outside and use outside facilities. For infidels, they were surprisingly clean."

"Have you found such a place?"

Abou answered carefully. "With Allah's blessing, something will come available."

Yasser made a vulgar sound with his lips and returned to his dinner. "Two days then. If you haven't found anything, I expect you to take the room I was so fortunate to find."

As Abou prepared his sleeping pad, Akbar brought him a large pot of steaming tea and was quite solicitous of his grandfather, although usually he took him for granted. "I will miss you," Akbar said as he prepared the cup, and Abou took the boy in his arms and said, "I will be nearby, young Akbar, to look after you, your baby sister, and your mother."

This seemed to satisfy Akbar, who nestled down into the security of his grandfather's arm. They sat together until it was time for the little boy to go to bed. As Akbar left the tent, Abou wished more than anything in the world that he could insure the little boy a safe and prosperous life.

The Fourth Darkfall

WHEN AKBAR FINALLY LEFT, Abou lay on his back, his hand clasped on his chest, and smiled into the darkness. He didn't feel at all sleepy, so it was a great surprise to see Cohen pull aside the flap and enter the tent. If anything, the angel's white suit was dirtier than it had been the previous night.

"Would you be insulted if I asked my daughter to launder your suit?" Abou asked.

The angel looked down at his clothing. "I'm on the road so much, I hardly notice how grungy I get. But I do have another suit somewhere. I don't want to bother poor Sophia with my laundry."

"I mean no disrespect . . . ," Abou began, but the sentence drifted off.

"I heard you today telling your friend about the tent. So, you think of me as a friend," Cohen said with a great smile, pouring himself a cup of tea without asking. "That is very flattering, Abou."

Abou propped himself up on his elbow. "Well, I couldn't say that an angel told me my tent had historic significance, could I?"

Cohen made himself comfortable on the chest. "No, I suppose not. But I must say, it made me feel great when you took my suggestion. That's what we're supposed to do, you know. Facilitate things. Give a different viewpoint. Offer alternatives." Cohen looked down, almost pouting. "You have no idea how often our advice is ignored. It makes us feel so . . . marginal."

"You are very good at it, Cohen," Abou said, using the angel's name for the first time. "You have told me many provocative things that I shall mull for years to come, Allah willing. Just today someone said my son-in-law envies me, and it was just a night or two ago you mentioned envy. I don't see the connection, but it is interesting that the concept has reappeared."

"Keep in mind what it's all about, Abou," Cohen replied, warming immediately to his task. "You need to eat to survive, and your children need to eat to survive and carry on your genes. Envy comes easily to humans, and in a way that's good for it is one of the bases of ambition, but it can turn real nasty. Yasser's is the worst kind of envy, for he imagines you to have all the wealth he so desperately needs, and you refuse to give it to him or die, you old rascal."

"He wants me dead?" Abou was genuinely shocked.

"Indubitably," Cohen replied without hesitation. "This is not a man interested in your welfare. Yasser is interested primarily in himself, and then in his son, and that's about it."

"Oh my," Abou murmured. "That's dreadful."

"But very common, old boy. Fortunately Yasser's a coward, so he won't, I think, do anything overt to finish you off, but for heaven's sake, don't depend on him to bring you your medicine. He simply isn't trustworthy."

"Should we be talking about him this way?"

"Certainly I shouldn't," Cohen agreed. "In fact, I should be visiting him and trying to get him on a better path, but I'll tell you right now, it would be a tough haul. I've worked with his kind before, and the failure rate is staggering. I mean, his kind just pulls down your stats, if you know what I mean. But, maybe I'll ask one of my associates to drop in on him."

"You take so much time with us," Abou replied. "We must be very difficult."

"It's mostly fun," Cohen replied. "At least it's fun now. In the beginning, before those wonderful Phoenicians invented soap, the stench was unbearable. Anyway, you people, even unwashed, give us meaning."

"Meaning?" Abou tried to understand.

"This is what we do. When we cease counseling humans, we cease being. When the last human draws a breath, I suspect we'll just disappear. I mean, we'll ask to be reassigned to another galaxy or universe or something, but there's nothing exactly like you humans, as far as we know, so I suspect our usefulness will be over. We'll just be laid off. Of course, we'll ask for retraining, but that's uncertain."

"I'm sorry," Abou said. "I had no idea."

"Pish," Cohen said with a casual wave. "Just think about yourself. Don't worry about us."

"We'll be gone too," Abou said, a little sadly.

"Faster than you think, if you're not careful," Cohen replied. "All humans should study the Easter Island civilization. Cut down the trees, exhausted the land, and suddenly, the last islander died and that was the end of them. I'm afraid today's humans are doing the same thing to the rest of the world.

Using up land, destroying trees, eating whole species into extinction. It's very depressing, Abou, because we, my associates and myself, have really come to care about you people."

"Are we so self-destructive?" Abou queried.

Cohen nodded. "I'm afraid so. Unless there is a remarkable change in your behavior, you aren't long for this world."

Abou was obviously distressed by the angel's candor.

Cohen cleared his throat. "I'm sorry. There's no reason I should preach at you like this. You are the nearly perfect human. You and your wife had one child, not fifteen. You have used very little of the world's oil reserve, except when you were driving taxicabs in New York, and even then you were only trying to make a few quid to send home. You have been very circumspect about what you consume. Sadly there are far too few of you."

"You embarrass me," Abou complained. "I am a simple man."

Cohen replied, "Well, believe me, you aren't perfect, and don't pull that humble pie routine, Abou. I know you too well. You people just don't make sense at times. Take meat, for instance. When there was little of it available, because your cohorts were just terrible at hunting, a small amount from time to time was a real shot of protein and was sorely needed, but now the human race is just gorging itself on it. You eat far more than you should and you know it. Of course, you aren't as bad as some. I understand they have even been forced to put sumo wrestlers on diets."

Abou didn't want to hear this. "You are confusing me, my dear angel. Your minds seem to roll from place to place like mercury. Remember I am but a humble servant of the Lord."

"Balderdash!"

"What?" Abou asked.

Cohen grinned. "I forget. I pick up slang from different eras and forget to drop it when appropriate, but the point I'm trying to make is that humans adapted to fat and meat consumption an eon ago, and you're still programmed to consume every bit you can get your hands on. You'd think that the whole race was a bunch of Eskimos eating blubber for energy. You eat everything! Whoever thought the shark would become an endangered species, but that's what is happening."

"Gluttony is a sin!" Abou replied with a degree of pomposity which covered his embarrassment, for he knew what Cohen was saying had a disquieting element of truth.

"True, true, but try telling that to a fellow who is sitting down to a tremendous meal." Cohen said with a giggle, then tried to sound serious. "I mean, I like to eat as much as the next angel, but what we see going on is just astounding."

"Just why do you eat and drink?" Abou asked, looking at the teacup in Cohen's hand.

"Well, we decided years ago that it made humans more comfortable if they could meet with us across a table and share a little bread and wine. I mean, all these apparitions standing on hilltops flapping their wings are a bit theatrical, so we decided to be more homey, and to tell you the truth we came to enjoy it. Your wine is superb and your food can be appealing, but the amounts you consume still astound us."

"I disapprove of wine," Abou replied.

"Yes, well that's your loss, old fellow. It's even good for your heart, I'm told."

About had read that and decided not to reply. "Yasser is gaining weight as of late."

"I like that!" Cohen exclaimed. "It has a ring to it. Have you thought of poetry as an avocation?" Then in a more serious tone, he asked, "Do you have any idea why Yasser acts as he does toward your daughter?"

Abou shook his head. "Not just Yasser. I have often wondered about the tension and hatred that exists between many men and women. I find it very sad."

"Maize and yams," Cohen said with certainty.

"Pardon me?"

"Agriculture. That's the key to the way you live. As I mentioned before, men were really rotten hunters, but if the truth were told, most of the food was grown by women and children around the camps and caves. All this hoopla about the hunting male and his need to be in the wild stalking his prey is a bit of bombast so that the men could get out in the woods and act like kids. Women did the real work, planting and hoeing small plots so they could all survive. When the men came to understand that farming was the only sure way to survive, they began to take over. They soon realized how powerful they had become, but their power depended on the domination of their families. Women's main function turned to having male children to work on the farms. There was more food, but the relationship between men and women changed."

"Just because of farming?" Abou sounded suspicious.

Cohen nodded. "And, sadly, because of the increased amount of food produced, women accepted the change. According to Gabe, that was their big mistake. He's developed a whole theory about human development. Really good stuff. Women became chattel, just like the cows and horses. Slavery, a cheap source of labor, flourished. A whole barter system of productive females and children sprung up. Even today men still act like farm managers, but they're sitting in cities instead of growing food."

"Gabriel, the angel?" Abou asked. He avoided any comments about Cohen's latest revelations. With the women's situation in the Middle East, the existence of child labor, and rumors that slave traders still operated in the Saudi desert, he saw no point in the discussion.

"Who else?" Cohen replied.

Abou raised an eyebrow. Cohen was casually talking about the most holy angel as if he were some sort of straw boss, just a hair more important than the rest of them, but this, according to Muslim teachings, was the angel who came to the Virgin Mary and who visited the Prophet and bestowed the holy Qur'an on the human race, as well as stopping in on numerous celebrities in the Hebrew Old Testament. Abou decided to go back to agriculture. "And that was the cause of male/female problems? For grain?"

Cohen laughed. "That, and water rights, as well as farm animals. First you got women and children to do most of the work, then you tried all sorts of animals. You got buffalo to haul for you, and more land was cultivated. And I must say, your ancestors were inventive little buggers. They came up with hundreds of tools for farming."

"Nobody farms any longer," Abou mused. "My father hated leaving the land and his herds, but there wasn't enough money in it."

"Ironic, isn't it?" Cohen agreed cheerfully. "Food is so plentiful in some parts of the world, it doesn't bring a decent price, and in other places there isn't enough, but those places are generally so poor the population can't pay for it anyway. Of course, you can't feed everybody. You humans reproduce too rapidly. The food supply just can't keep up, so you'll have famine and death from starvation. But, hey, given the joy and gratification you get from creating kids, you make up for these dips in population very quickly."

"Then there won't be enough food for all of us?" Abou asked.

Cohen shrugged. "Tell you the truth, I haven't done the arithmetic, but given another fifty years, I don't think food production has a prayer against your sex drive, my goombah. I mean, it isn't even a fair match."

"You make it sound very bleak," Abou mused, feeling sad for his grandchildren and their children.

"Oh, I don't know," Cohen replied. "If you figure out that you can't go on like you have been, I suspect you'll cut back on the kids a bit. We know how tough that is for you fellows, but if you can let logic overcome urges for a few years, you'll do just fine. You know, if each couple produced just one, the population would drop like a rock in a generation. The Chinese are doing something like that already, and I think the Gauls have lost interest in populating the planet with little Frenchies. Restraint is good."

Remembering the passion he felt with Salah, Abou knew they would have had many more children if she had lived. This discussion with Cohen was oddly discomforting. "I must rest. I have a difficult day tomorrow."

"Ah, yes, the great move," Cohen replied, rising from the chest. "I wish you well."

The Fifth Day

ABOU WAS UP AND ABOUT when Sophia brought his morning coffee. She saw the chest open and his folded clothing.

"Oh, Papa, I wish you didn't have to go," she said in a whisper. "The children and I will miss you so."

Abou gestured for her to seat herself next to him. He poured her a cup of coffee before pouring his. Without saying a word to each other, they sipped their beverage. Finally setting his cup aside, Abou said, "Families have these problems, dear Sophia. I did not want to move to a distant town, as you never know when the Israelis will close a checkpoint and I will be cut off from you completely. I have made other arrangements. Absollah has agreed to allow me to pitch my tent behind the bank in that empty lot, and he said I can use the facilities within the bank during the day, although I will have to go to the Camel's Hump on weekends and at night. But it will suffice, and I will be near you and the children."

Sophia fingered her veil. Abou looked at his daughter's lovely face with its miserable expression. "I don't know why

Yasser is acting this way," she said. "It is almost as if he hates you, and us, and doesn't want us to see each other."

Abou shrugged and turned to his shirts, which he began to fold carefully. Uncomfortable watching a man do such work, Sophia took up the task, packing for him. "People have different ways, dear child. I don't know what motivates Yasser, but I know I don't want to spend my last years separated from you."

"Nor I," she said. "I have some clean clothing of yours in the house. I will fetch it."

She glided out of the tent. Abou rolled his rugs and tied them with stout twine.

Absollah was true to his word; the bank's truck arrived at nine promptly. Three young men greeted Abou with deference and began to dismantle his tent. Sophia, holding the baby in her arms, stood with Akbar at the back door and watched the men work swiftly, removing her father from her life.

Finally, Abou took his daughter's hand in his. "I will be in back of the bank, as I said. We are going to invite schoolchildren to visit an authentic herder's tent, so Akbar might want to stop and visit me after school. You can ask your husband if that is permissible."

"I would like to visit, Grandfather," Akbar said in a clear voice.

Abou bent and kissed his grandson's head. "With your father's permission, little warrior. You are always welcome in my tent."

Sophia eyes teared above her veil. "We will come as often as we can."

Abou kissed the baby and got into the truck's cab. Two of the young men sat on the tailgate, making room for the ancient inside the vehicle. Abou thanked the driver.

"It is a great pleasure to do something for one of your age and dedication, Sheik Abou."

The lot behind the bank was open to the street, so the activity attracted a rather large group that pitched in when help was needed erecting Abou's tent. When Absollah explained that the tent would be open to schoolchildren as they came home from school, the crowd nodded approval, saying it was of great historic significance and would add greatly to the young ones' sense of history and view of themselves as a great and mighty people who had lived as one with the land since the beginning of time.

When the tent was up, Absollah led Abou through a back door to where a men's room, a water fountain, and a shower room for the employees were situated, for it was a very modern bank that had an ample spread between the interest paid and the interest charged, so there was money for such conveniences. Banks were frowned upon by the more conservative, as lending money with interest was really a function of the Lebanese and the Jews, but the profits were such that some forward-looking men, such as Absollah, overcame their aversions and entered the world of business. "It cannot all be trade," he explained to Abou and the others one afternoon over coffee. "Now a person needs capital to invest, and that means banks. Even the Saudis buy American bonds and happily accept the interest, and more than one has bought into major banks in New York and London."

Abou found the facilities delightful. "It is a fine thing to have iced water running from a fountain, the indoor lavatory is a blessing, and the chilled air is refreshing on the skin. You are indeed fortunate to work in such an atmosphere, my friend."

Absollah waved a dismissive hand, but his face showed how pleased he was by Abou's words. "We both remember more primitive times, Abou. We may have given the infidels algebra, but they have given us wonders in return. I have now installed air conditioning in my own home."

"Remarkable!" Abou was truly impressed.

"My mother-in-law objects. She says it makes her hands and ankles ache, but my wife has told her to be quiet and accept the modern ways."

They watched as the young men finished carrying Abou's chests into the tent, laid the rugs, and cleared the debris.

"There it is, Abou. I asked Hamid to come to the bank early this morning and arranged with him to circulate handbills to the school today after lunch. He seemed very enthusiastic about it."

Abou smiled. "May I take *you* to lunch, good friend?"

Absollah looked at him shrewdly. "No, it is I who should take you. Your friend, whoever he is, who suggested the historic value of the tent gave me an idea as to how we could make the bank seem a friendlier place to the local inhabitants. I owe him for this idea."

"I shall thank him for you," Abou replied, "although he probably already knows."

"How could he possibly know?"

"He seems to know everything that's going on," Abou said with a grin.

"What is his name?"

"Well, that presents a problem. Like me, he had a name which might be thought Jewish. It doesn't help to broadcast it about."

"But he isn't Jewish?" Absollah asked hastily.

"Oh, absolutely not," Abou assured him.

"And he's one of us?"

"Ah, not exactly," Abou evaded. "He's not of any religion, as far as I can make out."

"Oh," Absollah replied slowly. "Be careful, Abou. It isn't good to associate with people who have lost their faith. Be very careful."

"I never meet him in public," Abou replied. "We are very discreet."

Absollah nodded. "That's good. You can't be too careful. Just associating with such a person can be ruinous to your reputation, and you, Abou, enjoy a reputation far surpassing any other man I know."

Abou bowed his head. "It is very embarrassing. I would prefer to be known as Abou, the former goat herder, who enjoys his old age and tries to be kind to others, and that, my dear Absollah, is why I asked you to lunch, for you need sustenance."

Absollah laughed. "You are sneaky, old friend."

"It is part of my charm."

Hamid joined them at the Camel's Hump for a light lunch before he set out with his handbills. He was delighted with his task.

"Our postal people expect everybody to come to them. Going door to door with mail is much better. It is friendly. A service people appreciate."

"It will certainly be a service for the children," Abou said. "I will show them my tent each afternoon and tell them what it was like to sit with the goats on those long nights. I can tell them about the stars. I studied them endlessly, watching each one progress a bit each night. I can show them where Venus will be this very night in the southern sky."

"I would like to know that," Ammon, the barber, said, seating himself and accepting coffee and rolls from the waiter. "I have never had the patience to study the stars and I have often felt my children suffered from not knowing what to look for."

"It is a vast picture of beauty," Abou replied. "And the wonder of it is that the universe looks so static and yet is in constant motion. Stars are flying from the center at a fantastic speed. My father spent hours telling me which star was which. He was a kind and patient man."

"And very wise," Absollah said. "He had wisdom that he was willing to share."

Abou was pleased with the compliment. Hamid was hurrying his food, and when he finished, he leapt up. "I shall begin my rounds," he exclaimed happily. "If I am successful, you shall have students this very afternoon." He was off with a great flapping of robes and slapping of sandals, his leather satchel filled with the bank's publication concerning the historic herder's tent.

"Not only will the children come," Ammon added, "but I shall pay you a visit, too. Absollah has been busy this morning and everyone in the marketplace is talking of this project. Don't forget, there are many of us who have lived our lives in towns and villages. We know little of the old pastoral ways."

"You should get out into the country more, Ammon," Abou replied with a grin.

"I would be lost and lonely," the barber replied easily, sipping his coffee. "There is no chance to haggle as in the marketplace, make profitable business arrangements, and enjoy the fruits of one's guile." He said this last with a great laugh.

"You have a corrupt view of the world, my friend," Abou replied, sure that Ammon must be involved in business endeavors other than his barbershop.

LATER THAT AFTERNOON, Abou sat in the shade of his awning waiting for the children. At first he thought none would come, but after a time two little boys peered around the corner of the bank building and slowly came forward, curious but timid.

"Welcome to my humble tent, young scholars. Have you ever seen a herder's tent before?"

They both shook their heads, and then Abou noticed a little girl peeking from behind a large garbage can. He gestured for her to come forward. The boys scowled at her but said nothing.

"Males and females both must learn," Abou said. "It is good for both to come. Come inside and see my tent."

Within minutes, several more children had arrived and soon the tent was filled with small, searching eyes, following Abou's words as he described the meaning of the intricate patterns sewn into the panels, the use of the oil lamps, the small stove, and the contents of each chest and rug. He still had goats' bells hanging from the supports, which he hung on one of the children's necks to tinkle as the little fellow stamped around in a circle.

Finally, he told them all to hurry home but to return the following day and he would tell them more about herding under the stars. They marched off down the alley chattering about what they had learned. Abou sat on his rug with a great smile on his face. His late afternoon class pleased him immensely.

Absollah appeared and was pleased with the report. "Come home with me for supper," he insisted, but Abou declined.

"I want to eat a light supper at the Camel's Hump and retire early. It has been a very full day, for which I have you to thank, Absollah."

Walking to his new home in the dark, he was very satisfied with himself, sad only that Akbar had not joined the other children.

His only problem, he realized, was that he had made no arrangements for tea, and Cohen, if he came that night, would have none, but he shrugged it off and lay on his pallet, deciding that if he did appear, he would ask Cohen's pardon.

The Fifth Darkfall

THE ANGEL ARRIVED with a pot of steaming tea. Abou awoke immediately, smelling this unworldly aroma, a most heavenly smell.

"It's not easy bringing this stuff all that way and keeping it hot," Cohen said, setting the pot down and pouring them two cups. He wore a new, tight-fitting checkered suit, which was immaculate. "But you have been generous with your tea and coffee these last several nights, so I decided it was my turn to bring some."

Abou smiled. "You knew I forgot, didn't you?"

"Of course," Cohen replied, "but it really was my turn. Trouble is, it's so hot."

"It's delicious," Abou replied, sipping the cup he had been handed. "Hot, yes, but the best tea I've ever had."

"Well, we've had a few years to develop the blend."

"You should package it and sell it," Abou enthused.

"Do you think we could?" Cohen asked, immediately interested, and then shook his head. "No, that wouldn't be appropriate. And what would we do with the money?"

"Give it to the poor," Abou replied with a grin.

"Yes, I suppose we could do that. It would be something tangible. All this talk, talk, talk is hard to evaluate, you know?"

"I'm enjoying it," Abou replied. "Did you see my luncheon guests this afternoon?"

"Oh, yes, and we watched you with the children with great interest. What you said about the stove was fascinating, but you didn't explain how this little stove heated your tent during long, cold nights."

"Well, I can tell them tomorrow. And I thought the cooking information was very important."

"It was," Cohen agreed, and then, almost as an afterthought, he asked, "What do you think was the first use of fire by your ancestors?"

Abou considered this. He was somehow sure he was going to guess wrong, or Cohen wouldn't have posed the question.

"Keeping warm, I expect."

Cohen nodded. "Partly, but just as important was protection. They found animals stayed away from them if they kept a fire going at the mouth of the cave. When necessary, some smart rascals drove animals out of caves with fagots and then occupied them for their very own. Your ancestors needed something to scare these predacious buggers and that's when fire came in handy. After that, they realized they could get out and about in tents, houses, and whatever, because the fire also kept them warm. Opened up the housing market, so to speak."

Cohen settled himself on the chest, sipping his tea. Abou nodded as the angel spoke, encouraging him for, in truth, Abou had become intrigued in five nights by Cohen's stories. He asked, "And this use of fire was a long time ago?"

"Oh, yes," Cohen said. "A million and a half years, at least. Lightning would strike, and they would carefully save pieces of burning wood, carrying them back to the caves and leaving someone to watch over them. Very tedious job. They had no idea how to kindle a fire, so hoarding the burning sticks was the only way to keep things warmed up. There are some tribes even today who still do it the same way, and for that matter, there are people who just don't use fire at all."

"Don't use fire?" Abou was astounded.

"Yep. Pygmies don't, and there are some islands east of India called the Andamans where the people never used fire. They must be into sushi," Cohen added.

"They had terrible fires in New York," Abou mused. "Children trapped, whole buildings demolished. I always thought highly of the firefighters."

"Yes, sir, and there isn't one Pygmy firefighter in the world. Not one."

"They don't have forest fires?"

"What few they have, they avoid. Just sends a little more game scampering their way."

"I often wished we had more wood so that we could cook more."

"Yes, a common problem." Cohen nodded agreement. "The Chinese have made an art of cooking with almost no fuel."

Abou raised himself from his mat, staring at the angel closely. "You know a great many things . . . Mr. Cohen?"

"Just Cohen. We aren't big on titles," the angel replied. "And thank you. We try to stay current, but I must tell you, Abou, you humans are giving us a merry chase. I mean, the shark has changed very little in a hundred million years, but you human characters keep changing, adapting, and thinking up new stuff."

"Do you enjoy our cooking?" Abou asked. "You mentioned Chinese cooking. I had it once in New York."

"We love it," Cohen responded enthusiastically. "I mean, as I mentioned before, to fit in better we had to adopt some of your functions. How would humans greet an angel who wouldn't join them in a cup of tea? So we began eating and drinking as a social ploy. Of course, to avoid utter hypocrisy, we gave ourselves a sense of taste. Am I glad we decided to do that! Now, whenever one of us is near a Chinese restaurant, he or she orders takeout for the whole crew."

Abou hesitated. "But you don't do any of the rest?" He didn't quite know how to couch the intimate question he was asking.

Cohen shook his head with a smile. "Sadly, no. I mean some of it looks like fun, and the Greeks wrote tomes about gods coming down and seducing fair maidens, but we just don't do that sort of thing. We decided it wasn't seemly and would confuse our mission even more, so we decided against it, but I've often thought . . ." He let the thought drift off into space.

Abou nodded. "At least there is the food and tea to make your visits more pleasant."

Cohen grinned. "We need a little something to get through some of these sessions. You have no idea how uptight some people are."

"And me? Trying to find out how I stand in Allah's eyes? Is that unusual?"

Cohen laughed. "Not hardly. You want to be a good man, and you want to be perceived as a good man. Those are not the same, you understand. For most, perception is the crux of the matter. That's why you had this first dream. I'm just sorry I didn't have better news for you."

Abou shrugged. "I thought I was doing so well."

"You are! Don't lose heart, kiddo," Cohen admonished. "And keep in mind the odds are against you. As human population increases, it becomes harder and harder to be number one."

Abou brightened. "Well, at least I have these conversations."

Cohen examined his fingernails. "As you know, this is an experiment, Abou. We are not quite sure how these disclosures will affect you or humanity, if at all. But I was given the go-ahead, so here we are. I can answer anything you want to know."

"Why was I chosen?"

"That first night I sort of shot my mouth off, and when my associates and I talked about it later, it seemed a good idea to continue."

"Am I supposed to tell others?" Abou asked.

"You could," Cohen replied carefully, "but they might think you dotty, if you take my meaning. And your religious leaders might get really hostile. They don't seem too open to new ideas."

"Yes, that's true," Abou admitted. "Well, for now I'm satisfied with our conversations. I have all sorts of questions I'd like answered."

"Such as?"

"We were talking about cooking. Just how did it get started and why? I've wanted to know that ever since I was a little tyke."

"Accident," Cohen replied. "As a child were you told the story of the pig that fell into the fire and the little boy found it delicious? That was pretty much on the mark."

"It was a lamb," Abou corrected him.

"Ah, I forget all these fetishes about food. Of course, it would be lamb."

"You eat everything?" Abou asked.

"We can," Cohen admitted. "Just like you. Interesting. I never thought about it before, but you and the shark are the only animals that eat everything. It's probably for the best that you have developed dietary laws."

"The thought of eating pork repels me," Abou murmured.

"Only because you have been told since childhood that it is unclean," Cohen replied. "But the Americans have some hams you'd die for, and the Poles, too. And there is a Canadian bacon which is just superb. Ham and eggs is one of my favorite breakfasts."

Abou shook his head. "Do you enjoy hummus?"

"I love it!" Cohen exclaimed with enthusiasm. "And the variety! It is one of man's greatest achievements."

Abou found this response strange. "Really? I would have thought it was mathematics or something like that."

"Well, this is all subjective, you realize. Certainly your mathematics is wonderful, albeit deficient in showing you all the aspects of the universe, but what I find so extraordinary is your art, music, literature, and most certainly the cuisine you've developed."

"Do you read a great deal?"

Cohen nodded and smiled. "And we watch TV, listen to radio. We try to understand all human achievements, Abou, so we involve ourselves."

"I enjoy reading," Abou replied.

"We know."

"It is a source of great satisfaction to know things, isn't it?" Abou hesitated for a moment before adding an additional thought. "I would really enjoy sharing some of your information with my friends."

Cohen grinned. "If I were you, I'd go easy on that, and certainly I wouldn't mention me for now." He hesitated before continuing. "In general, people haven't progressed enough to assimilate all this information, even in the so-called "advanced" nations. Why, in America 90 percent believe in heaven, and 66 percent believe in the devil. The only people who have the slightest clue as to what's going on are the 72 percent who believe in angels. They, of course, are correct.

"Remember that I told you how this universe got started, by a massive explosion, and that matter formed, galaxies popped up, stars were created, planets congealed, moons developed, and all this took billions and billions of years?"

"Yes."

"Well, 65 percent of Americans believe this is untrue, that there was no 'big bang', as it is called. I think, if you were to spread the message around here, the figure would even be higher. Most people, for reasons we aren't clear about, seem to resist this explanation."

Abou didn't tell him how uncomfortable *he* was with that explanation. Instead, he said, "It isn't surprising. Americans are extraordinarily gullible. I found them in many ways a wonderful people, but on certain subjects they seemed ferociously stupid, as well as strangely artless."

"Point taken," Cohen replied with a nod, "but Americans aren't that much different from the rest of the population. And telling the truth can be rather uncomfortable in a world of fanatic idealists. Remember, you are surrounded by fundamentalists here, which seems to be a name for anyone who believes his views should prevail at the expense of all others. I think it would be unwise to broadcast our little chats. Better to act on your wisdom than to voice it."

"Well," Abou replied, adjusting his covers as he thought about all this. "Increased fecundity and fire," he murmured. "Was there anything else of this magnitude?" He had been reading that last word for years and finally could try it out.

"Well, not really," Cohen replied casually, flicking a speck of dust from his sleeve. When he saw Abou watching him, he grinned self-consciously, then added quickly, "Well, let me re-phrase that. Nothing as *fundamental* as those two. But later you had the development of tools, which was a biggie, and later there was mathematics and printing. All these conventions were immensely important, like the Scotch boiler and Scotch whiskey."

Abou relaxed, putting his hands behind his head and lean-ing back. "It's almost as if there were a grand plan for it all."

Cohen giggled. "A common human fallacy. People witness three random events in a row and all of a sudden they see a cosmic plan. Believe me, it was a combination of chance and a certain craftiness on the part of your forebears. You've got to remember, they were a tad brighter than other pongids."

"The what?" Abou questioned.

"Oh, you know. All those other fellows jumping around in trees. Early chimps, gorillas, whatever."

"Chance," Abou muttered.

"That English fellow Chaucer had it about right six hun-dred years ago," Cohen replied. "He knew that existence was all luck, but nobody took him too seriously. Now that I think about it, he didn't take himself too seriously, either. I mean, everyone knows he's a great writer and all that, but few con-sider him the most profound thinker ever. Even Einstein couldn't believe existence was a crapshoot."

Abou knew the game of craps from America, but he was sure Cohen was well aware how much he disapproved of gambling and had used the analogy to annoy him. "And what about evil in this world of chance?" Abou asked with disdain.

Cohen shrugged. "Evil is nothing more than bad luck or, if you prefer, bad happenstance. That's the way things are, just as Chaucer saw it. No great plan. Part of the charm of you humans is your belief that there will always be more to come. I suspect when your sun begins to collapse into a white dwarf and there are only two people left on earth, one will turn to the other and ask, 'What's next?'

"Collapse?" Abou questioned. "You mean our world will end?"

"Well, actually it's a phase with your sun becoming concentrated cold matter." Cohen replied. "The very structure of the universe is impermanence."

"And people?"

"Ah, yes, people," Cohen replied, considering his answer. "I don't wish to shock you, Abou, but your sun is tucked away in this obscure corner of the universe, really a backwater. I know how important human life is to you, but the very fact you die should tell you something. The whole point of the universe seems to be flux, change."

"How long do we have?"

Cohen pursed his lips. "Several billion years, give or take. That's not to say human life will last that long. Zipping along as you are, chewing up this and that, you'll be lucky to last to your year 3000."

"You are very pessimistic," Abou replied, "but I must admit that your billion-year estimate isn't very threatening to my family personally."

Cohen grinned. "You aren't under any real time pressure here," he said and then added, "Look, I have to dash off. I have another assignment. Are you going to be okay with your move?"

Abou shrugged. "I feel as if I am deserting my daughter and her children, but I know that's nonsense. It isn't as if I *wanted* to move from the orchard. I'll be all right. Will I see you again?"

Cohen threw his arms wide. "Of course, my friend. As soon as I get my other assignments squared away, I'll be back. To tell you the truth, I've come to really enjoy our natter."

"As have I," Abou replied and fell into a deep sleep.

The Sixth Day

ABOU SLEPT BETTER that night than he had in years. He awoke feeling fully rested, ready for the day, eager for human contact, and especially looking forward to the children's visit to his tent on the bank parking lot. His mind swirled with ideas as he washed his teeth in the bank's men's room and then showered. He had seldom showered since returning from America, and secretly it was one of the real pleasures of Western society he missed most, next to oranges. Middle Eastern oranges were sour and skimpy compared to the juicy fruit of California and Florida. Once, in a group of unemployed men whose main entertainment was denouncing the United States, he remarked casually that America had wonderful fruit. The men stopped and looked at him suspiciously. Saying anything good about the West, especially the United States, was frowned on, but one of them said, "Your mind was turned to mush by your stay in that abomination of a country, Abou. There is nothing good to say about it!" Abou still secretly missed the California oranges, but now he kept it to himself.

Emerging from the back of the bank, he found Sophia waiting for him with two large containers of coffee and baby Leila in her arms.

"I have come to inspect your new tent site," she said, as they walked side by side to the entrance. "I have just taken Akbar to school. He was the center of attention yesterday when some of the children decided to visit your tent after school and then told their playmates. When he came home, he could talk of nothing else, but his chatter seemed to annoy his father. He heard in the marketplace that you had moved to the bank site and it seemed to anger him, although I am not sure why."

"Perhaps he thinks I passed up a wonderful opportunity not taking the room he found for me," Abou suggested, holding a tassel over the baby, who grinned and attempted to bat at it.

"Are you happy here?" Sophia asked, taking a deep draft of coffee.

Abou smiled at her. "I miss you and the children. I feel I have deserted you."

Sophia looked shocked. "But you haven't. Yasser forced you away! I am so sorry, Papa."

"It is not your doing, my daughter," he replied gently, "and I have running water and a lavatory, rare luxuries for an old man such as me."

"Akbar wishes to come with the children this afternoon," Sophia said. "He was afraid to ask his father, so he asked me on the way to school."

"He certainly can," Abou said with great happiness. "He knows how I enjoy talking with him about his day. Will Yasser object?"

"Probably," Sophia replied, "but I will talk to him. Now that you have moved from the orchard, he is angrier than before.

But I will tell him others will talk if he keeps Akbar away. He always worries what others say about him."

"He is a troubled man," Abou said, sipping his coffee and looking at the baby, who was beginning to fret. "Perhaps his business isn't doing well and he's worried."

"He says nothing to me about his business," Sophia replied, turning away and uncovering herself so that her baby could suckle. "She needs her breakfast."

Abou grimaced, feeling uncomfortable with his daughter nursing her infant in his presence, but at the same time somehow liking the idea that she felt she could. He averted his eyes as any decent Moslem man would, although there was absolutely nothing to see.

Abou finished his coffee. It was cold but still quite good. "I will eat lunch with Hamid, Ammon, and Absollah today."

"You eat with them every day," Sophia reminded him. The baby had fallen asleep. Sophia rearranged her gown. "What is so different about today?"

"I have plans," Abou replied. "The children enjoyed their visit to my tent yesterday. I should have more children, including Akbar, this afternoon. I must begin to think of a program for them. That is what I want to discuss with my friends."

Sophia smiled and touched his hand. "And you should. You are doing a very important thing here, explaining the herder's ways to these children. Our ancient customs would be lost forever if it weren't for people like you." As an afterthought, she added, "Have you ever thought of how much lore *has* been lost? Even in tribes where stories were handed down with care, details must have been left out, gone forever. We can be thankful for books, so our children will have some record."

"And computers," Abou reminded her. "Everyone will have access to so much knowledge."

"I would like Akbar to attend university. I would like him to be an engineer."

Abou touched her hand. "Perhaps he will. And the baby? Do you want an education for her?"

"It is almost too much to ask," Sophia replied in a whisper, as if someone were listening outside the tent, "but yes, I would like her also to attend university. More and more women are, you know. Every child should have a richer life than his or her parents."

"It is a good thing. We need so many educated people to make our country strong. Doctors, scientists, engineers, businesspeople . . ."

"Not lawyers?" She grinned at him.

Abou shrugged. "Perhaps we have enough lawyers. They seem to create as many disputes as they settle."

"But bloodless," she reminded him. "Our ancient ways of settling disputes must end. Court decisions are better than feuds."

Abou was impressed with his daughter's insights. He realized he had never seriously thought of her as having a cognitive mind. In many ways he, too, was still mired in the old culture.

"I shall leave you to your tasks," Sophia said as she rose. "I am not happy you have moved your tent, but I am very happy that you have found this project. And I want you close to us. It was wrong of my husband to try to send you to a distant town."

Abou saluted his daughter and watched her move across the lawn in front of his tent. She had suddenly become unique. Still his beloved daughter, of course, but a new person who thought and acted independently of him and her husband. He suddenly felt very proud of his Sophia. Certainly, he decided, his contact with Cohen was changing him. . . .

It was just after noon prayer when Abou walked with Absollah across the square to the Camel's Hump. Ammon and Hamid were already at a table sorting flyers.

"My friends!" Abou exclaimed. "Still busy?" He was secretly disappointed that all the flyers had not been distributed as yet, and that he had managed to miss midday devotions again.

"We have just returned," Hamid said happily. "As his business was slow, Ammon left his shop in the care of his wife and helped me circulate these to all the schools, and he has given them to merchants to hand out to customers. You are going to be a very busy man, Abou. I have only a few stops this afternoon and everyone will know of your project!"

They ordered lunch and ate with relish, for they were busy men with good appetites. Once the coffee was served, Absollah lighted one of his long Egyptian cigarettes, which he smoked with obvious enjoyment. Abou cleared his throat, a sign to the others that he had something he thought to be important. "I have been thinking about yesterday, and I have decided that the children may become bored with my simple stories about the life of a herdsman. In America there is a ubiquitous restaurant called McDonald's which often has a play area for children attached to it. What if we could have such a place where the children could come and play, and then listen a little while to an old man?"

Absollah beamed. "What a splendid idea! The bank's back lot has been dreary far too long. We will turn it into a children's playground, where a wise man can impart his learning but children can also play. I will call this very afternoon and see if I can order some play equipment. Of course, we would need a little sign saying it was donated by the bank."

Abou was pleased with the ready acceptance of his first idea. Everyone was smiling at him around the table. He carefully cleared his throat. "It also occurred to me that my tales of ancient times might not be exactly what the children need, that the advice of others might be more useful. Perhaps we could find an engineer, a banker," (a wink at Absollah) "a doctor, and maybe even a policeman to tell the children about their work. And I think we should ask the children if their parents would come to talk to the whole group, too."

Ammon simply gaped. "Would the children be interested?" he finally asked.

"I think so," Abou replied. "This idea that you work only at what your father worked at, and his father too, needs change. Children should have many avenues to explore."

"All those people coming to participate," Absollah murmured. "It would be wonderful for . . ." His voice faded, but they added the word "business" in their minds.

"Perhaps I could explain what a postman does," Hamid offered. "I am not a postman, but I know what they do."

"Fine," Abou replied. "And perhaps you could circulate the names of the guest speakers to the schools."

"I would be honored," Hamid looked greatly pleased.

Absollah spoke again. "It is a great idea, Abou. I would like to think about it some more and talk to some other businessmen about it. Perhaps we could broaden the program by inviting them to participate and help with the funding. Maybe we could even offer the little ones some food, if their parents didn't object."

"I could give a free haircut a day and show them how to cut hair," Ammon offered.

"Children hate haircuts," Hamid observed. "They always cry."

"Not in my shop. I give them dates and sweets sometimes."

Hamid laughed. "It is the dates they love, not your haircuts."

"Gentlemen. Gentlemen," Abou intervened. "All children love dates, as well as candy, and I'm sure they all love Ammon's haircuts. We will certainly find out if he offers to cut hair free and someone volunteers, won't we?"

Absollah was so excited he rushed off after paying the bill, forgetting his usual parting amenities.

"I believe you have managed to turn our banker into a flappable duffer in one lunch." Ammon was grinning from ear to ear.

"Oh, it isn't that bad," Abou observed, finishing his coffee. "He is just a bit excited. I must admit I was too as I thought of some of these ideas. My grandson is to visit me this afternoon. That makes me very proud."

"As it should," Hamid concurred. He rose and shouldered his pack. "I shall continue my rounds, my friend. Thank you for trusting me with such an important task."

Ammon said he had to return to his shop. In the excitement of the previous few days, he claimed his trade had suffered from his absence and he found himself a bit short of dinars. Actually, Abou had noticed no change in his business, which was sluggish at best, but he said nothing to his friend, not wanting to insult him or pry. Abou made his way to the market, where he purchased a large bucket of dates. The talk of haircuts and dates had given him the idea that the children might enjoy a taste of the fruit that afternoon.

The children began arriving just after three and continued filling the small lot until four. Abou was delighted with the crowd, as was Akbar, who sat next to his grandfather and glowed in the limelight. Abou told the children about goats, their eating habits, how they cared for their young, and even gave a passable imitation of a male goat looking for his dinner or something else. He didn't go into that "something else", but several of the older boys snickered and nodded knowingly.

The girls hung back at the edge of the crowd listening, but not asking any questions. Abou tried to draw them out, but they were timid with so many boys about. But the dates, which Absollah supplied, were welcomed by all. Hamid, who arrived a bit late, expounded on the mail and, to Abou's surprise, was quite eloquent about how necessary and important communication was between humans.

"Weren't you lonely sitting out there with your goats all the time?" one little boy with soulful eyes asked Abou.

Abou hesitated. "Yes, I was," he admitted. "I wanted to stay in my village and play with the other children and go to the occasional film, which was a great treat in those days. I knew I had to help my father, but I wanted more than sitting with goats on a hillside. My father taught me to read and supplied me books to keep me occupied, and now I realize how wonderful those days were."

"Did you eat your goats?" another boy asked.

"Oh, yes," Abou admitted, "but their milk was so rich and the cheese so wonderful that we kept them alive as long as we could. But we wasted nothing. We were very poor and had to use the whole animal."

Parents began arriving to take their children home, but not before Ammon, who had arrived just moments before, pointed out that the Americans called their children "kids", as if they were baby goats. This, for some reason, caused great glee, and the children trooped off calling each other "kid" just like the Americans did. "Hey, there, kid," and "What's for dinner, kid?" and "How many kids in your family?"

Abou sat before his tent holding Akbar on his knee, and when Sophia arrived, she asked her son how he had enjoyed his afternoon.

"Grandpa told everyone funny stories, and Hamid told us about the post, and Ammon, the barber, told us that the Americans call their children kids, as if they were goats."

"They must love goats very much to use their name for their children," Sophia observed.

Abou frowned. "Actually I never saw a goat in America, and it was very difficult to get goat meat, although they had wonderful, tender sheep."

When she and little Akbar had gone, Hamid and Ammon helped Abou clean up, although the children had been very careful and had dropped almost nothing.

"They are good children," Ammon said. "I wish mine had been as well mannered."

"Your children are fine, as are your grandchildren," Hamid replied, a tad out of sorts, for he had never married and had no offspring.

Ammon nodded good-naturedly. "I suppose, but the grandchildren never seemed as interested in things as these children were this afternoon. All they want to do is watch TV and play games on small computerized machines. But I'll see if they want to join us." It was well-known that Ammon was a generous father and grandfather, who bought his offspring many expensive gifts.

They walked Ammon half the way to his house and then Abou and Hamid stopped for a light supper.

"I thought you were good with the children today," Abou said.

"I wanted to be a teacher, but there was no money for education in my family." He laughed suddenly. "There was no money for food either, for that matter."

"Do you ever visit your village?"

Hamid shrugged. "Not for many years. I have one remaining brother and a sister who married a well digger. He's not very successful, but they ask him to search for water in straight lines so that they can use his holes to build fences after he's gone." Hamid looked down at the dust his sandals caused as he moved them under the table. "I have been thinking about my home of late. When we were young, it seemed so right to fight the Jews. They came and took our land. We swore we would push them into the sea. How foolish we were to think we could defeat them so easily."

Abou nodded. "It is a shame we couldn't have found a better way. The Jews are to be pitied for what they have suffered, and they are an energetic people who do wonders with the land."

Hamid looked at his friend sharply. "You may be right, Abou, but we should be careful talking like that."

Abou shrugged. "We could have shared Jerusalem."

"Perhaps," Hamid muttered, looking about to determine if anyone was listening. "Certainly things have not worked out well for us as it is, but people of different faiths do not live comfortably together."

"You may be right about that. Maybe we were better off when we were small tribes meeting each other casually every few years in some far corner of the desert. We are too crowded in this little land."

"Were we ever like that?"

Abou flushed. He knew he was drawing inference from what Cohen had said to him. "So I have been told," he added lamely.

Hamid relaxed. "You read too much, my friend. I am usually satisfied with my mail. Dreaming of where it is from is enough for me."

The Sixth Darkfall

ABOU DRIFTED OFF QUICKLY, but Cohen was late arriving and seemed oddly out of sorts. Abou offered him tea, which the angel took gratefully. He had on his new checkered suit, but it was now looking a little worse for wear, like the white one.

"We have so little power," he complained. "We can only suggest and cajole, and most humans, although respectful, really do what they want. It's most discouraging."

"I'm sorry," Abou replied. "Is there anything I can do?"

"Do? How could *you* do anything? I can't accomplish a thing and you expect to do better?" Cohen snapped.

"For you, I meant."

Cohen looked chagrined. "How tacky of me. What you don't need is an ill-tempered angel. I apologize, Abou. I shouldn't have snapped at you, but I visited the most difficult man today."

"From what country?"

"Oh, America."

"Do I know of him?"

Cohen shrugged. "Helms is his name."

"He rejected your entreaties?"

"He asked me if I was a Democrat! He was absolutely insulting. He kept insisting I had been sent by some subversive organization. Can you imagine an angel who is a member of a political party? How droll."

"Gracious," Abou replied mildly.

Cohen slumped on his perch. "It's so frustrating," he said with a sigh. "I mean, humans have unbelievable variations of responses. Whole different cultures develop, as well as languages and political forms. It's just fascinating what you have done over the last fifty thousand years. Simply terrific! But then you meet somebody like this senator and you wonder . . ."

Abou was anxious to tell Cohen about the children, but he didn't want to interrupt. Finally, he said, "I met with the children today and we had a wonderful time."

"Oh, yes, I watched you for a while during a roll call vote. It was great to see the children so interested. I must say, Abou, you are blossoming. Perhaps you will head the list yet."

Abou shrugged. "It doesn't matter really. I was being selfish. Former President Carter certainly has done many beneficial works."

Cohen grinned. "I would say that, yes! He, like you, is a good man, and you'd be surprised how many good people there are in this world. Kindly people who genuinely want to help others. It is most gratifying to watch them doing their deeds. Most gratifying!"

"But there are those who seem bent on harming others," Abou observed and immediately wanted to retract his words.

Cohen gave a great sigh. "Sadly, a great many. We must talk someday about why some people behave so well and others are as mean as a skunk. And the most frightening aspect of hate is that you humans have developed such remarkable tools of destruction." Cohen sat back, a bit more relaxed, and sipped his tea. "If you think that all this technology started with the simple stone weapon, then human destruction began about two and a half million years ago. I mentioned the poor Neanderthals. They were distinct but similar to you. But now they're gone. Very sad, in a way. They were interesting, gentle brutes who showed great promise."

"They had tools?"

"Oh, yes. Quite sophisticated. Fire-hardened spears five hundred thousand years ago. Really advanced stuff for the time. State-of-the-art."

"I don't understand why spears and stones were so important," Abou remarked. "They seem too primitive."

"Exactly," Cohen replied. "But you kept improving them. I mean it took time, lots of time, and, on top of that, you developed other uses for your weapons, but you did manage to improve them over time, and that's what is so important. And the development of adventitious uses of these devices was just extraordinary. The use of the spear for both attack and defense was interesting, as was the first stone knife, which could be used to kill a fellow human and wound or kill an animal, as well as to butcher and skin a beast. In fact, flint knives were first used to cut meat and dress skins, but other uses soon came to mind."

Abou laughed. "It just shows how versatile we are."

Cohen studied Abou for a moment, then responded gently, "Humanoids were destined, if I may use that word, for extinction. They were the most fragile of a vulnerable lot, with no natural protective devices, expelled from the haven of the forest, forced to live on whatever they could garner—from acorns to small rodents. When we looked at them early on, we thought they were goners, but what we misjudged was their will to survive and their adaptability. Very early on, you recognized your most dangerous enemy wasn't other animals or the natural elements, although they took their toll, but your fellow man, and you've been butchering each other ever since. It was one thing to meet a tiger who wanted supper, but when meeting another human, you met an enemy who possessed arms, food, women, furs, shelter, and hunting grounds, and these were worth killing for."

"And when I was designated as one who loved his fellow man?" Abou asked. "Does that mean only that I wanted to kill my fellow man a little less than others?"

Cohen smiled. "You're a rare one, Abou. You really don't seem to want to hurt anybody."

"I have hated others!" Abou objected.

"Oh, yes, but not to the point of eliminating them or even wishing them dead. You are not a vindictive soul, Abou."

"Am I normal?"

Cohen considered this. "No, I would say not. Not in this world. Human history is replete with atrocities against others. Maybe all this nation against nation, race against race, religion against religion, is just an excuse to secure a stable food source for yourself and your kin, but we suspect there is more going on than that."

"What about rape? I have read that dreadful behavior occurs in every war." Abou was shaking his head.

"Ah, rape! Such a primitive and dreary device to expand the gene pool. Really in bad taste, especially because humans seem so bent on expanding the pool voluntarily with extraordinary vigor. But boys will be boys and they do want to impregnate every female they meet. I suppose you wouldn't be such a successful species if you behaved better, but I must say that rape is one of your least attractive aspects."

"I find it painful to hear of these incidents," Abou replied thoughtfully. "Sometimes I think I understand very little about the people around me," he admitted.

"Such as?" Cohen asked.

Abou nodded absently. "I never cared to hunt," he murmured, thinking back on his boyhood. "Others found great satisfaction in tracking animals all night. It simply disgusted me, killing just for sport, and not even hungry. I never understood it."

"Ah, well," Cohen replied with a sigh. "Now you're talking about another trait embedded in the psyche of man. The hunt! Once he had a few weapons, the hunt was everything. And not only the hunt for food, but the hunt for women. Did you know they recently resumed bride-stealing in Kazakhstan?"

"But women hunt too, in a way," Abou replied. "Not here, of course, where we keep our women covered and secluded to prevent such behavior, but in New York, I saw women return smiles, and I drove them to bars to meet and drink with men."

"Sinful, isn't it?" Cohen said with a grin. "In Cairo, they also have wonderful meeting places where dancing women can be viewed and worse."

"I have heard," Abou admitted, "there were such places in Istanbul, but I never visited one while I worked there."

Cohen eyed him skeptically, one eyebrow arched.

"Well, once, with my fellow dockworkers, to show I was not a prude," Abou admitted.

"I know," Cohen nodded. "But that's a form of hunting, too, Abou. Bands of hunters would go out searching for food, come upon another tribe, attack them if they had the advantage, and take their women, as well as their food. They satisfy their need for fat and marrow and expand their gene pool at the same time."

"Yes, I suppose you're right." Abou hesitated and then added, "I am always surprised how primitive we remain."

"Put it in perspective, dear friend. Sixty-five million years ago, the reptiles were dethroned by an asteroid and you mammals became the dominant creatures. You fellows have only been around for a *soupçon* of time, a few million years. I know that seems like a lot of time to you, but it isn't. You've really done wonders in a very short time."

"Do you think He is satisfied?" Abou asked with a crafty expression.

Cohen shrugged. "He? Oh, that anthropocentric crap again. Who knows? We certainly aren't privy, if that's what you want to know." It surprised Abou that Cohen seemed irked by the question.

"Certainly you must have some idea about Allah's will," Abou persisted.

"Not a clue, old chum," Cohen replied. "Not a bloody clue. It's as big a mystery to us as it is to you."

"Aren't you interested?"

"Certainly we are, and we're confused about it, too. This planet has taken some terrible hits—we thought life was finished for sure four or five times. And that last big one, the one that knocked the dinosaurs on their butts, wasn't the worst by any means. There was a whopper about 370 million years ago that made the earth look like a fried meatball, but life somehow managed to come back stronger than ever." Cohen hesitated, shrugged, and then added, "Besides, it *would* be nice to know who your employer is. This job security thing really bugs us."

Abou murmured, "You mean we'll be hit again?"

Cohen shrugged. "Hey, we don't know. Probably. Will it mean the end of man? We simply don't know. There's a lot of flying rock out there."

Abou was dejected. "I never thought my grandchildren and their children might someday not exist."

"Listen, I don't want to upset you," Cohen replied, "but you're feeling the old gene pool tugging at your heart-strings. Sometimes I forget who I'm talking to. It's like you're one of us."

"An angel? Oh, I don't think so."

Cohen smiled. "We have become kind of chummy, haven't we? I told you, no angel has ever chatted up a human like this before."

"Well . . . that's very flattering," Abou replied.

"Piffle! You know our conversations are the greatest. Who are you kidding?"

"Well, for me they have become insightful. When I asked about my status, I never imagined we would end up each night discussing the development of mankind."

Cohen suddenly held up his hand as if listening to an inner voice. "I have a long day tomorrow, old fellow. My appointment book is filled. I'm afraid we'll have to continue some other time." And with that abrupt, almost rude, farewell, he disappeared.

The Seventh Day

WHATEVER THE REASON for the angel's early departure, Abou was grateful the next morning. Sophia was at his tent just after dawn. She made small noises, a slight ululation in the back of her throat to express her distress. Abou came off his pallet and found a soft cushion for her. She was somewhat disheveled, a condition alien to Sophia, who prided herself on her neatness both when in public and, for that matter, when in private.

"I have no refreshments for you, my daughter," Abou whispered, kneeling in front of her.

She waved her hand, letting her veil drop, and he saw tears in the corners of her eyes. "Yasser was horrible, Father. Just horrible! He screamed about me bringing Akbar here yesterday afternoon. It was as if he were demented. I cannot describe how he behaved. The children were terribly upset."

"And you? Did he hurt you?"

Sophia looked down at the floor. "He beat me. He beat me for nothing."

Abou sat down on the floor, the wind taken out of him. "What did he say?"

"Only that I had not obtained his permission to bring Akbar here. Was I so wrong?"

Abou shook his head. "No, you weren't wrong. Akbar's visit was not the reason, I suspect, although I don't know what it is. He said nothing else?"

"Only that," she replied, "but he was in such a rage."

Abou considered his next words carefully. "Do you wish me to find you and the children a place to live away from him?"

Sophia looked at her father and then away, at the far side of the tent. "I have been a good wife, Father. I do not deserve such treatment. But it is a husband's right to correct his wife if he believes she has behaved improperly. No, if I were to take the children, he would just come and seize them, and you know they would be given to him."

Abou nodded at the truth of what she was saying. "Yasser may be mentally unbalanced. He has worries about his business, or so I hear."

Sophia looked at her father. "He tells me nothing of this, but he has always been . . . how shall I say it? Demanding. But last night went far beyond that." She shrugged. "He is the father of my children."

"That is not an answer, Sophia. In a good marriage, affection grows over the years."

"Is that how you felt for Mother?" Her voice was almost wistful.

"Your mother was my whole world, my daughter," he replied. "She made my life worth living. My great sadness was that I was away from her for all those years. There was no work here, and I didn't want us to live in poverty, but so many years were lost. Her greatest joy was still being able to have you."

"My birth killed her."

"But she felt she had been blessed. She was so happy those months as she carried you. She seemed to glow from within. It was a wonderful time for me."

"I only wish Yasser thought of me like that."

"He should," Abou assured her. "You are a wonderful creature who has given him two beautiful children, more than any man could ask. He should feel blessed in this marriage."

Sophia looked away. "If only he did," she murmured and rose. "I should not trouble you with my problems. I will return to my house and feed him and get Akbar ready for school." She stood with the ease of youth, without the creaking of bones and awkwardness of limb that Abou experienced.

"Are you sure, my daughter? I do not like the thought of you being beaten."

She shrugged. "He is my husband," she said, and with that disappeared through the tent's flap into the early dawn.

For Abou, sleep was finished. He lay on his thin mattress looking up at the last stars of the night, faint in the breaking light. He wished for Cohen to appear to discuss this problem, but he knew this wish was absurd. He should be turning to his friends for counsel, but he also knew exactly what they would say. It *was* the right of a husband to chastise his wife. Sophia was wrong in not seeking Yasser's permission, although Abou secretly never quite understood when a wife was supposed to know that permission was needed in their world of arbitrary rules and capricious dicta.

When he heard movement inside the bank, Abou rose and dispatched his early morning necessaries quickly, even bathing again in the shower, for he wanted to be clean for the children. Then he hurried across the bazaar, stopping to watch the smaller vendors setting up their stalls. Those with stores in the buildings along the end of the market could arrive later, remove the window guards, and open for business, but the less successful hauled their goods to the square early each morning, carefully setting their merchandise out and then sitting in the shade all day, protected from the sun by a small scrap of canvas.

Abou wished to catch Absollah on his way to the bank, to inquire if the play equipment had been ordered and, if so, when it would be delivered. He imagined a playground around his tent with children laughing and playing in the late afternoon, with storytellers spinning tales and perhaps tutors helping them with their studies.

Absollah marched importantly across the square, a huge, fixed smile on his face as he greeted friends, customers, even strangers. When he saw Abou, his expression changed. The false, fixed smile of the businessman was replaced by the warm gaze of a friend.

"Ah, Abou, you are up early this day. If I were you, I would stay abed and get enough rest for the afternoon onslaught."

"I had to know about the play equipment you were going to order."

Absollah stroked his mustache. "Today, my friend! It will be delivered this very morning. By three there will be a wonderful playground behind the bank. I only hope the parents appreciate the tremendous expense the bank has incurred for their children's pleasure."

"Oh, they will! They will!" Abou exclaimed, delighted with the news. "This is the most exciting thing I have done since the birth of my Sophia!"

Absollah stopped on the steps of the bank and looked deeply into Abou's eyes. "You are a good man, Abou. The children are very lucky to have such dedication. Go with Allah, my friend!"

In the area behind the bank, Abou and Hamid, whom he met at the post office, found four men assembling swings, climbing bars, and a gigantic slide that would accommodate two children abreast, or aseat. Abou watched with delight as the structures took form. He wondered if Absollah would allow him to keep a few goats at the far end of the lot so the children could come to know these animals as he had learned about them. And he would explain how cheaply the animals could be purchased now that the Israelis had begun to push the last herders off grazing land near the river Jordan.

AFTER NOON PRAYER, Abou and Hamid ate their lunch. Absollah didn't join them, and Ammon dashed by, saying he had an appointment. Abou nodded, waved, and began to read some of Hamid's mail aloud. Usually Abou found the mail, if not depressing, at least boring, but today Hamid had two letters, both in French, offering new magazines on the politics of the Middle East. It was strange that they would both come the same day, but there they were, one pro-Arab, the other sympathetic to the Jewish state. Abou's French wasn't the best. In fact, it was almost nonexistent, but he tried to translate the letters for his friend as best he could.

"Tear that one up!" Hamid blurted out, pointing to the advertisement sympathetic to the Jews. "If we are found with that document in our possession, we will be stoned. Please, give it to me. I will destroy it immediately."

Abou held the letter away from Hamid's grasp. "The editor is a man named Kareem, hardly a Jewish name."

"Who can tell?" Hamid replied. "Look at you, Abou. You have that cursed *Ben* in your name."

Abou felt too good to be annoyed by Hamid's remark. "It means no more than I am the son of Adam, as are we all. A little paternal whimsy, I suspect."

"I know, I know," Hamid replied. "But it is dangerous, Abou, to joke about such documents. You are only curious about the writers, but believe me, my friend, possession of that letter will not be viewed in a kindly fashion. These are perilous times."

"I suppose," Abou admitted, "but it seems sad that we can't look into the minds and hearts of our enemies and read them, too."

"For you," Hamid snapped, "but just remember it is my name on that letter. I wish to have it."

"Well, at least you can keep one letter," Abou answered, handing the remaining missive to his friend. "Not as exciting as the other, but safer, I suppose."

Hamid hurriedly stuffed the offending letter into his cowl, then folded the other carefully and put it in his satchel. "Much."

"Come, let us return to the bank," Abou said. "We have a busy few hours before the children arrive."

They walked silently across the marketplace, avoiding the shoppers hurrying here and there and the strident merchants hawking their goods. "We all play the simpleton at times, Hamid," Abou murmured to his friend, who looked at him with interest. "I read but don't discuss for fear of offending. I want so much to ask questions, but I dare not. I suspect you are the same."

"So many things," Hamid agreed. "But who is there to ask?"

Once the two friends returned to Abou's tent, Hamid took his leaflets and struck out toward the west end of the village. Abou sat in the shade and ruminated. He wanted to strike a balance between what interested children and what they should know, and it was difficult to decide what was important but boring and what was unimportant but interesting. He felt safe with the general area of animals, specifically the goats, as well as the stars and how to read them, and certain occupations, although this last was fraught with danger. Accounting could be dull, as was history, and mathematics seemed to be anathema to everyone except a chosen few. Absollah, for instance, had loved math in school. While others suffered, he shone, dedicated to solutions, those perfect solutions that pleased him so.

Hamid returned at a little after three with a rather long face and a dejected demeanor. "The merchants weren't willing to hand out our leaflets. They seemed reluctant, although a few took them and promised to give them to customers."

"Well, no matter," Abou replied, feeling the elation returning. "The children are what matters. It will be a deluge, if yesterday was any example."

But the deluge never came. Instead, three little girls appeared at the corner of the building and stared at them.

Abou waved them over. "Come! Play on the slides. Use the swings. They are for you."

"Where are the boys?" the tallest girl asked.

"I don't know," Abou replied. "I thought they liked it yesterday."

"They did," the smallest girl replied. "My brother and his friend said it was great fun."

Abou nodded. "He must have been kept in school this afternoon."

"No, he went home. My father came to the school and told him to go home immediately, not to stop here."

"But not you?" Abou asked. "You didn't have to go home?"

"My father seldom thinks of me," she replied with a shrug and went to the swing. She was joined by the two others, all delighted to have the gym equipment to themselves.

Abou and Hamid sat on their small stools and watched the three girls swing, then go to the slide, and then use the seesaw and finally the jungle bars, where they climbed like little monkeys.

"Are you interested in the stars, girls?" Abou asked.

The three nodded, so he showed them a chart he had made up of the night sky.

"Tonight you must find the north star," he said.

They agreed, flattered that they had been given an assignment.

When Absollah emerged from the rear door of the bank, he looked at his watch and said to the girls, "Time for you to go home and help your mothers with the preparation of the family supper. Don't want to disappoint your father or brothers, do you?"

They scattered like chaff in the wind, racing homeward.

"We must talk," Absollah said, standing before the two seated men.

Abou knew something was wrong. "Shall we go to the Camel's Hump?"

Absollah looked from right to left. "No, it would be better if we talked inside the tent."

Inside, in a low voice, he said, "Yasser has been very busy today. He has spent the whole day spreading terrible rumors. I began getting calls this morning from customers, but I waited to see if the children came anyway." He hesitated and looked up at Abou. "Banking is difficult enough in this climate. Bankers are necessary but often detested because we won't lend money when it is really needed, and we

112

charge interest, which some think is against Allah's will. The holy men would love nothing better than to have us outlawed, but we are needed for commerce, so we are tolerated, but . . . but we hang by a delicate thread, my old friend. You understand that."

"I do," Abou replied. "But what is it that Yasser has said?"

Absollah looked away. In a thin voice, barely audible, he replied, "That he was forced to ask you to leave his house because of his son."

Both Hamid and Abou were momentarily struck dumb. Hamid finally blustered, "And he was believed?"

Absollah shrugged. "Everyone assumed he meant unwanted attention to the boy."

"Everyone assumed," Abou repeated. "Nobody forced Yasser to be more explicit. He's allowed to defame me with words too vague to be called an allusion."

"It is the way with these rumors," Absollah agreed. "He said he was too embarrassed, too hurt, to say more."

"And you, my friend? When you heard these words, what did you say?"

Absollah spread his hands. "These are my customers, Abou. They know we have known each other for years. I could say nothing."

"Nothing!" Hamid almost shouted. "Why is that, you scoundrel? You know this accusation is not true. We all know Abou. He is too decent for such acts!"

"Poor Sophia. Poor Akbar," Abou murmured. "To live with this abomination is beyond the pale."

"Is that why none of the children appeared today?" Hamid asked.

"The girls came," Abou said in a faint voice. "They had nothing to fear."

"Abou, please," Absollah pleaded. "This will pass. But in the meantime, I . . ." He stopped, unable to finish his thought.

"In the meantime?"

"It is damaging the bank," Absollah responded, looking away. "I must ask you to move from your tent, Abou. At least until this matter is forgotten."

Abou looked at his childhood friend. He could remember sitting next to Absollah listening to the imam's lessons. They had played together in the marketplace and the alleys. Once, only once, they stole an orange from an old vendor. Abou looked at the face of his friend but saw nothing but impassive determination.

"So be it. I will make other arrangements in the morning."

Absollah stood. "Good. I am sorry, my friend. I think this matter will be forgotten within a day or two, but who knows?"

"And the children?" Abou asked.

Absollah looked about him. "The idea is still valid. Our customers like the idea. I hope to find somebody else to carry on tomorrow." As Absollah turned to the tent's opening, Abou asked, "One question, Absollah. Do you know how much money I have in my savings?"

"American?" Absollah responded, his eyes crafty.

Abou nodded.

Absollah glanced at Hamid, shrugged, and said, "About sixteen thousand." He hesitated, deciding that a protest against a withdrawal would be in poor taste, even for a banker. "Goodbye then," he said and slipped out of the tent.

"What will you do, Abou?"

Abou shrugged. "Who knows? I will think about it tonight. Do you want to have a bit of supper with an old pervert?"

"It would be my pleasure," Hamid replied.

As they emerged from the tent, they were met by Ammon. Hamid blurted out Absollah's betrayal.

"Yasser has been busy today, Abou," Ammon said. "He has betrayed you. Such treachery is unforgivable."

"We are off for a light supper," Abou answered. "Will you join us?"

"My wife expects me home," Ammon replied, then thought again, "but I will have coffee with you. A man accused of buggery must have support."

Abou grinned. "I should be flattered that people think I am capable, given my age."

At the Camel's Hump, other customers stared and whispered, but the waiter took their order without incident. A table of local merchants hurriedly paid and left.

"What is your next step?" Ammon asked, sipping his coffee with relish and smiling at acquaintances around the room. They rapidly looked away.

Abou felt a warmness toward Ammon. It was almost as if he didn't need the townspeople's business to survive. "I want to talk this matter over with a friend."

Both Hamid and Ammon looked interested.

"A friend? Besides us?" Hamid asked.

Abou smiled. "I don't believe you know him. I consult with him now and then about my difficulties."

Ammon was intrigued. "Who is it, Abou? You must tell us."

Abou was a bit sheepish. "It sounds absurd, but you know that angel who visited me years ago in a dream?"

"Yes, we know," Hamid replied, having heard the story several times over.

Abou knew he had bored his friends before, but he felt he needed to discuss Cohen. "Well, about a week ago, I said a prayer and at the same time asked how I was doing."

"Asked who?" Ammon questioned.

"Why, Allah, of course," Abou replied. "And he sent this emissary, a strange fellow, but quite likable."

"He came to you in a dream?" Hamid asked, obviously excited.

"Yes," Abou responded. "In fact, he's been visiting me quite regularly, telling me amazing stories and giving me advice. It helps me sort out my thinking."

"I do that," Ammon replied. "Sometimes in my sleep I find a solution to a particularly difficult problem."

"Yes, something like that," Abou answered. "Anyway, I want to review all this with him tonight and see what we can work out."

"You are being visited by an angel?" Hamid repeated. At times it seemed he was a bit slow.

"Well, I don't know," Abou answered. "I could just be dreaming this. I mean, I am dreaming this, but I could just be making it up. It may not be a real angel. I can't really tell."

Ammon grinned. "Yasser better watch out. Anybody with an angel advising him will be dangerous to taunt."

"Don't josh," Abou warned. "And the angel made it quite clear he couldn't interfere directly in any problems. He just suggests solutions. He was quite clear about that. We must make our own way in the world."

"I suppose that's true enough," Ammon agreed. "Nothing seems to improve our lot except diligence and skullduggery."

Both Hamid and Abou laughed. "You are becoming quite the cynic," Abou said, clapping his friend on the back.

"I'm a realist," Ammon replied, "and I was thinking of Absollah."

"A great disappointment, but I suppose really not unexpected," Abou agreed.

Hamid ordered still another coffee. Ammon rose and stretched. "I must be getting home." He waved farewell, leaving coins on the table for his coffees.

Abou and Hamid sat enjoying the cool breeze from the desert. The other customers drifted away, apparently made uncomfortable by the presence of a scapegrace.

"It seems we are quite alone," Abou observed. The waiter was skulking in the doorway, casting malevolent eyes upon his two remaining customers.

"Do you think I might have another cup of coffee? I suspect dinner is out of the question," Hamid queried, looking at the shadowy shape and raising his hand timidly. The shape turned away, ignoring him. "Apparently not," Hamid murmured and turned his cup upside down in disgust.

"It will just keep you awake, my friend," Abou said and rose. "Come, let us walk together for a few minutes."

The streets were empty, but Abou and Hamid both kept eyes open for cutpurses. "When the streets are empty, I fear being set upon from a dark alley, and when they are filled, I fear being set upon by a passerby," Hamid murmured.

"Have you ever been robbed?" Abou asked.

"Not as yet," the pseudo-postman replied. "But it pays to be vigilant."

"It certainly does," Abou agreed. "Why don't I walk you to your door, Hamid?"

"That would be very kind of you, but who will walk with you once I have gone inside?"

"Allah will care for me."

"I wish I felt the same about Him. These muggers don't seem to be aware of Him."

Abou smiled softly. "It is strange how they can ignore Him with impunity, while we seem to suffer if we violate His will."

The Seventh Darkfall

ONCE BACK TO HIS TENT, Abou lay on his pallet and looked up the smoke hole at the stars. He wondered what the next day would bring.

Cohen sat on the chest, his usual perch, and examined his nails, which were always dirty, or so they appeared to Abou. Cohen was wearing his white suit again, but it looked a bit cleaner. "A bad day, old friend?" It was really a rhetorical question.

"It was," Abou agreed.

"That was very decent of you to tell those two that you wanted to talk it over with me, but I noticed you didn't identify me. Are you uncomfortable with my name?" Cohen grinned slyly.

"You know they wouldn't understand." Abou sighed. "In fact, I'm not sure I do. But that doesn't solve my problem. Yasser told abominable stories about me, and evidently everyone thinks them true, and no one knows he beat my daughter."

"Yes, he's a brute," Cohen agreed readily. "But he certainly knows how to manipulate language. We listened to him today and he never once said directly that you were corrupting Akbar. Subtle use of language. A long way from those screaming sounds made by your ancestors to alert the band to impending danger. You know velvet monkeys do the same thing today . . . use different sounds to identify different dangers?"

"And Yasser is my little velvet monkey screeching about what a danger I am?" Abou replied bitterly.

"No, no, you know that isn't what I mean," Cohen replied. "Your forebears have been talking for a couple million years, and even Yasser has learned the sophisticated use of speech as a weapon, as well as a mode of communication. It's like everything else you people do—the upside is you couldn't have survived without being able to speak to each other, or so it seems to us; on the downside, you've learned to use language for other reasons than simple communication, and that has become hurtful at times."

"What can I do?"

Cohen considered this for a moment. "Why did you ask Absollah how much money you had in his bank?"

"I was thinking of paying the taxes and casting Yasser out into the street, but my daughter, ever dutiful, would probably leave with him. I would have a place to stay, but she and the children wouldn't."

"There is little a father can do in your society." Cohen was talking slowly, as if thinking the matter through. "I think I mentioned to you that this male-domination thing is a rather late development. Not that humans haven't always been somewhat skewed toward males. I mean, it was the honcho who decided who got the best cut of meat, but it was fair in a way. Other hunters got their share, and they divided it between their women and children, so the most able and his kin got the most."

"But?"

"Well, once the men took over procuring the whole food supply, meat and veggies, so to speak, they became unbearable. They got other animals to do all the work. I mean, the ox and the buffalo really helped these guys out, but the men strutted around like they put food in the pot."

"You mentioned that before, but it doesn't help me."

"Did I?" Cohen thought for a moment. "Well, I had some point to make."

"Yasser has destroyed me with his vile words, and what can I say? That I love my grandchildren and would never do anything to harm them? That I find men being intimate with other men alien to my temperament? That I am too old to be a pedophile?"

"Ironic, isn't it," Cohen said with a slight nod. "So much damage done with words, and almost nothing to offset it."

"I wish we were all mute," Abou said bitterly. "Yasser used words to destroy me."

"Hey, you threatened him," Cohen said, opening his hands in an expansive gesture. "What can you expect?"

"Me? What could a seventy-odd-year-old man do to him?"

"Well, you could make him feel inadequate. He can't feed and house your daughter or their kids. He's scared, and you've got to admit it, you're a formidable old codger."

"Me?"

"You read a lot. You know a lot. He doesn't. You make him feel puny in front of his wife and children."

"I have been careful to avoid any unpleasantness," Abou replied.

"Yes, and you've done wonderfully, and if you were on the same level as he, there would be no problem. He had only one weapon and that was to slander you. He may not be bright, but he is a clever, malicious villain."

Abou looked down. He saw the teapot. Putting some kindling under the vessel, he lit it.

"Tea?"

"Yes, that would be nice. That delicious green tea, if you still have some."

Abou found his small supply of Japanese tea and carefully spooned it into the heating water. He never let the water boil. It gave the tea a bitter taste.

"Sugar?"

Cohen held up his hand. "No. No. I really must cut down. This weight problem is making getting about difficult."

"Is there nothing for me to do?" Abou asked, as they waited for the tea to steep.

Cohen nodded sagely. "Look, humans have free will, except for your genes, which are working all the time and trying to control your every action. But generally, you humans can do what you please, if you put your mind to it. Conflicts are developing, of course. Look at the dispute over abortion and contraception. Reproductive genes, if they had minds, would want to outlaw abortion and ban contraception, whereas many women want to choose the number of children they have. Free will versus genes. It's really quite a flap!"

"I wish Salah and I could have had more children," Abou replied wistfully.

"Of course you do! That's normal. You're supposed to want as many as you can have. Ten, twelve, eighteen. That's the way you were designed by good old nature, if you want to use that word. But remember, old buddy, you first had to go off and work in foreign lands to support your wife and children. You were concerned about how they were going to be fed."

"Sophia should have brothers to protect her," Abou added.

Cohen wasn't really listening. He was on a verbal binge. "And these people who blather on about the sanctity of life! As if life were sacred! It's like saying breathing is sacred, or death is sacred."

"I find the idea of killing babies repugnant," Abou replied in his sternest voice. He didn't like it when Cohen made these outrageous remarks.

"You're supposed to. Life, more life! That's your genes talking."

"Sophia is the dearest thing in the world to me, and the grandchildren are next." Abou was finding the angel suddenly annoying. He even considered waking up.

Cohen raised his arm in protest, ready to respond caustically, and then suddenly let it drop. "I'm sorry, Abou. Of course you do, and you provided for your daughter and you're trying to provide for your grandchildren. You can't do better than that."

The old man shrugged. For some reason, he didn't want to admit being offended by Cohen's last statements. "It is nothing. And I know what you are saying. It is detestable to see starving children, friendless children, children wandering the streets of cities stealing for food."

"Yes, you understand, don't you?" Cohen replied, his voice lower. "You have no idea how distressing it is to see what you have just described. You have enough sadness around here, but look at the rest of Africa, cities in South America, the slums in Manila. It's just so pitiful."

Abou was struck by Cohen's compassion, and he suddenly understood that Cohen's outrageous statements came from his detestation of the inhuman conditions that afflicted so many. "Are your associates so tenderhearted?"

"Oh, yes," Cohen replied. "Especially Gabe. He is very sensitive. It's so hard to explain. We have been privileged to witness this fantastic development over millions of years with so many interesting twists and turns, and now we see such extraordinary self-induced privations and sadness, at least in part. We would weep if we could."

"You can't weep?"

"For what purpose? We took our human form so as not to frighten you people, but there is no point in cluttering up our existence with superfluous accouterments. We have the shape we need and the faculties we must have to communicate. The rest isn't really de rigueur, as you can see."

"But if you can feel pity and compassion, shouldn't you have an outlet?" Abou insisted.

Cohen considered this carefully. "You know, you may have something there. I'm going to bring it up at our next staff meeting. But would you poor humans enjoy a multitude of blubbering angels?"

Abou was beginning to weary. "What about my problem? What can I do?"

Cohen shrugged. "Repressive society. I mean, if you attack Yasser, it will look like you're defending yourself. If you let his lies slide, most will think what he has said is true. A real pickle."

"That isn't very helpful, Cohen," Abou replied, using the angel's name for the first time. But oddly, the frailty of his advice made Abou feel closer to the celestial being.

"I know. I know. We're good at handing out simple advice. I mean, you shouldn't kill anybody, especially during their reproductive years, or unless they're about to do you in during your reproducing years. That is really simple stuff, but this false witness stuff is bad news."

Abou frowned. "What are older people to do? Kill themselves?"

"Well, to be frank, for the good of the species, recycling would be best. I can see why you might not like the idea, but protein is in short supply already. If you humans don't slow down your reproduction, you are going to have to consider using cadavers as an alternative food source. That, or have more of those starving children we were talking about."

Abou didn't care for the drift of the conversation. "I thought you liked me."

"Of course I like you. We all do," Cohen insisted, trying to understand. "Oh, there's nothing personal in this, Abou. When you die, we will miss you terribly."

"I see," Abou replied, hardly mollified.

"Look, Jonathan Swift alluded to the subject of starvation almost three hundred years ago," Cohen ruminated. "If I remember, he recommended eating babies because they were tender and succulent."

"This hardly helps me with my problem," Abou complained.

"That's true, and I'm sorry about that. I don't know what's going to happen about all these goings-on, as we can't see the future, but it doesn't look good, Abou. It just doesn't look good. Yasser, as despicable as he is, has all the cards just now."

"Then I am going for undisturbed sleep for the remainder of the night," Abou replied and pulled his robe over his head. He heard Cohen mutter, "I don't blame you," and then there was silence.

The Eighth Day

THE PROBLEM ABOUT his new living quarters was solved for Abou when Sophia arrived at the tent flap early the next morning with her two children in tow. At least Akbar was in tow. She carried the baby.

"What is it?" Abou asked, the sleep still in his eyes.

"My husband is a madman, father! He beat me again and threatened to kill all of us. I ran out of the house with the children. He will kill us!"

"He has beaten you before," Abou observed, "and you returned to him."

"This time it was far worse. And he chased after Akbar with a knife at one point."

Abou sat up. He had to urinate immediately. "Excuse me," he began, but Sophia interrupted him with, "I took no money or clothing. We will starve. He is insane. He said you had ruined his business by speaking of him in a derogatory fashion in the marketplace."

"I spoke of *him* in a derogatory fashion?" Abou muttered, retreating to the tent's opening, hoping to make it to the rear, where he could relieve himself.

"He said you said vile things about him!" she continued.

"Excuse me," Abou muttered, trying to edge out.

Sophia became indignant. "You don't want to be bothered with us, do you?"

"Please, Sophia, take pity. I am an old man. I cannot contain myself as I did when I was younger. I must go!"

He then ducked outside and fumbled with his clothing as he hurried around to the rear of the tent, freeing his member just in time to wet the earth. He looked up to find three little girls staring at him.

"Excuse me," he muttered and stuffed his penis away. "I meant no affront."

The threesome turned and, without a word to him or to one another, disappeared down the road.

Abou, shaking his head, sure his reputation was now completely in tatters, made his way back into the tent. Sophia was holding her children, all three crying.

"He will know you came here," Abou said. "We must get you to a safe place. I am leaving here today myself, so we shall find a place first thing. But have you eaten?"

Sophia and Akbar shook their heads.

"Well, let us go for some food first," he said in the cheeriest voice he could muster. "Allah will forgive me for forgoing my morning prayer because of this emergency," he muttered, reminding himself that he had been letting his devotions slip far too often as of late. He wondered absently, as he stuffed clothing into an ancient portmanteau, if his talks with Cohen were somehow affecting his piety. He cast the case over his shoulder and the thought out of his mind as he took Akbar's hand and the foursome hurried away from his tent.

Abou pondered his daughter's danger as they had a hurried breakfast at a street vendor's. He was almost sure that Yasser would not harm Akbar, although he wasn't sanguine about the baby girl, and he was certain that Sophia was in danger. He would never forgive himself if he did nothing and Sophia was injured or killed by this madman. He decided to take his small family to the one place that Yasser would never think to go, the small room he had found for Abou that the old man had found so offensive. The little troop caught the first bus to Shomi, only twenty-odd kilometers away but because of the deplorable roads and the age of the bus, a ride which often took more than an hour, if they weren't stopped by the Israelis. It was demeaning to flee, but Abou could think of no alternative.

After the bus bumped along the dusty road past dismal hovels and mangy dogs, it stopped at a roadblock about five miles short of the family's destination. Abou's heart sank when he saw Israeli soldiers at the checkpoint. All passengers were forced to debark and stand in the sun while the young soldiers tried to sort through the papers presented to them.

When the bus stopped, Sophia had been nursing the baby in the back, so she was separated from Abou and little Akbar, and once she found herself half a bus length away from her father, she began to cry. A burly trooper, with a jaunty beret and a walrus mustache, demanded, "What are you crying about? What have you to hide?" The baby immediately began to yell. The soldier became more agitated.

Without thinking, Abou stepped out of the line to help his daughter, and another soldier, just a boy, although quite formidable in size, immediately struck him on the head with the butt of his assault rifle, knocking him to the ground.

"Papa!" Sophia screamed and the Israelis looked about.

"Who is your papa?" another soldier demanded.

Sophia pointed to Abou, who was trying to rise but was unable to get off his hands and knees.

"That is your papa?" the burly soldier shouted. He seemed given to shouting.

"Yes. You have killed him!" Sophia screamed hysterically.

The other passengers were becoming restive and the soldiers began fingering their weapons, but the young soldier near Abou laughed, trying to break the tension, and called out, "Not quite, I'm afraid. He has a wonderfully hard head. Come, help the old fool up. And tell him when he recovers that when we say stay in line, we mean stay in line. We didn't know he wanted to visit his grandchildren."

Sophia helped her father to his feet. Abou's head was bleeding and he was dazed. Sophia threw her arms around him.

"Papa, can you hear me? Do you understand me?" she cried.

"I have a terrible headache," Abou moaned. "Your yelling doesn't help."

"Yes, I suppose so," she replied, trying to regain her composure by adjusting her head scarf and dusting off her father at the same time.

After an exhaustive check of papers and the detainment of several passengers, the rest were allowed to board the bus and continue their journey. Within twenty minutes, they were in the village of Shomi and Abou was making a futile attempt to bargain with the landlord over the price of the room. They finally settled on a week's rent, as Abou said he was not sure they would like living in the decrepit dwelling.

"What's not to like?" the landlord asked suspiciously. "It has all the conveniences. A toilet, running water. What else is needed?"

Abou waved his hand vaguely. "A new town. We don't know if we will like it. The room is fine."

Abou left money with Sophia for food and promised he would return as soon as he took care of some business. With some hesitancy, he reboarded the same bus as it bumped and swayed its way to the checkpoint, where the passengers were again told to get out, line up, and show their papers.

"It is the old man with the hard head!" the young trooper reported to the others, as they went through the papers of every passenger. "Lose your daughter and her kids?"

"I settled them into their new home," Abou said wearily. His head still throbbed from the drubbing.

"Head hurts?" the young soldier asked.

"Yes."

"Here," the boy said, and handed Abou two aspirins and his canteen.

"That is very kind of you," Abou said, throwing the medication into his mouth and greedily drinking the water.

The young soldier took back his canteen and went to the next man in line, whom he treated with derision and contempt, finally having the man step out of line. Abou marveled how the young man could be so kind to him and so bellicose with another for no apparent reason.

They were back on the bus within an hour and the driver apologized. "It is very difficult to keep a schedule with the checkpoints. And you never know when they will stop you. Sometimes they just wave you on, and other times they aren't here at all. Politics is confusing." Everyone on the bus murmured agreement, except for two probable Hamas or Mossad agents in the back, who scowled and said nothing.

Back home, Abou made his way to the office of Hafez, the tax collector. They had known each other for years.

"Israeli checkpoint," Abou said, touching the matted blood in his hair.

Hafez nodded. No more had to be said. In fact, no more should be said, for you were never sure to whom you were talking or, for that matter, who was listening, for spies and listening devices were everywhere. Some said secret microphones were inserted into the mouthpieces of almost all the telephones in public buildings.

"I understand my son-in-law, Yasser, owes considerable back taxes on his house."

"That is true," Hafez replied, taking down a huge ledger and opening it, his rapacious eyes gleaming. "Are you considering paying these taxes?"

Abou hesitated. "I would want the title transferred if I were to do that."

Hafez loved intrigue. His little eyes were alight with the ramifications. "Just whom would you like to have title?"

"I think my daughter," Abou replied.

Hafez sat back in his great chair and stared at Abou. "You want me to transfer title to your daughter? A woman! Won't that offend her husband terribly?"

"He threatened Sophia and the children last night and he beat her," Abou replied. "This is intolerable. I must have someplace where she can be safe."

"I see," Hafez replied, looking through the ledger, "but won't this make the situation worse?"

"Perhaps, but what else can I do?"

Hafez shrugged. "Well, for $1,251 American I can transfer the title to Sophia, but Yasser can claim the property as her husband."

"What if I were to transfer the title to Akbar, with Sophia as his guardian?"

Hafez shook his head. "Yasser would only demand custody of his son, and he would probably get it. He would be right back in the house."

"Then there is no purpose in my paying the taxes, is there?"

Hafez became agitated. "May I make a suggestion? Take title yourself. See a lawyer about willing your estate to your daughter. I'm sure a good attorney could do something."

Abou drew in a deep breath. "That is a great deal of money. I am not sure I have that much."

Hafez looked at him shrewdly. "Perhaps something could be done, Abou. It is costly to foreclose and resell the property. Perhaps a reduction of 10 percent?"

"I think I would need at least fifteen," Abou replied. As distressed as he was, he couldn't help bargaining.

"Twelve is the best I can do," Hafez replied.

"Perhaps we could settle at twelve-five. Then we both would be satisfied."

"You are a difficult man, Abou, but I will accept $1,100 American."

Abou calculated swiftly in his head. "$1,094."

Hafez sighed. "$1,095."

"So be it. I will go to the bank and get the money. You will draft the correct papers?"

"They will be here when you return."

"And will you notify Yasser that you have foreclosed and are taking possession of the house?"

"I foreclosed yesterday, Abou. I gave Yasser until tomorrow to vacate with his wife and children. I will tell him again today so that there is no misunderstanding. You will have title to the house by this evening and possession tomorrow."

133

When Abou arrived at the bank, Absollah rushed out. It was obvious that Absollah feared Abou was about to close his account, and he was greatly relieved that it was only a withdrawal. Absollah oversaw the drafting of a bank check to the tax collector for the delinquent taxes.

"I will move the tent tomorrow or the next day, Absollah," Abou told his former friend.

"There is no hurry. We have hired a storyteller to greet the children this afternoon and the tent will play a large part in his stories."

Abou nodded and took the bank draft with him. Two doors away, he stopped at the office of Marwan, the attorney.

"I thought you might be coming to see me," Marwan greeted him, his eyes avoiding the bloodied mat in Abou's hair and the dirty condition of Abou's robe. He was a portly man who ate well from the tribulations of others. "Some terrible things are being said about you, my friend."

"Allah's ways are mysterious," Abou replied. "Perhaps good will come from all this." He then explained about willing the house and bank account to Sophia.

"It can be done, dear friend," Marwan answered. Abou was surprised by the "dear friend" as he barely knew the man. "But you must understand that, as long as they are married, it matters little what you direct to your daughter, for on your demise her husband will control it, manage it in her name. That is the law."

Abou sat back and looked at the fat lawyer. "She can't decide to pay her taxes so that she doesn't lose her house? She can't decide to keep money in the bank? These acts don't seem to take much financial acuity."

Marwan laughed. It was a bit forced, but it was an acceptable attempt at being jovial. "But again, trying to avoid the rules governing paterfamilias is contrary to our laws, as well as an affront to Allah."

"I can't believe Allah condones Yasser abusing his family and mismanaging his business."

Marwan sat back and looked at Abou in a speculative fashion, wondering. Abou had the sudden thought that Marwan suddenly found him interesting now that these hideous rumors were being circulated. Abou also realized that some people in the village thought his reporting of an angelic visitation years before was bizarre, as well as heretical.

"I can draw a will," Marwan said. "We will assume your daughter is no longer married to Yasser, so it will be worded as if she were divorced or a widow, although without specific language. I will make the children her heirs, per stirpes, but when the baby daughter marries, her share will come under the control of her husband. There is nothing I can do about that."

"As it normally should be," Abou agreed. "Will it take long?"

"Tomorrow. Bring the title of the house with you," the attorney said with a huge smile. "And don't pay Hafez the full tax. He will settle for less. I am sure you can get 5, maybe 10 percent off." At these moments he loved his clients as well as the unique situations they presented. Abou muttered "Probably," as he departed.

He hurried back to the tax office.

"I have the money, Hafez."

"I was about to leave for lunch," the tax collector replied, rising from his desk. "You took so long, I thought you had changed your mind."

"I wanted to think more about it," Abou replied, a calculating gleam in his eye. "I still am not totally convinced. It seems to me that paying the whole amount, even with this discount, is an unfair burden on me. With your office having title, you will now have to sell the property as well as manage it until a sale develops. As you said, this will be a great expense for you."

Hafer looked at him with respect. "I will give you one-fifth off."

Abou nodded. "I am most grateful."

Hafez resumed his seat. "Why don't we just sit down and take care of the paperwork now?"

"You are too kind," Abou replied and sat in the offered chair. He pulled the bank draft from his cloak.

"Yes, yes, all is in order." Hafez forced a smile as he set the check aside and began scribbling on this sheet and that, stopping to stamp a paper now and then with huge, official-looking instruments. He inked the stamps carefully and then gave a mighty stroke, as if afraid that if he didn't exert his all, the imprint would someday fade into oblivion, and all his good work would be for naught.

Finally gathering up the papers, filing some, setting aside others, he said, "You will have to sign here, and here, and here." He pointed to various lines in the documents. "You may read them if you wish."

"I am sure they are all in order," Abou replied.

"I note you brought a draft for the full amount we agreed upon earlier."

"If I had to, I would have paid, but I thought it excessive."

Here is a receipt for the money you paid," Marwan exclaimed, "and this is the title in your name, and this document states the taxes are paid up to date through next year. I think that is everything."

Abou waited.

"Oh, the change! Yes, yes, I forgot," Hafez continued. He went to his safe and withdrew a packet of money. Carefully, he counted out Abou's portion.

After leaving the tax collector's office, Abou checked the bus schedule on the wall near the stop and found he had several hours before the next bus to Shomi departed. At a table outside the Camel's Hump, he saw Hamid reading a letter.

"Good day, Hamid," Abou greeted his friend as he slipped stiffly into a chair.

"You are having a difficult day?" Hamid asked, carefully folding his letter.

"Extremely."

"Yasser?" Hamid asked, looking at the wound on his head.

"Oh, this," Abou replied, "no, an Israeli roadblock. A slight misunderstanding."

Hamid nodded. He was thoroughly experienced with the misunderstandings that the Israelis seemed to vigorously engender. Avoiding Abou's eyes, Hamid said, "Hamas has informed Absollah he may not run an after-school program without its supervision."

"And?"

"He agreed, of course," Hamid answered. "Hamas workers are there now. They are enjoying your tent."

"I hope they don't become too fond of it," Abou answered and signaled the waiter. He had to take the bus back to Shomi, or Sophia would be alone all night. "I intend to move it tomorrow."

Hamid shook his head back and forth, a habit that made him sometimes look like a fool. "I would be careful, Abou. Speak to Absollah. Hamas is not an organization to take lightly."

Abou sniffed. "I don't take it lightly, but it is my tent and I want it. I will have a place for it tomorrow."

Hamid shrugged. "As you wish."

Abou's lunch arrived. He had goat curd and greens in a pita. Taking a bite, he said, "I will talk to him. You are right. Hamas takes affront easily, but it is my tent."

"Absollah may not have made that clear."

"I'm sure he didn't," Abou agreed. "He probably donated it to the group!"

Hamid grinned. "You are becoming as acerbic as the rest of us."

"And you are becoming as cynical as Ammon," Abou replied with a grin to match his friend's. He rose and bid Hamid farewell, making his way to the bank, where he deposited a good portion of the money he had saved at the tax office. It was never wise to be carrying too much money when traveling in the Strip, he thought, as he made his way to the bus stop. He hoped the Israeli soldiers would be gone from the check-point, but of course they weren't, although the one who had given him the aspirin smiled at him.

"We are beginning to think you are a smuggler, old man," the soldier said.

"I wish I were doing something so profitable," Abou replied as he trooped out of the bus. Another hour was lost as the soldiers checked everyone's papers, arrested one man who had an extraordinarily evil face but who carried papers that looked to Abou to be in order. "How can someone who looks like this be legitimate?" the Israeli officer said and they held the man, allowing the rest of the passengers to board the bus and continue.

Sophia was waiting docilely in the room with her two children.

"I thought you would not be back this evening," she whispered.

Abou forced a smile. "These Israeli checkpoints. They are endless with their checking of papers. They took a man standing next to me out of line with perfect papers—too perfect, they said. For years, they have been arresting those with small flaws, not realizing that a provocateur who really wanted to infiltrate their territory would not have smudged papers that were difficult to read or clumsy forgeries to cover a bad date."

Sophia nodded. It was obvious she had little interest.

At a small nearby eatery, over lentil soup and pita, Abou said to Sophia, "I paid the taxes on your house and had the title put in my name. I am making a will that will leave it to you."

Sophia looked at him for several minutes. "What will Yasser think?" she finally asked.

"I have no idea, my daughter. You must have a place to live. He cannot provide it. Paying the taxes is a present to you and the children. You knew he owed money?"

"He often yelled about how confiscatory the taxes were," she admitted, "but then he yelled about how unfair other businessmen were. He claimed they cheated him and drove his customers away. Is that true?"

"I doubt it," Abou replied, suddenly aware that he had to be careful about what he said. Akbar would not take kindly to criticism of his father, and perhaps even Sophia would resent it. "Something else must have caused his loss of business," he added carefully.

"What of the room you have paid for here?" Sophia asked.

Abou shrugged. "The landlord can rent it to another. In the morning, we will tell him we don't want it any longer." He finished his cup of coffee and signaled for another. "Do you think I could move my tent back to the orchard tomorrow?"

Sophia looked at him for a moment, her expression grave. "Yasser wouldn't approve."

Abou said nothing.

Sophia nodded. "I don't suppose he will be there, will he?"

"No. The tax collector ordered him to vacate today."

"Then you could stay in the house. There is no reason for you to live in your tent."

"Except," he said with a smile, "I like my tent very much. I feel comfortable there."

"As you wish," she murmured.

"No, it is your house now, Sophia. If you think my being in my tent is troublesome, then I will make other arrangements."

"It is not troublesome," she said.

They slept on small pallets on the bare floor of the dismal room in Shomi. Abou could hear the steady breathing of sleep, first from Akbar and finally from his daughter. Little Leila made only small mewing sounds.

The Eighth Darkfall

COHEN APPEARED SUDDENLY, looking about for a place to sit. He finally settled for a spot near the wall, sitting uncomfortably on a bucket that he turned upside down.

"It's you," Abou observed sourly. "I had rather hoped for an undisturbed night's sleep."

"Actually, I came to apologize. What I said about the elderly was callous."

"But you still believe it's true," Abou observed, pulling himself up to a sitting position. "And you can't lie," Abou added.

"No. But that isn't to say I'm not sorry. It seemed so reasonable to me at the time. You know, it isn't easy thinking about you as human. I forget myself. It's like I'm gabbing with my colleagues." The angel looked about and added, "Boy, is this a dump."

Abou nodded agreement.

"Well, it's a test of human adaptability, one of your more remarkable traits. Other animals have a deuce of a time making do, but humans seem to be able to adjust to almost anything. A unique quality."

"I have no intention of adjusting to this," Abou replied stiffly.

"No, of course not," Cohen replied, looking around. "But still, you did think of this place when you needed a place to hide, didn't you?"

"Only until I can work out some other solution." Abou hesitated and then added, "I am only a humble goat herder. Solutions don't come to me too readily."

"Humble, my ass!" Cohen replied with a great laugh. "You're not a run-of-the-mill person and you know it, Abou. Most humans we deal with haven't thought about things as you have—haven't thought about anything, for that matter, as far as we can tell. You're aware of the world around you, and you're obviously conscious of your own thoughts and feelings, as well as those of other people. We don't really know what goes on inside the human mind, but we see from their actions, and you ain't no ordinary guy. That's for sure."

"And what have you observed about my situation?" Abou asked.

Cohen shrugged. "You're in a real bind, Abou. This Yasser is a dreadful person and could be dangerous to your daughter and the baby, although, at least, he seems to love his son. Society's laws and mores are certainly stacked in his favor. But you have advantages. He appears to be crafty, but you're smart, which means you have a better developed thinking process, as well as a moral center."

"None of this seems to be helping much now," Abou replied.

"No, I don't suppose it does," Cohen admitted. "I wish we knew what you were thinking. All we've seen is human development from the outside. From the first time humans used their right hand more than the left, from the first stick man picked up as a tool, we've known something was going on inside your noggins, but we were never sure just what. Did you know chimps use either hand indiscriminately?"

"Really," Abou replied. "Is that significant?"

"We suspect so. It showed some sort of ordering of your brain. It seemed the first step in a process—awareness, consciousness, speech, thought and, finally, logic."

"Unfortunately, Yasser is right-handed, too."

"Come on, Abou," Cohen replied with a shake of his great head. "Don't be like that. I did ask your pardon."

Abou nodded his head in agreement. "Then why aren't I doing better with my problem if I'm so intelligent and Yasser's such a dolt?"

"Nobody said you're perfect," Cohen replied. "Your consciousness evolved, as did language, imperfectly at times, incompletely in some individuals, more complete in others. But a thinking person with a well-ordered mind has an edge in solving problems."

"Incompletely?" Abou questioned. In spite of himself, he was intrigued. He had hoped to focus on Sophia's problems alone, but Cohen's comments, as always, were tantalizing and, in a way, seemed related.

"Man's a work in progress, Abou," Cohen said. "You well know that language doesn't always explain what you mean or feel. Well, your consciousness is much the same. There are things humans do for no rational reason. Unexplained acts. You've had that experience, haven't you?"

Abou nodded, still a bit put out, but interested. "I suppose I have."

"Right!" Cohen exclaimed. "The reason is that human consciousness isn't quite developed yet. You still have a jumble of instincts and urges which control many of your actions. Lots of time you're on autopilot—when you walk, greet people in the market, eat a meal, have sex. And, as hard as you try sometimes, logical solutions can elude you."

"Where are we going?" Abou asked. "I mean, are we ever going to be . . . perfected?"

"Beats me," Cohen replied. "I've got to tell you we were all a little bit surprised the human race got this far. I mean, logic started because you had slightly bigger brains than your fellow . . . fellows. There you were scared half out of your wits, hanging on to life by a thread. You made the adjustments I mentioned, walking, being able to fornicate and procreate whenever you wished, and using rocks as tools and weapons, and you finally got a handle on fire as a protective device and for warmth, as well as a way to tenderize food, but still it wasn't enough. You people were being eaten with a ghastly frequency. You had nothing really adequate to defend yourselves with, and you'd given up the safety of the trees, so you were just there, little bitty snacks for whatever animal had a craving."

"One wonders how we survived," Abou answered dryly. He hadn't forgiven Cohen's intrusion and, Abou admitted, his comments about the elderly.

"It was a wonder. You began to hunt in packs, or troops, if you will. And you learned to express your ideas in language. We're still arguing among ourselves whether talking got you thinking, or thinking got you talking. You banded together for protection in bigger and bigger groups. First, it was with immediate family, then with other relatives, and finally with distant kin and even strangers of the same ilk."

"Until we ended up in situations like the one I'm in," Abou responded with some bitterness, waving his hand about. "All this progress hasn't done me or my family much good, has it?"

Cohen thought about this for a moment. "I really don't know how to answer that, Abou. I know your situation looks impossible to you now, but all this progress, this will and effort to survive, is astonishing, and the key to successful surviving is thought and reason. Of that we're sure."

"Yet, we live in an unreasonable world of hate and turmoil. My family is being torn apart. Frankly, I see little hope, Cohen. Little hope."

"Oh, Abou, don't say things like that," Cohen replied. "Don't lose heart. Mankind is trying, in spite of what you see around you. Think of what you've accomplished."

"What?" Abou asked in a low voice.

"Well, man has tried to develop a moral code of sorts," Abou replied. "Of course it's taken years and there's been a zillion lapses, but once you banded together, you developed some rudimentary ideas about killing and stealing. I mean, you couldn't live in a troop and kill each other, could you? And you couldn't steal from each other, because you didn't want to be stolen from. The first commandments were right there, and other groups developed similar rules of conduct. Moses got their order a little confused, but he was a little *meshuga* from all that climbing up and down mountains and yelling at the Red Sea to part. Anyway, you learned you didn't mess with somebody else's man or woman, because you certainly didn't want to be feeding somebody's else's kid. Another commandment taken care of. A primitive moral system was developing."

"And you didn't covet your neighbor's wealth," Abou added, returning to the problems Yasser presented.

"Right! You got it. The better hunter got more and there was no use pining away for his food or his furs. You went out and got your own or you did without. Of course, it didn't stamp out jealousy and envy, but it curbed them a little.

Well, in most people. Yasser missed out on a few moral lessons along the way."

Abou sat with his back to the opposite wall, thinking about Cohen's words.

"I should have brought some tea," Cohen replied, looking around. "Getting out of here tomorrow, aren't you?"

"Allah and the Israelis willing."

Cohen looked down. "Your head must hurt like the dickens."

"The soldier was kind enough to give me medicine."

"They're a strange lot, aren't they? Whack you in the head and then give you a tablet for your headache," Cohen observed. "You don't understand how other people think either, do you?"

"My own people have occupied my tent and Hamid thinks I will have trouble getting it back."

"Do you want it back?" Cohen asked.

"Yes, I was quite content living in the orchard. I was near Sophia and the children but left alone enough to please me. It was very pleasant."

"I hope you get it back."

"As you said, your own tribe should not steal from you," Abou observed. "I should expect honesty there, at least."

"Tribes have become unwieldy," Cohen replied. "They are no longer homogeneous."

"You mean our ancestors had a better grasp of honesty than we?"

Cohen laughed. "Far fewer people with fewer conflicts was more like it. Actually, they were simpler beings, with an ill-defined sense of self, hazy feelings for their mates and their children, and a much looser bond with members of their tribe, but they did establish basic rules. They warned each other of danger, and they fought together against predators, but their memories were weak. A dead child seemed to be forgotten within a week."

"Sounds so . . . what is the word I want? Simpleminded."

Cohen laughed aloud. "Perfect choice of words! What I have described took a million years. But with each new thought, each new word, the smarter, more adept ancients reasoned better and the others fell by the wayside. This caused another problem, but being able to think was absolutely necessary for survival."

"And what was that other problem?" Abou asked. He knew Cohen well enough to respond to these little verbal ploys.

"As the brain got bigger, the head had to grow. I touched on this before. The baby had to be born sooner to pass through the canal, so these ancestors of yours were saddled with infants who needed long-term care after their births. Being bright has its drawbacks, but still, mankind's strength rests in his ability to think clearly."

"That's all I have?" Abou asked. "Some sort of faulty logic?"

"Let me ask you something, Abou. Why did you pay the taxes on the house?"

"To provide a place where Sophia and the children could live. Not a perfect solution, as you know."

"But you're moving ahead to solve the problem. That's good, Abou. You have to try to work out a solution."

"I suppose," Abou replied, his voice expressing both doubt and a little hope.

"Maybe this has been a little helpful," Cohen said. "It's times like this I wish we could intervene directly, but that would lead to an awful mess, too. At least I was able to explain human weaknesses to you. I hope it helped. And you have to keep trying to think through your problems. Don't let anger and revenge divert you."

147

"Thanks for coming," Abou replied. "I'll try to work something out."

"Good boy! You have to use your intelligence to outwit these dullards," Cohen said as he rose. "I think I'll toddle off now. No offense, but this place depresses me. Good luck getting your tent back and be careful." With this, the angel vanished, knocking the bucket over as he departed.

The Ninth Day

WHEN ABOU AWOKE, he was miserable. His head ached, he felt absolutely filthy, and he desperately wanted his morning tea. Remembering the water spigot outside the building, he took Cohen's bucket and walked toward the door. Sophia was already up and nursing the baby in the far corner. Averting his eyes, Abou hurried down the stairway, where he found Akbar playing with a rather rough-looking group of boys. Abou hurriedly descended the steps to wash himself, but the faucet emitted only an odorous trickle of umber water, and the boys raced about taunting him, especially when he tried to wash behind his ears.

"Sophia, when you are ready, we can go for something to eat and then we shall take the bus home," he called up the stairs.

She came to the door adjusting her clothing, her head scarf hanging over her shoulders, as if it were proper for the world to see her body and face. As she came down the stairs, she managed to pull her veil across her features and Abou relaxed a bit, wondering why such customs were so important to him. He decided he wanted Sophia to be well thought of by the people who knew them, and being seen dishabillé would certainly set tongues wagging. At the same time, he remembered that in America nothing was thought of women showing huge portions of their bodies, and he had been told that in France, in the south especially, even more was shown on the beaches. But for Sophia to uncover her neck and chest was too much where they were in the heart of Islam. It just shouldn't be done.

Abou watched as Sophia slowly descended the stairway, holding the baby close, protecting the infant, and then she spoke sharply to Akbar, and strangely, the other boys stopped their clamor at the sound of her voice. Abou puzzled about this, too. Muslim women, who had absolutely no status in adult society, were, for some reason, listened to by young boys. But even they, once they became adults, would find it somehow wrong to listen to, or depend upon, women for advice.

"You boys hurry home for your breakfast," she told them sternly.

One boy, obviously the leader, snarled, "What breakfast?" and another, a small ferret of a boy, yelled, "What home?"

Sophia was taken aback. "You boys have no homes?"

"Here," the larger boy said, spreading his arms grandly. "Our home is right here in the streets," and they ran off.

Later, on the bus, Sophia said with a deep sigh, "They should not have to live like that. Children should have a home and parents."

Her choice of words, the plural "parents", sent a chill down Abou's back.

Mysteriously, the Israeli checkpoint was abandoned. Candy wrappers and cigarette butts were all that remained of the contingent that had occupied the position the previous day. Abou touched the wound on his head and thought how one day could make a great deal of difference in a person's life. Because those on the bus avoided the inconvenience of the search and examination of papers that the Israelis performed so meticulously, Abou and his party arrived back in Helar early and set off for the office of Hafez, the tax collector.

"Ah, Abou," Hafez greeted him, taking the old man aside. "That Yasser is a nasty one. He gave me no end of trouble yesterday and didn't want to surrender the keys to the house. I finally had to call a constable."

Abou fully expected to receive more bad news, but no, Hafez was simply explaining how difficult it was to be an official in such troubled times. He handed Abou the ring of keys. "Here, my friend. Take your daughter and live peacefully in your house. I will see you next year at tax time."

Abou saluted the official and gathered up his family. They walked to the office of Marwan, the attorney.

"So this is Sophia and the children!" the monumental lawyer said with gusto. "It is truly a pleasure. I have the document ready for your signature. You must keep this in a safe place. I can keep it here for you in my safe if you wish, or you can take it to the bank and rent a box at great personal expense."

"We will leave it in your safekeeping, Marwan, but I will need a receipt, so that if something were to happen to you, your successor will know I have left the will here in your care."

They both knew that what Abou really wanted was proof that the will existed, so that when he died, Sophia wouldn't be cheated by Yasser, who could and probably would try to use bribery to destroy the document. Marwan smiled at his new client's sagacity.

"Very wise, my friend. It will help my successor locate these papers."

Abou nodded and signed the document.

"Have you explained all this to your daughter?" Marwan asked when Sophia was distracted with the children.

"Some. I must go into greater detail." Abou was not entirely comfortable with the situation. By telling Sophia that the only way she could keep possession of the house was to be divorced defied established custom. It was, Abou admitted sadly, a dubious solution, but most human efforts were uncertain. He laughed to himself, thinking how much he was beginning to sound like Cohen.

Over lunch, Sophia said, "It is terrible that we must abandon those homeless boys to their fate."

"It is Allah's will," Abou replied, using the phrase to partially satisfy his feelings of impotence. "But I wish I had vast wealth to help poor souls like those boys. We are losing Palestine's youth to poverty and turmoil."

Sophia smiled gently at her father and put her hand over his, a gesture so warm that Abou almost cried. "You are a good man, Father. You help all you can, and you have helped me in my misery."

Abou, much to his surprise, for he was not a demonstrative man by nature, covered Sophia's hand with his own and said, "Your misery becomes my misery, for I wish for your happiness more than anything in the world."

"I know you do," Sophia replied and withdrew her hand.

The house, which stood locked and deserted, seemed strangely forbidding, but in spite of this, Abou warmed to the sight of its bright blue color, the small garden inside the gate, and the red tile roof. Abou fumbled with the gate key. Inside, the house seemed hollow, although most of the furniture remained, and the rugs were still on the floor, as if Yasser planned on returning. Abou wandered down to the grove and looked at his tent site. Even that gave him little pleasure as he realized that as despicable as Yasser was, he did belong with his family, and oddly, as an elder in this culture, Abou did not. He sat on a rock and pondered this. Older people did live with relatives throughout the village, but they were really superfluous, baby-sitters, arbiters, handy for small errands and helping with the shopping and cooking, but really not worth much, and older females were far more valuable than males, for they helped with the children and caring for the houses. The old men spent vast portions of their days gabbing in the marketplace, smoking and drinking endless cups of coffee or tea. It was a role they seemed to enjoy and, if truth were told, Abou had become somewhat accustomed to it, too. Yet, he told himself he couldn't allow his daughter to suffer more at the hands of Yasser, this malicious incompetent. Abou wondered why, during those interminable marriage negotiations, he had not seen the flaws in his son-in-law. The happy thought of his daughter being married and having children had clouded his judgment.

"Papa!" Sophia's voice disturbed his reminiscence.

He hurried up the path to the house to find his son-in-law in the courtyard, his face contorted by a fierce scowl. Sophia stood in the doorway with the baby on her hip. Little Akbar had run to his father.

"What do you want?" Abou demanded.

"I came for my prayer rug," Yasser snapped.

Abou looked at his daughter. "Please find it and bring it here," he said, and then turning to Yasser, continued, "You are not welcome, Yasser. Your behavior toward my daughter is unpardonable."

"You mean my wife," Yasser snarled, correcting Abou. "She is primarily my wife, not your daughter, and she's only upset because she got a small slap for being difficult. The spoiled cow doesn't know how to be loyal to her husband. She must have everything her way."

"Please leave," Abou said, taking the small rug from Sophia and handing it to Yasser.

"You were unable to provide a home," Abou continued, knowing full well the young man could easily turn violent. "A true man provides food, clothing, and a home for his family."

Yasser's face paled; he was stunned by the insult but managed to cover his shock very quickly. "Perhaps not the lavish home she wants, nor all the food she can eat, but I provided."

"And love," Abou added. "A true man provides love. You are a mean-spirited man who has only enough love for himself."

Abou knew he had gone too far, that no relationship between them would ever exist again. Yet, telling the truth satisfied him profoundly.

"My children are my life," Yasser sputtered. "My son is my soul."

Akbar clung to his father, crying.

"Then you should have worked harder to provide food and a home, son-in-law. You have failed and I have been forced to pay your taxes so that my daughter and my grandchildren have shelter."

Yasser spun around, shaking loose his son's clinging hands, and rushed to the gate. He turned and said, "You could have helped me, old man." He slammed the gate and was gone. Sophia and Akbar were both crying. Only baby Leila seemed unmoved, a sunny smile on her face as she eyed her mother's breast covetously.

LATER THAT AFTERNOON, Abou set off for the marketplace. Although marketing was usually a woman's job, Abou had agreed to go, glad to be away from the unhappiness and confusion of the household. He was deep in thought when Ammon, razor in hand, hailed him from the door of his shop.

"I am off to the bank," Abou said. "I wish to reclaim my tent and have it moved back to the grove."

Ammon looked around furtively. "I have heard the tent is a big hit at the day care center. Be careful, dear friend. You don't want those Hamas people taking anything amiss. The bazaar has sensitive ears."

"A good phrase." Abou grinned at the remark. "Especially in this village." And then he added, "The tent is mine. Absollah had no right to give it away."

Ammon shrugged and said, "Possessions have little value if you can't enjoy them."

"Meaning?"

"You must be alive to sleep in your tent," Ammon replied with what Abou considered some brutality. "Just be careful what you say, or you may enjoy watching the children play in your tent from up there." He lifted his razor to the sky.

Abou was taken aback. "You think they would murder me?"

Ammon shrugged again. Shrugging for many was a safe way to respond without committing to words. "It has been rumored Hamas is rather heavy-handed in solving problems."

"With the Zionists, perhaps, but not with its own people."

"Oh, Abou, you are such a naive man. How did you get this far in life?"

Abou drew himself up, indignant at the suggestion he wasn't worldly. "I have managed by not stealing tents from others."

Ammon smiled. "Do not be angry at me. Just be careful. I need good company over lunch, something more than Hamid's incessant talk of mail and Absollah's interest rates."

Abou nodded, putting his hand on Ammon's arm in a gesture of friendship. "I have been having a bad couple of days. Forgive my temper, old friend."

Abou made his way toward the rear of the bank building. He was taken aback by the activity—children laughing as they played, others listening attentively to a scholar, and still others enjoying food at a table the local Hamas group had set up. Abou finally asked a large man who was standing beside him who the leader was.

"That would be Khaled el-Qut. He is the man with the graying beard feeding the children back there."

The Hamas leader was standing next to a large pot, ladling up soup for the youngsters. Could this be the man who had allegedly killed hundreds of Zionists in lightning attacks, his wrath merciless, his savagery legion? He worked among the children with a benign expression, a newspaper folded under his arm. One handsome little boy laughed when the warrior's beard brushed his face.

Abou saw that behind the tent men were working, painting and scraping, hammering and plastering on an old building in the lot behind the bank. This was something new. Such activity was rare in the relatively torpid villages such as Helar, where accommodation to the sun was more common. Abou approached Khaled el-Qut.

"I am Abou Ben Adhem," he began, saluting.

Khaled put aside his giant spoon when he was sure each child had enough soup. "I must tell you, Abou Ben Adhem, I have heard of you since I was a boy, and not for one minute did I believe those vicious rumors that were floating about this last week."

"It is good to be respected. A person's reputation is all he really has."

"That is true," Khaled replied, stroking his beard. "And this was a worthwhile project you started here, much needed, and I am ashamed that I did not see the need as you did. Unfortunately, we have been preoccupied with the Israeli settlement-building on our land and have had little time to think of the needs of our own people. It is good that men such as you are filling in when we become derelict."

Khaled gestured to the building renovation in the rear, as well as the expanded play area for the children. "These children need such a place. We are going to make this area a permanent place for the children to play and learn."

"It was a small effort," Abou replied in a low voice.

"And the donation of your tent was a brilliant stroke. How will our children know how their ancestors lived without seeing such artifacts? We are now looking for other treasures to use for the children's education. Perhaps we could start a museum. The building back there, donated by a benefactor, will serve as classrooms for our activities when the weather is bad. There may even be enough space for a small museum."

His enthusiasm stymied Abou for a moment.

"It was about the tent that I came."

"The tent?"

Abou nodded, looking down at the dusty ground. "I had the tent moved here when I could no longer use it behind my son-in-law's house. It is where I live. I had intended to move it to some vacant ground when land became available."

"Weren't you explaining to the children how you and your father lived in such a tent? Weren't you telling them of the stars?"

"Yes, it seemed a wonderful way to keep the children occupied after school, and Absollah thought it would be a useful way to spend my time while I was staying on the bank's property."

"I see," Khaled el-Qut replied, the smile gone, a hard glint appearing in his eyes. He slowly opened the newspaper he had folded under his arm. "Did you read that the Israeli government demanded the resignation of the head of Mossad because he botched an attempt to assassinate one of our leaders? And this is not the first time they have done such a thing. No remorse that they attempted to kill a man, just worried that the Mossad appeared amateurish in the eyes of the world. A seriously disturbed government."

Abou shook his head. "I have not been reading the papers these last few days. I have been looking for a place to live."

Khaled nodded slowly. "I must have misunderstood Absollah. The children have become quite taken with your tent, and we are planning a whole series of projects about how the ancients lived. It would be a centerpiece."

Abou felt his will wilting, but still he persisted. "I understand. I wish I could give it up, but I don't really have a place to stay. Well, that isn't really correct. I could stay with my daughter, but her husband doesn't want me around, but then . . ." His voice drifted off, wondering if he should tell Khaled that Yasser was out of the house but might return at any moment. "Well, I certainly can leave the tent here for a time," Abou added. "Perhaps, when you have finished your program, and the children are no longer interested, I can reclaim it."

Khaled smiled. "We will return it to you, Abou Ben Adhem, and we will even set it up for you wherever you wish. And we want you to return here and tell of your goat herding days. The children have asked about you."

"But the rumors?"

"Bah! We will tell everyone they were false rumors spread by amateurish Zionists who were bent on ruining the reputation of a great man."

Abou decided not to explain about Yasser. "I have a friend, Hamid, who was helping me," Abou suggested, hoping Khaled would respond positively.

"Bring him with you. He is welcome. He is the one who is interested in the mail system and wants the children to know how wonderful it is to be a postman, is he not? The children must have professions when they are older. No more hanging about in the streets throwing stones and being indolent, although the stone throwing has been very effective publicity for the media. We will expect you tomorrow." With this, el-Qut turned back to the children and offered more soup to depleted bowls.

As Abou made his way back to the marketplace, he pondered the latest turn of events. True, he didn't regain his tent, but he was going to be with the children again, and that pleased him. It was a great honor for such an organization as Hamas to accept the help of non-members. Abou suspected the group was so overextended with its other activities that it needed help with its social programs, but whatever the reason, Abou knew it was a unique opportunity.

At home, he found Sophia in the kitchen, singing softly to herself as she prepared *imam Bayeldi* for their supper. He realized it was the first singing he had heard in the house in years. He watched her with tenderness until Akbar came upon him and yelped in delight at his grandfather's return.

"Ah, Papa, you are home," Sophia said with a smile. "I am preparing your favorite."

"I smell it," he said happily.

They ate with great appetites, careful not to mention Yasser or his visit. Abou told Sophia about his tent, although he insisted it was the joy of the children playing that had convinced him to give up his claim, not the fearsome reputation of Khaled el-Qut.

When Akbar was safely in his bed and the baby asleep in the wide bed with bolsters, Sophia sat next to her father. "You shall stay in this house," she said. "It will be as it was before I married. Except for the little ones."

Abou hesitated for a moment and then said, "What I said to Yasser today was foolish. It only made matters worse. It demeaned him."

Sophia nodded. "What you said to him was true, but I'm sorry it was said in front of Akbar. A boy should not hear such words about his father."

Abou retreated to a small room off the kitchen. He rolled out his pallet and lay down, feeling improperly chastised.

The Ninth Darkfall

"THIS IS REALLY MUCH BETTER," Cohen said, perched on a sugar bin in the far corner. "A bit too cozy, but not as dismal as that place last night."

Abou smiled at him, rubbing his eyes. "Let me get us some tea."

Cohen held up a container. "I got it on my way in."

They sat facing each other, sipping their tea, a familiarity and friendliness now firmly established.

"I was quite craven today," Abou finally said.

"Expedient."

Abou laughed. "I was so full of myself when I met this man who thoroughly intimidated me. I never realized how afraid of authority I am."

"A reasonable response."

"Why do you think he told me about the Israeli bureaucrat who resigned?"

Cohen shrugged. "It was meant to tell you many things. How stupid his enemies were. How powerful Hamas has become. How right el-Qut's cause is, and most important, how necessary it is to do terrible acts at times. All that conveyed in a little story from the paper. Mostly I suspect it was the last—to intimidate you."

Abou nodded. "He managed that. His organization frightens me, as does the Islamic Jihad, Hizbullah, and all the rest. I like to think they don't, but I'm deluding myself. They control our lives."

"You're normal, Abou. Just remember, when your ancestors were feeding in small bands, they had no protection, only sentries stationed on the perimeter of the troop, and when an alarm sounded, they all just acted without thinking. Millions of years, billions of times, until you reacted instantly to save yourself. You became attuned to authority, to the voice of a leader who was really the only thing between you and destruction."

"Sounds like the little velvet monkey you mentioned," Abou replied. "The beginning of language."

"You got it!" Cohen was delighted. "I wasn't sure you were listening to all this stuff. These early bands of prehumans selected sentries while feeding and sleeping, and they reacted to calls of alarm. You've been programmed, so to speak. No wonder you responded to Khaled. He is an imposing man. His methods are deplorable, but within his own context, he is doing good." Cohen replied, rolling the tea over his tongue in enjoyment. "I must get more lemon next time. Do you like lemon in your tea?"

"I like goat's milk in tea," Abou admitted, "but it marks me as a bumpkin if I admit it to anyone."

"Goats are a much neglected creature," Cohen mused. "In America, in the South, they have a weed called kudzu which grows at an alarming rate. Imported from Japan originally, if I remember. Goats could take care of it, but Americans don't really like goats much, so the weed is strangling the entire lower portions of that country. I think Americans must develop a taste for goat or this weed will bury them."

"I realized today that Sophia needs a husband," Abou interrupted, "but someone other than Yasser. I would die happy if I knew she had found someone who thought more of her and the children than himself."

"You are such a sentimentalist, Abou," Cohen replied. "In your world there are few men like that. In fact there are few people like that—male or female. Generally, humans take care of themselves first, then their children, and finally their mates, if they have enough energy. Yasser, like so many who have limited energy, can just keep himself functioning. Most people are like that, just spending all their lives trying to survive, and then, if they can manage it, trying to secure a better place for their children." Cohen hesitated for a moment and then added, "But, for each million Yassers, an individual comes along who does something really remarkable."

"Remarkable, huh!" Abou sniffed.

"Evolution is a laborious process," Cohen replied with a grin. "Just think of how long it took the giraffe to grow a long neck and how limited an achievement that is and you get some idea of what you humans have done."

"But I have to know what to do about Yasser and the problem Sophia has," Abou complained.

Cohen nodded, then shrugged. "I know, and there is really no immediate answer. We presume the Yassers of the world will be weeded out someday, but that's a long time off. But that isn't to say what I've said is a bunch of bullshit, I hope you understand. Of course, we worry about polluting the atmosphere and nuclear waste, but generally you have solved most problems as they've come along, and it's impressive." Cohen thought for a moment and then smiled sardonically. "That's not to say you couldn't err and wipe yourselves out, but we should try to look on the bright side, shouldn't we?"

Abou was unimpressed. "Today, I wished to have money enough to feed some hungry boys."

"Yes, and that's a human dilemma. If they grow up to be productive people, it is a good thing, but if they drain resources, it isn't. But, you know what was said in the *Atrahasis* a few thousand years ago?"

"The what?"

"A Sumerian epic," Cohen replied nonchalantly, screwing up his face to remember the exact quotation he wanted. "It went something like this: *The people became numerous / The god was depressed by their uproar / Enlil heard their noise / He exclaimed to the great gods / The noise of mankind has become burdensome.*"

"The gods complained of overpopulation?" Abou questioned.

"Those Sumerian gods did. Prickly fellows!" This brought a great laugh from Cohen. Abou sensed Cohen enjoyed teaching.

Abou hesitated for a moment, then asked, "And what about Allah?"

"Allah?" Cohen repeated the word as a question. "I've told you all we know. It's a presence. A sort of aloof CEO, if you know what I mean."

"But you know about these other gods," Abou insisted.

"We know what was ascribed to them," Cohen replied. "That's all."

Abou smiled sadly. "I must tell you, my angelic friend, that your coming here and tantalizing me with tidbits about humankind, only to tell me we should stop talking about this or that, is criminal."

Cohen grinned. "A criminal angel. I believe we have an oxymoron there."

"You know what I mean," Abou replied. "I would like to understand what is happening to me and my daughter. I would like to know why we humans behave as we do. Why men hate and fight and kill. That is what I want, Cohen, and you have opened up that possibility for me. Perhaps I can better understand Yasser and Khaled el-Qut. And I want to know what I should believe and trust. That is all I want."

"That is all," Cohen answered with an expansive opening of his arms. "You are insatiable."

"Probably because I *am* human," Abou replied easily. "All I really want is to understand, so I can leave my daughter secure and happy. What can I tell her and the children?"

"It sounds so simple when you say it like that," Cohen replied, "but nothing we say ensures solutions to your present problems. We can only explain and guide. You're living in a complex, illogical society driven mostly by urges and instincts millions of years old, and there is nothing we angels can do to change that. We can argue for a curbing of sexual appetites, but who would listen just now? Well, the Chinese are trying to do something. . . . We can suggest some of you eat less, but you saw how much Americans ate. I will talk this over with my partners and see if there is something more immediate we can do, but I don't think so. In fact, I sure we can't."

Abou interjected, "Are your associates all men?"

Cohen laughed. "No, as I explained at the outset of our discussions, we take all forms—every ethnic group, religion, sex, age—whatever seems appropriate, but we gave up the religion gig."

"I've become so used to you, Cohen," Abou admitted. "I wouldn't trade you in for any other angel."

"Why thank you, Abou. That's really nice."

Abou thought Cohen blushed a little.

The Tenth Day

Abou slept late and his head was clear when he opened his
eyes. Hearing a sudden cry, he rose and hurried to the small
kitchen, where Sophia was hunched over the table weeping,
holding a letter from Yasser. It said he intended to divorce
Sophia and wanted custody of his son. There was no mention
of baby Leila.

"I will go to the mullah today." Abou consoled his daughter,
putting his hand awkwardly on her shoulder.

"Papa, he will take little Akbar from me," she wailed.

"No, we will not allow that," Abou replied as calmly as he
could. "The mullah will not allow a man who has no home and
little income to take a child."

Sophia wasn't consoled. Still weeping, she left the room to
tend the baby. Akbar appeared, upset by his mother's tears.

"What is wrong, Grandfather?" the little boy asked.

"It is something that has upset your mother but doesn't concern you."

"She is crying," Akbar persisted.

"Yes, but she will get over it," Abou replied. "She must feed the little one."

Abou prepared his grandson's lunch, spreading hummus generously on pita.

"You are giving me far too much, Grandfather."

"You need nourishment, my grandson," Abou replied and put more of the succulent spread on the bread. "You must have strength to learn."

"We are visiting your tent today," Akbar replied. "Hamas arranged it with the school. We are to spend the whole afternoon learning about goat herding and other things."

"And I shall be there to greet you," Abou said and hurried the little boy off to school.

He found Sophia sitting in her darkened room. She had not even opened the shutters to air out the room. On her lap, the baby cooed in a loose embrace. "The clerics will take him. They always decide for the father."

"This is different, Sophia. Yasser cannot feed or clothe him. The mosque will not support such a plan."

In a low, dreadfully intense voice, she whispered, "They don't care as long as their beloved male world is kept intact. You will see."

Abou was stunned by her words. "Ours is a fair and kind religion," he said lamely. "I have always believed that."

Sophia turned back to Leila and gently began crooning to her, a song Abou had heard at the knees of his own mother more than seven decades before. Abou retreated to his room, washed himself, and trimmed his beard. With unsteady steps, he proceeded to the mosque to see the mullah, Anis Malluk, a man Abou had known since boyhood. Malluk was the consummate temporizer who, when forced to make a difficult decision, often showed a mean side, which hardly comported with his usual unctuous smiles and ingratiating words.

Wanting above all else to become an imam but lacking the wisdom and scholarship necessary, Malluk struggled day in and day out with the small village mosque. Yet, Abou admitted, Malluk had always been fair with him and had seemed particularly impressed years before when Abou told him of Yousef's visitation.

The mullah was in a small cubicle, where he did his thinking about matters spiritual, and where he secretly fed information to the Israelis from time to time for a small monthly stipend, an avocation not uncommon in the village.

"Abou, my friend," he said with a smile, rising slightly from his desk to show just the right amount of respect, but not too much. When entertaining, he liked to sit on the floor cushions, as the Bedouins did long ago, although as far as Abou knew, Malluk had no desert blood in his veins, having been born and raised in the city, as were his father and grandfathers.

"I hope you are well," Abou began, inquiring about the mullah's family and his family's family, as protocol demanded. Abou stopped listening to the answers as Malluk prattled on about this cousin or that uncle, some now in America, which he was sure was of great interest to Abou, who everyone knew had lived for a spell in that country of infidels.

"America?" Abou asked politely.

"My uncle has a restaurant on Court Street in this Brooklyn. I thought he lived in New York City, but he keeps writing *Brooklyn*."

"It is a borough of the city," Abou replied and then knew he would have to explain. "A section of the city. But it is very big. Millions of people live in Brooklyn."

"Imagine," Malluk murmured. "A neighborhood with millions of people. Unthinkable!"

"Yes, well," Abou replied, trying to redirect the conversation, but Malluk continued to drone on about the history of his family throughout the world.

Abou realized all this was a delaying tactic, which meant that Yasser had already visited the mullah and received tacit consent for the divorce. Malluk would never come right out and give approval, but Yasser must have left with some idea that he would look benevolently on the divorce.

"My son-in-law has lost his house for back taxes," Abou interrupted rudely.

"I heard," Malluk replied stiffly, cutting off the tale of his third cousin twice removed, who lived in Cairo and had a thriving import and export business—supposedly olives, but Abou had actually heard the cousin trafficked in opium.

"I am sorry to be so abrupt," Abou explained carefully, "and I long to hear of your family, but today I have little time. You understand, being a busy man yourself. Yasser has informed my daughter he desires a divorce, which is his right according to the Qur'an, but he wants custody of his son, whom he can't even feed."

Malluk scowled. "We don't know that, Abou. Yasser has been to see me and has admitted he has suffered some temporary reversals in business, but he certainly can feed and clothe his son. And he is being generous. He has not asked for the baby."

"Could he nurse the infant?" Abou asked.

"Now, you sound bitter," Malluk replied, sticking a sickly smile on his face that he imagined to be compassionate. "Couples have these problems these days. It is not like when we were young and we stayed married, regardless."

"Regardless?" Abou asked, truly not understanding.

"Well, every male tires of his wife eventually," Malluk explained, as if he were talking to an idiot.

"That never happened to me," Abou replied coldly. "I hope that isn't correct."

"You married so late and you were away so long," Malluk replied, "and your wife died in the birth of your daughter. You had no time to become weary."

Abou replied, "The world is filled with Yassers who are still children at heart and will not care for their families."

Malluk was interested. "You think Yasser has found someone else?"

Abou shrugged. "It makes no difference. He will, and he will have more children. If there is a male child, he will wallow in the pride of that accomplishment, and then he will again fail to care for that family, just as he is now failing to care for this family."

"He claims you could have helped him," Malluk suggested slyly.

"Supported him, you mean?" Abou asked, and then added, "He wanted me out of the house before he disgraced himself."

"I think you give him too much credit," Malluk replied. "In any case, he seems to have decided he no longer wishes to remain married."

"And he wants the boy," Abou added.

"As is his right. It is his son."

Abou looked at the mullah carefully. "You are going to subsidize him?"

"We have made arrangements," Malluk replied coldly.

Abou stood. "In other words, you are in this with him. You will feed and house him as he continues to shirk his duty as a man. And to do this, you will use contributions to the mosque? This is despicable."

Malluk rose. "We knew you would come and cause a scene, and that is why we spoke to the imam."

Abou was speechless. The chubby canon was looking at him with a small smile. "Perhaps your beloved angel can help you understand."

"My angel?" Abou was stunned. For a moment he thought the cleric knew of Cohen.

"Who came to you years ago and told you how you loved your fellow man. Offensive! And you not even a holy man. We all know that nobody sees an angel but the Prophet, not even a cleric, yet you somehow had one visit you. We only hear them, but you see them!"

"All these years. You've felt this way toward me all these years?"

"Servants of Allah have toiled for years in His service, only to have you emerge suddenly and tell this ludicrous story. Your name led all the rest!"

Suddenly Abou shook his head as if to clear his mind. "All these years. I had no reason to lie about it."

Malluk hesitated.

Abou simply waved his hand in vague dismissal and turned. "It doesn't matter. Jimmy Carter is at the head of the list now," he said over his shoulder as he walked away.

ABOU WANDERED AIMLESSLY, his hand as always on his purse to prevent it from being stolen, but his mind was far away, trying to fathom the depth of his fellow man's envy. He was appalled at Malluk's cruel words, and that the imam agreed with the mullah was unbelievable. After all these years, he was faced with suspicion, dislike, and dishonesty. It was almost too much to bear, and what would Sophia, Akbar, and the baby do?

Almost magically, he found himself at the Camel's Hump, and with a sudden feeling of relief, he saw Hamid, Ammon, and Absollah sitting over their lunch. Abou rushed forward to greet his friends, an oasis of kindness and understanding in a malevolent world.

"You shouldn't have been surprised. Years ago when you told about your dream, many were dubious, but they were afraid to say anything. A possible visit from an emissary of Allah is nothing to dismiss lightly, but everyone knew the clergy's nose was out of joint," Absollah responded after Abou had explained his dilemma. "I didn't," Abou replied sadly.

"You gained respect," Absollah reminded him, "but you also gained the enmity of the clergy, it would seem."

Abou studied Absollah. He was still hurt that Absollah had betrayed him with Hamas, but talking to his old friend was comforting. He decided to change the subject. Abou told them about Khaled el-Qut's request that they resume their teaching.

"Not that I can take time from my shop, but I would love to tell the children about my profession," Ammon said pompously. His three friends laughed.

"You are hardly ever in your shop now," Hamid observed. "Your wife and your assistants run it for you."

"I arise at dawn to sharpen my scissors and razors for the day," Ammon replied.

Absollah clamped his hand on Abou's shoulder. "We should not laugh at Ammon. He is the only man I know who can run a successful business without working. He is an absolute genius!"

"It is not easy," Ammon said defensively and then quickly asked, "But what can we do for Abou and his problem?"

There was a silence as they pondered.

"How am I to tell Sophia?" Abou asked.

"I wouldn't," Ammon suggested. "There is nothing to be gained. Just tell her that you explained the situation to Malluk, but there has been no decision."

"I feel that is dishonest," Abou replied.

At that moment there was a commotion at the end of the square. Several men with a portable radio were talking wildly, and finally one broke away and raced past the table where Abou and his friends were seated. Hamid, who was always the first to find out what was happening, jumped to his feet and grabbed at the fleeing man. The man focused on Hamid. He grasped his hand and shouted, "The Israeli checkpoint outside of town has been attacked. The radio said all the Jews were killed. They think it was Hamas. There will be Israeli troops here in minutes. Maybe tanks! I am going to board up my shop. Last time I was looted. It took me two years to restore the lost goods."

Absollah rose. "I must return to the bank. I will call around, but I think I may close for a day or two, just to be safe."

"Would you tell Khaled that Hamid and I won't be with the children this afternoon? I should be with Sophia," Abou asked Absollah.

Ammon agreed. "I too must hurry. I am glad I installed the steel gate to cover my window and door. These are parlous times."

Hurrying up the hill, Abou wondered if the young soldier who gave him the headache tablet was one of the dead. He was greeted by Akbar, who had arrived home from school only minutes before.

"In school, we were told you will be at the bank in your tent telling stories, but we were to go directly home today, not to stop because of some great emergency," Akbar said with excitement.

Sophia eyed Abou with suspicion when he produced the succulent lamb and the wonderful tomatoes, as well as the onions that he had purchased at a favorable price just as the market was closing. "Did it go well with you today?" she asked.

"The Israeli checkpoint was wiped out," he replied, not wanting to address her real question. "Everybody in the village is closing their shops."

Sophia was interested. "Hamas?"

"So it is said," Abou replied, relieved that he could put off telling of his conversation with Malluk.

Sophia put the lamb into a marinade of spices and oil. She looked at her father from the corner of her eye. "Malluk wasn't helpful?"

"Oh, Malluk," Abou replied. "I had forgotten about him with all the excitement. He heard me out, but you know how he is. No commitment. He will look into the matter."

"Papa . . . ," Sophia began, then reconsidered. "Well, in any case we will feast tonight. I made pita today and we have soured goat's cream, so we shall have a banquet!" Her cheeriness seemed a bit forced, but Abou said nothing, feeling guilty enough about answering her question with an untruth. Instead, he took another path. "As Khaled el-Qut has asked Hamid and me to resume our teaching behind the bank, tomorrow afternoon I shall be there, the Israelis permitting."

After the tasty dinner, they purposely didn't listen to the radio until after Akbar and the baby were in their beds. The news reports were ominous. The bodies of the soldiers had been found. The Israelis, who had not threatened retaliation for a while, were silent, but Palestinian newscasters speculated that there would be a dire price to pay for the Israeli deaths. Again, Abou found himself hoping the soldier with the headache tablets had escaped the massacre.

"Do you think these are the same men who stopped us?" Sophia asked, knitting a cap for the baby.

"I believe so, although the checkpoint was vacant when I passed through yesterday."

Sophia looked down at the needles in her hands. "They were very young."

"I wish both sides would stop fighting," Abou said. He was usually very circumspect about his utterances, as were most in his part of the world. He suddenly wondered if the young trooper had a grandfather who was mourning him, as Abou would mourn in similar circumstances.

"They will not stop," Sophia replied, looking up from her mending. "It is the way of mankind. Enemies are needed to fill some void in the human psyche. Sadat was the only wise man on our side for the past fifty years. He was our only hope and he was butchered."

Abou looked up in surprise. It always amazed him when women in the Arab world expressed opinions. They were so obsequious, seldom vocal about politics or religion, and suddenly his own daughter was telling him that mankind, meaning men he supposed, were profoundly defective.

"You will never get another husband talking like that."

She grinned. She actually grinned. It warmed his heart. "My luck wasn't so good behaving like a scared mouse, so maybe I should just say what's on my mind."

"Your mother did," Abou replied.

Sophia leaned forward, the sewing basket falling from her lap. "What was she really like, Papa? Was she interesting?"

"She thought me very funny and wise, which doesn't speak well for her acuity, but she made me laugh, as well as think. She was provocative."

"Not a troublemaker?" Sophia said in a questioning voice.

"Oh, no, but strong-willed. I asked her once if she would like to return to America with me, but she refused. She wanted you born right here in her native land."

Sophia was interested. "I did not know you wanted to return to America."

Abou shrugged. "Work was plentiful there. It was just a passing thought." He wanted to share his secret with her that he had become an American citizen, but he didn't.

"Would she have recommended that I try again to live with Yasser as his wife? Would she think that a wise course in order to keep Akbar?"

"We don't know . . . ," Abou began but stopped when Sophia looked up at him with those sad eyes.

"I am not a fool, Papa," Sophia said in a low voice. "The mullah gave you no hope. I saw it in your eyes. Yasser will divorce me and take my son, but he will leave me the baby, for he has no use for a female. Akbar will grow to manhood with all the hate and malice his father can instill in him. My only choice is whether I live with Yasser and try to mitigate the damage."

"Oh, Sophia, I am so sorry," Abou began. "I have thought about it all day. We could emigrate. The United States is composed of immigrants," Abou replied.

"Would we want to raise Akbar and the baby there? Could I find some sort of work?" Just the way Sophia asked the question sounded to Abou as if she were considering the possibility seriously.

"They would grow up differently. There are free schools. Women are in every profession. They have women in their army and navy."

"Like the Israelis?" Sophia asked.

"Yes, I suppose so," Abou replied, looking at her sideways. He didn't really want to leave his homeland at his age, but the thought of giving Akbar and the baby, as well as Sophia, a new life suddenly filled him with enthusiasm.

Always practical, Sophia asked, "And would it be possible to get the necessary papers with Yasser opposing such a move? And why would the Americans want us . . . a woman with two children and a . . ."

"An old man," he finished the thought for her. "I don't know the answer to that, my daughter, but if you are interested, I shall try to find out tomorrow. I will go to Marwan, the attorney, and ask his advice."

She neither agreed nor disagreed.

The Tenth Darkfall

SHORTLY AFTER, Abou felt fatigue overtake him. When he finally slept and the angel materialized and sat casually on an overturned basket, Abou smiled at him warmly.

"I am glad you came," Abou whispered. One of the reasons he wanted to sleep in the storeroom was that he was afraid he might talk in his sleep.

"You had another bad day, didn't you?" Cohen asked.

"Very depressing. I never knew that when I spoke of Yousef's visit years ago, I offended so many people."

Cohen grinned. "The human condition. Hating is by far easier than loving. Envy is more natural than benevolence."

Abou raised himself on his elbow. "What luck to have a cynical angel."

"I am a realist," Cohen corrected.

"Can I make you some tea? I'm sure everyone has gone to bed by now. We could sit in the kitchen."

At the kitchen table, Abou offered the angel some of Sophia's sesame cookies, a delicacy to which Abou was addicted.

Cohen sipped his tea and nibbled at a cookie. "These are exceptional, Abou! Ambrosia."

Abou sat across from him and sipped his tea. "Today wasn't good."

"We saw."

"I know in your mind there is no relationship between the clergy and Allah, but I was shocked by the mullah's response."

Cohen ate his third cookie. "A sordid bunch. In Teheran the clergy has taken to outright thievery, filling Swiss accounts."

"There must be some good men practicing their religions," Abou replied.

Cohen sniffed, pushing the cookies away. "There are good men and women doing everything in this world, just as there are evil people involved in most endeavors. But humans expect more from their clergy, as they should."

Abou poured more tea and pushed the cookies closer to Cohen, who took another. "Are you answering my question of the other night? Is there Allah?"

Cohen considered his answer carefully. "Look Abou, we sympathize deeply with your need for an answer. It is a profound yearning in most humans, and we gave careful thought about how we should answer this question, and you must remember our answer isn't definitive, although we have a somewhat larger perspective than you. There is no Yahweh or Allah or any particular god that we know of. There seems to be a force, an enormous energy which pushes the universe along. We don't really know if it's intelligent or not or, for that matter, what its intelligence is. We don't know if there is a purpose to the force. We know *our* purpose intuitively, and we can't explain how we know what we are supposed to do, but we do. That is the best I can do."

"No Allah?" Abou questioned.

"Nothing is gained by destroying your faith, Abou. One of the main causes of turmoil in the human race is this belief in a particular god. It has driven men to extremes in the belief their god is the only god. We don't see that." Cohen hesitated for a moment. "Take this desecration by the Taliban, the destruction of those beautiful statues of Buddha. They were beautiful statues and should have been left alone. All this is so pointless."

"And there was no Muhammad or Jesus Christ or Buddha or Joseph Smith?" Abou interrupted.

"Oh, sure. Nice guys. Hearts in the right place and all that, and they really believed what they taught."

"But not messengers of God?" Abou asked.

Cohen sighed. "Abou, listen to me. All this strife has come from the idea of a human as a messenger from God. Differences between religions have led to slaughter. Even differences within a particular religious group have caused all sorts of dissent. Your mullah is a petty man. His mosque is an organization which can dispense money unfairly, but all I am saying is keep your perspective. You know more about God right now than he does."

"And Muhammad wasn't a prophet?"

"Can energy have a son? Can energy designate a prophet? I mean, get real."

Abou rose and set the pot back on the stove, which had been banked for the night but still contained considerable heat. Without turning, Abou said, "And that means we really have no reason for being, no purpose."

"Being alive is purpose enough, Abou," Cohen replied cheerfully. "Having kids. Living happily. That seems to be quite something to us."

Abou returned to the table and poured hot tea into their cups. "But we simply live, procreate, and then die. Nobody remembers us after a generation or two."

"If somebody remembers you for fifty, sixty years, that's pretty good, and look at Shakespeare and Plato. Those guys' reputations really stuck. People don't want to dwell on death anyway, except maybe the Egyptians, who seemed at one time to get a real bang out of it. The whole idea of mummies is really kind of weird."

"A cynical, *irreverent* angel."

"Well, I feel like I can let my hair down with you," Cohen admitted. "Decay is good, Abou. Can you imagine the clutter if you didn't have it?"

"But for no purpose," Abou mused.

"Look, living ain't half bad. You have a great time eating, playing sports and . . . well, having fun with females, and for the most part they have a great time with you. Raising kids has its moments, although when people realize that's all there is, they can get very depressed, but the art and music humans have created is really amazing, and the world's literature isn't anything to sneeze at, unless you're dealing with musty books and then you can't help but sneeze." He slapped his knees in delight at his joke.

Abou gave him a disapproving look and Cohen held up a hand. "Look, buddy, you're looking at this thing all wrong. There are things of unimaginable beauty in the universe, and you are just beginning to find out about them. I've got to tell you, Abou, watching the death of stars, the birth of constellations, the density of black holes, is beyond the imagination. And now you humans are getting a chance to peek."

"Makes us very inconsequential," Abou lamented.

Abou shook his head. "I wouldn't say that at all. You humans are extraordinary. In many ways you're more fun than watching a supernova."

"Then tell me why we invented a god, if He doesn't exist?"

Cohen shrugged. "No big deal. Humans seem to need a reason for living. Just being alive doesn't seem to do it for them. I mean waking up and knowing you're alive is a miracle, in a manner of speaking, but that just doesn't seem to be enough for most of you. Look at it this way—stars die, galaxies crumble, and they don't complain. Just accept the situation and move on."

Abou looked at Cohen, waiting for further explanation. Finally he asked, "That's it? We needed gods so we created them?"

Cohen shrugged. "Well, of course there's that need for authority and all that other stuff we talked about."

Abou sat holding his cold cup of tea. Finally, he said, "I would have thought there was more to such a universally held belief. It seems so . . . well, pedestrian. According to what you say, our concept of leadership and religion is mixed together, and it all comes from a few barely competent sentries standing over a band of sleeping animals millions of years ago."

Cohen grinned. "Pedestrian? Not a word the average goat herder uses."

"I must think about this carefully," Abou replied. "I must say, I'm not convinced by your explanation. I'm not prepared to give up Allah so easily."

"Ain't that the truth," Cohen agreed cheerily, grabbed a few cookies, and disappeared.

The Eleventh Day

ABOU HAD NOT FORGOTTEN his promise to investigate the possibility of emigration with Marwan, the attorney. He left the house without his morning tea, but remembering his dream, he did stop to pray. He felt almost guilty that he had listened to the angel without stronger objections. Of course, Cohen had not actually said Allah did not exist, only that He might exist in a different form, and this, in itself, was perplexing, for Abou had always imagined Allah as a great, wise father. What he did know, and what he had suspected for a long time, was that he could not expect any intervention from Allah to solve his problems, that he and Sophia would have to work out their own solutions.

He rushed down the cobbled street greeting neighbors as he went. Some, not having heard of his redemption by Hamas, snubbed him as a pedophile, but others greeted him with smiles of acceptance, now that they had been assured that the tales about him were Zionist inspired.

Marwan was seated in a camp chair outside his office, warming himself in the morning sun before setting off in his endless pursuit of litigants. He loved nothing more than strolling through the market looking for a wayward donkey nipping an unsuspecting customer while he or she was selecting succulent fruit from a vendor's stall. Marwan would rush over, examine the wound, and offer his services and his card to the injured party. Some days he would accumulate six or seven souls who had been bitten, kicked, bumped, or otherwise inconvenienced by their shopping experiences.

When he heard Abou's hail, he opened one eye and examined him critically. "Ah, Abou, back again? And rushing about. You should rest. Bring a second chair from my office and take the sun with me. I can send my clerk for mint teas."

"Oh, that I could," Abou lamented, "but I have far too much to do today. I have but one question for you."

"It is?"

"How difficult would it be for my daughter and her children to accompany me to America?"

Marwan sat up. There could be a sizable fee involved in this. "A visit?"

Abou hesitated. He had not decided how candid to be with the attorney. The truth was very dangerous and he had kept his American citizenship secret for over twenty years. "We had thought about a permanent stay."

"You want visas and work permits?"

"Ah, yes, I suppose so," Abou replied. "No, work permits won't be necessary. We can live on my social security that I get from the American government."

"Social security," Marwan mused. "You they might let in, but what can Sophia do? You need a sponsor to emigrate, a promise of work."

"A visit then?" Abou said weakly.

Marwan didn't even open his eyes. "A visit is possible, but Sophia will need Yasser's permission to take the children out of the country, even for a visit. Does she have his permission?"

"Not as yet."

"I thought not," Marwan replied, "and the Americans will want to know who you are visiting and why, and if it isn't a good reason, they will figure you will probably stay on as unregistered aliens. At one time, they didn't seem to care much about this, but now they are more careful, and they don't like Arabs anyway."

Abou still hesitated. He really wasn't at all sure he should say what he was about to say. The danger to both him and Sophia was immense if Marwan were indiscreet. "I am a citizen," he whispered.

"A citizen?" Marwan questioned, sitting up. "Palestine?"

"And America," Abou admitted. "I took citizenship while I was there. I have never told anyone else, except my beloved wife."

"Don't!" Marwan warned in a whisper, holding up his hand. "It would be most dangerous if people knew you were an American citizen."

Abou nodded. "I know. It seemed like a good idea at the time. I was thinking Salah would enjoy living there, but she didn't want to leave our village."

"I understand," Marwan replied. "As for your question, I will have to find out the answer carefully. I cannot ask other attorneys near here or even Gaza City. That is far too dangerous. I will telephone colleagues in Jerusalem, but I would say that, as an American citizen, you are entitled to return to America and probably can bring your daughter and grandchildren. Have you an American passport?"

187

"It expired years ago, but I still have it."

"Consider a trip to Egypt or Jordan to renew it, but don't do anything until I can give you an answer about your status. This is a very interesting problem."

Abou nodded, turned away, and began walking slowly back toward the square. When he had taken about ten steps, Marwan called after him, "I saw Yasser in the marketplace last evening after prayer. He was greatly subdued."

Abou returned to where Marwan still sat. He didn't want the conversation spread about the bazaar. "In what way was he subdued?"

Marwan shrugged. "Oh, I don't know. You know how he usually is. Loud. Opinionated. He just stayed by himself and drank his coffee."

"I heard that the mullah is lending him money," Abou replied, seeing an opportunity to undermine Malluk's plan.

Marwan sat up. "Money? He is giving Yasser money from the mosque?" Then, cautiously, suspecting he was being drawn in, he added, "I had no idea."

"That is what Malluk told me yesterday."

"He did," Marwan mused. It wasn't even a question.

AFTER LEAVING THE ATTORNEY, Abou wandered the town thinking that the threat of an immediate Israeli incursion seemed to have lessened. People were shopping, talking, and taking care of everyday business. Abou knew that the Israelis would certainly retaliate for the attack on their checkpoint, but the form of that retaliation was always a question.

In any case, Abou planned to be outside his tent at three to greet the children. Sitting on a bench near the village well, where gossip flowed far more freely than water, he watched as the women filled their pots and pails, some indifferent to the amount or purity of the liquid, as the occasion was only a social event for them. For others the trip was necessary, as there were still many homes in Helar without a water pipe. He half listened to the babble of the marketplace, his mind wandering over his insoluble dilemmas.

"Abou?" Hamid emerged from the crowd, his ersatz postal bag slung over his shoulder, a huge smile on his face. "Is that you?"

"Who else?"

"I am surprised, that is all," his friend responded and sat next to him on the bench.

"And what are you doing?"

"Playing mailman," Hamid admitted cheerfully and plunged his hand into his satchel. "Handbills for the play center. Khaled el-Qut asked me to hand them out so that the center is filled with youngsters today and tomorrow. He plans special events."

"Such as?"

"He didn't say, but he expects you to be there today."

Abou nodded. "Certainly I will be there. In your travels, have you heard anything about the Israelis?"

"No, nothing," Hamid replied, shaking his head slowly. "And it is strange. There has been nothing. No attacks. No overflights. Nothing on the radio."

"They are probably still arguing in Jerusalem," Abou replied with a shrug of indifference. "Believe me, when they have finished debating, they will think of something horrible to inflict on us. It is their way."

Hamid rose. "Will you help me hand out flyers?"

"Why not?" Abou replied. "Let us hand them out and then you and I will have a fine lunch at the Camel's Hump. Agreed?"

"Agreed!" Hamid replied with enthusiasm, immediately delivering a sheet to a startled woman who was dragging her son behind her.

A little after noon, after they had finished their devotions, they entered the Camel's Hump and found Ammon and Absollah sitting at a far table in the courtyard.

"The Jews have not come. Maybe Hamas has convinced them that their stupid tit-for-tat policy is futile," Absollah said with a smile.

"Somehow I doubt that," Abou observed as he arranged his robe and sat in the shade of the building. "They have long memories."

"As do we," Ammon replied.

Abou talked about the morning's distribution. Absollah was suddenly enthusiastic.

"Khaled el-Qut wants the center to succeed," Absollah confided, acting as if he were the Hamas chieftain's confidant. "And it has been wonderful for business. Since you began this, Abou, our savings accounts have increased 7 percent, and our loans 9 percent. It has been very good for the bank." Absollah went on, "And I was told today that Yasser's landlord has padlocked his shop for nonpayment of rent."

Abou found this sobering. "In spite of all he's done, I feel pity for him. But, perhaps matters will improve for him. Just yesterday it seemed everyone was against *me*, and now I am accepted."

Absollah smiled. "I wouldn't be surprised it wasn't the doing of Khaled el-Qut. He was very annoyed when those hostile rumors started. I think he might have quashed them."

"If that is true, I should thank him," Abou replied. "I am not smitten with his organization, to tell the truth, but he seems a decent sort."

"For Allah's sake, Abou, please keep your voice down," Absollah hissed, and even Ammon nodded. "You can get us killed."

"Killed?" Abou replied in a much lower voice. "I don't think so. Hamas is powerful, but it is not beyond criticism, and some of its practices are questionable. We all know the members are sincere, but some of their activities seem inappropriate."

"Don't be naive," Ammon interjected. "If for a minute they thought you were harming their cause, they would eliminate you. Please keep your opinions to yourself, my friend, or we will all be tainted by your words."

Abou thought of Cohen's warning about divulging his visits. "I must be extraordinarily guileless," he admitted, turning to his lunch.

Ammon changed the subject. Years earlier the four of them had agreed to avoid politics in their meetings, but slowly, over the years, the immediacy of the turmoil had overridden their caution. "I heard this morning the Labor Party is badgering Sharon about his policies on restoration of our lands."

"A fat lot of good that will do," Absollah replied, his mouth stuffed with pita and hummus. "Likud couldn't care less."

Abou was subdued by the rebuke from Ammon, but Hamid said cheerfully, "As long as Arik blabbers, he won't bomb us."

"Ha!" Absollah blurted. "I suppose the Palestine Authority will protect us?"

Hamid replied softly, "Arafat is a good man."

"He is a dunce," Ammon replied. Helar was Hamas territory, so some criticism of other organizations and their leaders was tolerated up to a point. "Nobody pays any attention to him except the Americans, who seem to be fond of leaders that the people detest. He encourages our youth to throw rocks and then tells the Americans he can do nothing. He thinks he is cunning, but he is only a fool."

Abou looked out at the multitudes in the marketplace, the shrouded women, the men with expressions of wonder, greed, merriment, and dejection, their clothes dusty from the day's travail, the sun forever overhead. He sighed and turned to his friends. "Barak, Arik, Bibi—they are all the same. Peace is never any closer."

Absollah looked at his friend with interest. "I didn't know you thought much about politics, Abou."

"I think about survival," Abou replied in a weary whisper. "The Israelis build apartment houses, Hamas slays a few soldiers, the Israelis send their tanks in and kill a few dozen people, Hamas has the children throw rocks at the soldiers, and nothing really changes. It is the strutting of peacocks."

"They *must* withdraw from the West Bank!" Ammon declared, also intrigued by Abou's sudden declarations on the situation.

Abou shrugged. "It takes a great people to return land they have won in war. The Israelis gave the Egyptians the Sinai. But I think they will find it very hard to give back more land."

Absollah and Ammon nodded, their faces long. Hamid shook his head. "Arafat will convince them."

Abou patted Hamid's knee. "I hope so, old friend. I truly hope so."

They finished their lunch in silence.

KHALED EL-QUT GREETED THEM in front of Abou's tent. Abou noted that there were no workmen in the building behind the lot, but Absollah had reopened the bank.

"Ah, I am so glad you came, Abou Ben Adhem. And you brought the trustworthy Hamid with you. My men and I are very busy today and must be away for several hours, and we only have a few volunteers to help you and your friend. I can leave these men," he said, gesturing at several standing by the food pots. "The food is prepared and is ready to hand out, but, as you can see, more people are needed. Can you help us distribute the food?"

"That is why we came, Khaled el-Qut."

"Because of yesterday's incident, we may not have too many children, but you can never tell. The more who can help, the better. Have you prepared anything to teach them this afternoon?"

"My father once told me that after man tamed the wolf, he domesticated the sheep and goat next. I don't know where he got such information, but it seemed a worthy topic of discussion, how animals became our friends and what we have gained from them."

"Admirable," Khaled replied. "Be sure to note the diseases man has contracted from animals. The poxes especially."

Abou looked at him skeptically.

"No, no, I am serious, Abou. These children should understand that everything good can have a negative aspect, that we humans must decide what we want most, the meat and eggs of the chicken, or do we avoid the animal because of its pox? This will show them what man faces each day in this world."

"These are very young children," Abou replied. "I am not sure they are ready for such lessons."

"Younger is better," Khaled answered. "They must know that life is choice, and some choices are very difficult."

"True," Abou agreed. "I shall find some felicitous way of saying it."

"Ah, yes. Felicitous. These children are in better hands with you, Abou. I am an old desert rat with little couth." Khaled laughed and turned to Hamid. "And have you a lesson, postmaster?"

"I want to explain the importance of writing, how spoken words disappear on the wind, but the written word is here forever."

"Ah, a thought worth developing."

A man approached. Abou saw a weapon under his robe. He whispered to Khaled, who nodded his head. "I must go. What you have planned is very good. And tomorrow? Will you be back tomorrow?"

"Certainly," Abou said. "Will you be here?"

"For a time. I may be called away. These are very difficult times we face, and the situation changes from minute to minute."

Abou watched as the burly Hamas leader strode out of the center, his men in tow. He decided that if he were to continue this project, he would have to prepare material other than his father's tales.

Abou introduced himself to the three men Khaled had left behind to help with the food, lower-echelon Hamas warriors, or so they described themselves to him. They seemed a good lot, although hardly the stuff from which warriors were made.

The first child appeared a little after three, and after that there was a flood, some fifty to sixty children, both male and female (Hamas would not allow segregation, saying that both sexes were needed in the fight against the Zionists), laughing, delighted with the food and entertainment. Sophia came with Akbar, who was timid at first but within minutes had joined the rest, gobbling the food like little rabbits, their mouths twitching in delight at the dates and bread, spread with thick honey, a real treat.

After the food was consumed, the children settled in. Hamid described eloquently the miracle of communication between people, the different languages around the world, and the varied people who spoke them. The children were insatiable in their quest for information, particularly about movie stars and famous musicians. Abou was astounded by how much they already knew—far more than he—about celebrities in almost all countries. Their society was not as insular as some thought, he observed as he watched Hamid chatting easily with the children. And even more surprising was Hamid's intimate knowledge of inconsequential world events and the participants in them. Who were the Rolling Stones? He knew. How much were Nike shoes? He knew. Were there actually women who danced in the cafés of Cairo? Hamid hesitated, looking sheepishly at the girls in the audience, and then told the gathering, "It is an art form we do not allow in our town of Helar, but yes, women dance for male audiences."

The children giggled about this, and the girls whispered little-girl secrets to one another. Hamid quickly changed the subject, returning to the adventure of receiving mail. Knowledge about strange and wonderful things came from this very medium, the mail, Hamid explained, producing from his satchel letters about magicians' paraphernalia, the control of cockroaches, and a sale of lederhosen to young Bavarians.

When his time came, Abou showed the children the pictures of goats that his mother and grandmother had woven into the fabric of the tent wall, and he explained how important these goats were for the survival of not only his family but hundreds more in the vicinity. Most of the children had drunk goat's milk and many had eaten goat cheese, although it had become quite dear these past years.

When he described the llama and imitated the sound it makes, which he had heard in a zoo in America, the children laughed and clapped, but they scoffed at the idea that llamas were cousins of the camel, living half a world from them. Abou promised to try to find pictures of all the animals he talked about for those who had never seen them.

And then it was time to go home. Khaled appeared suddenly, a great smile on his face, followed by his aides, as he called them. He walked among the children, patting heads and laughing with them.

"But you must be off," he boomed with a deep laugh. "You must get home and do your chores, your homework, and get your supper. On Friday, you can stay later, if your parents agree. We will have many storytellers here then, as well as Abou and Hamid. It will give your parents time to visit the mosque for the evening service."

The children began to disperse and Khaled turned to Abou and Hamid, saying, "You were remarkable with the children. They will remember what they learned here for years to come. I was very lucky to find you men for the center. I would wager each one of them will be back tomorrow, with friends, to hear your tales."

"I hope so," Abou said, and Hamid nodded vigorously.

As they set off toward home, Akbar said, "It is very nice that you tell us these stories, Grandfather."

"It is our pleasure, isn't it, Hamid?"

Hamid shifted his mailbag and smiled down at the little boy. "Over the years people have thought me silly for caring so much about mail. It is good to find children who think it is important."

"It is *very* important," Akbar replied with a serious, little-boy demeanor that delighted both the men.

"Perhaps you would like to become a mailman?" Hamid suggested.

Akbar looked at his grandfather's friend with large, contemplative eyes. "I wish to be a bullfighter, but if it were not for that, I would be a mailman."

"A bullfighter!" Abou exploded with a laugh. "Where did you ever hear of that occupation?"

"In school," Akbar replied evenly. "I saw a picture. I was quite taken with it, as were some of my friends."

"I would think it takes many years of training," Hamid said as he bid them goodnight.

"Yes, I think so," Akbar replied, his eyes serious. "But it is very graceful when the bull passes the man with the cape."

"I believe he is called a matador," Abou said.

"Matador," Akbar repeated. "That is a nice name. I shall tell my friends. We will be matadors."

They walked a bit in silence, and then Akbar asked, "Do you love my sister?"

Abou was taken by surprise. "I . . . yes, but she is very small."

"I love her, and Mama loves her, but nobody else seems to pay any attention to her."

"She is very small," Abou repeated, beginning to feel uncomfortable by the turn in the conversation.

"She laughs when she sees me. She thinks I am foolish with my silly faces and the funny noises I make, but she smiles at me and makes nice sounds. I wish she could talk."

"Oh, she will. Within a year she will be filling your ears."

"A year is a long time," Akbar replied. "But I suppose I must wait. There is nothing I can do."

"No, you can't make them talk sooner or walk sooner. Babies take their time about these matters."

"She is getting very heavy. Mother is having trouble carrying her."

"Is that a fact?" Abou said. "I had not noticed."

"She is very big. The women in the marketplace say she is very big for her age. I have a very big sister."

"You sound proud," Abou said with a smile.

"I am, but I don't want her too big. I don't want others to laugh at her."

Abou realized how much he enjoyed holding his grandson's hand and talking to him. At the house door, Akbar stopped and looked up at Abou. "I am very proud that the other children think you are so interesting."

With that, he opened the door and greeted his mother, who was chopping onions in the kitchen.

"Have you schoolwork?" she asked.

"Sums."

"Do them before supper, little warrior," she said, and he ran off to his room.

She turned back to her chopping. "Yasser was here today."

Abou's heart sank. "And?" he asked cautiously.

"The mullah said he would help him reopen the shop. He wants to come home, but he is worried about you."

"Me? What about you and the children?"

She shrugged. "He said his worries about money made him behave badly."

She turned and he saw her eyes were red, but he wasn't sure if it were due to the onions or not. "The children and I have nowhere to go, Papa. I have nowhere to go."

"You have me, little one. I am old, but I am healthy and I have this small income. You don't have to go back to him unless you wish to."

She turned again to her chopping and he knew he had his answer. She needed a husband to sustain her relationship with her friends in the marketplace, and she needed a man in her bed. In their world a woman without a husband was almost nothing. This was the reality. She didn't need an ancient father who could only feed and clothe her and the children. "I think he misses the children . . . Akbar at least, these past few days. And I know Akbar misses him."

"Akbar said nothing to me today," Abou answered, sounding a bit peevish, as if the boy had bared his whole mind on the walk home.

"He confides in me," Sophia replied. "He cries at night for his father."

Abou kept his silence.

"This is my fault, Papa. I should not have brought my problems to you."

"Yes, you should," he answered softly, putting his hand on her arm. "That is what fathers are for. And if reconciliation doesn't work out, I expect you to come to me again. I want you and the children happy, Sophia. That is all I want."

She nodded and blew her nose. "Would you call Akbar for supper? I will set the bowls out."

He found Akbar working diligently at his sums, his little hand barely able to manage the pencil. When he made an error, which he had done just as Abou entered the room, he scrubbed the paper earnestly, as if wanting to obliterate the inaccuracy completely. "Wash, Akbar," Abou said softly and his grandson looked up with his great eyes. "It is supper time."

At the table, Akbar babbled happily about his success with his homework. He knew he had done well and when his mother reviewed it after supper, he would be rewarded, if things went as well as he expected, with a piece of rock candy. Abou realized, as he watched, how much family life was taken up with children.

Sophia had gone off to nurse the baby.

"Your mother has worked very hard today and we can help," Abou explained to Akbar, scraping scraps into a waste bin and placing the dishes in a pan.

"I help her when we are alone," Akbar admitted.

When Sophia returned, her face lit up with a smile at the sight of her table with only a bowl of oranges and dates in its center. "You are too good to me," she murmured, gliding to the sink.

"We could dry them for you," Akbar offered. "Grandpapa tells me he helps you too when Papa and I are not about."

"That is true," Sophia replied. "But I think it would be better if you showed your sums to your grandfather to see how well you did your work and if your work is correct. I may have missed something. You don't want the teacher to find an error tomorrow."

The little boy hurried off to get his workbook.

Abou again felt the warmth of his daughter's world and it saddened him to know he would soon be excluded. "I will step out in the back and enjoy my evening cigarette, away from the children, who, I have read, could get cancer."

"I hope that is not true," Sophia replied. "Yasser smokes in the house all the time."

In the cool garden, sitting on an overturned washtub with his Marlboro, Abou thought how pleasurable the aroma usually was and how wonderful the feeling of light-headedness each cigarette afforded. Just one cigarette in the evening, surrounded by the rich taste and smell, and he felt transported to a world of momentary opulence, as lucky as the richest sheik. But tonight the cigarette was strangely bitter and unsatisfactory, yet years of parsimony prevented him from casting it aside. Only when Akbar appeared was he willing to extinguish the stub beneath his sandal.

"It is my bedtime, Grandfather."

"Am I to check your sums?"

"Mother did it. She gave me another candy." He happily displayed the piece of candy between his teeth.

Abou hugged the little boy. "Sleep well. Tomorrow you will excel in school, and afterward, if your mother is willing, you will come to the center to listen to Hamid's stories."

After he was gone, Abou looked at the stars. When he was in America, he had been deprived of the stars. The city lights obliterated them. Sitting on the roof of his rooming house on Atlantic Avenue, he had thought of the stars at home, of Salah and what his life had become. The next day he would drive extra hours to earn more money.

When Sophia joined him, she asked, "May I have a cigarette?"

"I didn't know you smoked," he replied with surprise, fumbling in his robe.

"Secretly," she replied, exhaling. "Not often. It is very expensive."

"It has become so," Abou agreed. "Once it was the poor man's pleasure, but no longer."

"I like American cigarettes the best," she said, drawing deeply. "Yasser sometimes came home with a pack."

"He doesn't know you smoke?"

The tip of the cigarette glowed in the dark for a moment as she inhaled. "No, he doesn't know. He doesn't approve of women smoking. He doesn't approve of women watching soccer. He doesn't . . ." Her voice drifted off.

"Is reconciliation worth it?" Abou asked.

The light from her cigarette suddenly became brighter. She replied, "A woman with two children who has forced her husband into the streets has no place in this world. Other women would see her as a temptation for their sons and husbands, a disruptive force, even though they know full well why she rid herself of her husband. There would be no life for such a woman."

"Even if she were living with her father?"

Sophia didn't answer. The tip of the cigarette brightened again. Finally, she sighed. "He misses his son terribly. Yasser sees himself in Akbar, although I can't imagine how. Akbar is so innocent and loving. But Yasser, if he returns, will mold him into something offensive, I'm sure. I don't think he will really want to do that to Akbar, but he won't be able to help himself. Little boys can grow up into monsters. Still I think it is better if he returns."

"I will make arrangements tomorrow," Abou said as he rose. "I do not want to be here if he returns."

She didn't object. He left her there in the darkness smoking her Marlboro.

The Eleventh Darkfall

ABOU SENSED THE PRESENCE of the angel, and when he opened his eyes, he found Cohen sitting in an upright chair near the door of the cubicle.

"You heard?" Abou asked.

Cohen nodded.

"Why do you think Sophia decided to have him back?"

The angel shrugged. "I think you have to take her at her word. We have no greater insight than you in human motivation, Abou. We only know what a person says or does, and Sophia strikes me as a very honest human."

"She is. She is," Abou murmured, "but often people don't know why they say certain things."

Cohen nodded. He was wearing his checkered suit again and was cleaning his nails with a small penknife. "I know, but speech preceded thought, and both are still evolving. In a more primitive society, Yasser would hunt or till the soil while Sophia raised the children. With less stress, he might even be a nice guy. In this society, it isn't so easy, and in others, more advanced, in many ways it is harder still."

Abou snorted. "Where, I'd like to know?"

"Any industrialized nation. The traditional male role is distorted. There are too many children being raised without two parents. They need both of them. I know that isn't fashionable, but it's the way of the world from our observations. Happily, in America there seems to be a small reversal, where there are now more families with both the husband and the wife living together."

Abou thought about this for a time. In a small voice, he said, "I want Sophia happy."

"Certainly you do," Cohen replied. "And having children and seeing them grow makes her happy. She would be happier if Yasser did his part, but she isn't absolutely miserable, either. I think that is what she was trying to say tonight. And above all else, she wants to be a part of Akbar's life."

"Why didn't she say that to me?"

Cohen considered this for a moment. "I don't think she is capable of abandoning her son totally to Yasser. She just can't chance it, but she can't tell you why, either. It is a feeling inside her that overwhelms thought and language."

Abou thought about Sophia's feelings as he prepared green tea.

Cohen accepted a cup. "This is delicious," he said. "Do you happen to have any more of those sesame cookies?"

Abou shook his head.

"A shame," Cohen replied, looking deprived. Abou relented and reached up and took the children's cookie jar from the shelf. "Just leave enough for Akbar's lunch tomorrow."

"Oh, yes," Cohen replied, munching happily. "These are just extraordinary! Tell Sophia."

"Shall I tell her the source of the compliment?"

Cohen shrugged. "Why not? Well, maybe not. It's one thing to have an isolated visitation with an angel, but a protracted discussion is something else. This gets out and you'll be glad Arafat has spent absolutely nothing on mental health facilities in Gaza. They would pop you into a mental ward if they had one."

Abou ignored Cohen's last remark. "How can she go back to him?"

Cohen smiled. "There is very little pure logic with humans, Abou. Your math is the nearest you get to it. Logically, Sophia should cut her losses and move away, find another mate, and have more children. That way she would keep her baby at least."

"That's not . . . ," Abou objected.

"I know. I know," Cohen agreed. "You have this ill-conceived notion to slip out of the country with Sophia and the two children, but honestly, do you think that's going to work? In the meantime, Sophia is doing what she thinks is best for her children. It may not be rational, but it is the best humans can do and you have to respect it."

"What you're really saying is that many of us are so stupid, we can't solve our own problems," Abou replied heatedly, secretly knowing that Cohen was probably correct in his assessment.

"Stupid? I never said that. Abou, to repeat my words of these last few nights, humanity is a work in progress. Some of you are more advanced, more logical, but most of you are a bunch of crazy, mixed-up primates floundering around, screwing up all the time."

"So most of us are incapable of logical conclusions?" Abou was genuinely perplexed.

"You don't seem to have the foggiest notion whether your conclusions are logical or not. Look at this mess you're forced to live in. The British decided the Palestinians wouldn't mind having a Jewish nation plunked down in their midst. Talk about fuzzy thinking. And consider what the Brits could have done, given the stranglehold they had on the region. They could have declared Jerusalem an open city to all three major religions."

"Then you agree with us!" Abou concluded.

"Naw," Cohen replied. "There's no right or wrong to this. The British goofed. The Arabs misjudged the determination of the early Israeli settlers. The Israelis thought it was a simple matter of defeating an Arab nation here or there and they wouldn't have to make any compromises. Just goofy thinking all around. What we have is impaired minds trying to solve difficult problems."

"Then Sophia has an impaired mind?" Abou said.

"She is trying to solve her problems and her children's," Cohen replied, sneaking another cookie and accepting a refill of tea. "She's protecting her own the best way she can, albeit hopelessly. She's willing to accept a life of misery to help her children. Laudable, but not reasonable."

"There's no hope for us," Abou moaned.

"No, no, no," Cohen replied, "I never said that. As humans, you're making progress. War is a dreadful drain on natural resources, as well as a rather drastic way to end your tenure on earth if it gets out of hand, but you're trying to control it. Conservation has become accepted by many. Uncontrolled population growth is now seen as a danger by many and must be somehow controlled, but not by atomic weapons—that's a little much! Individually, people must face their day-to-day difficulties the best way they can. If you find you can spirit Sophia and the children out of the country to escape Yasser, more power to you. I don't know if she will go along with it, but it gives her an option. As of now, she sees no options, and that is crushing to a human's spirit." And with this pronouncement, Cohen snatched a last cookie and finished his tea. "I must be off, good buddy."

Abou, lost in thought, almost forgot a question he wanted to ask. "Wait! I made a promise to the children today, Cohen. I said I was going to procure a picture book of animals and I have no way of knowing where to get such a book. Can you help?"

Cohen smiled. "Well, it may be bridging a confidence, but talk to your friend Marwan, the attorney. He has a fine book on exotic animals in his home library."

Abou smiled. "Thank you for the suggestion."

"And buy a computer, Abou. You could find a lot of information on the Internet," the angel replied as he disappeared.

The Twelfth Day

ABOU WAS GROGGY when he awoke, still sleepy yet unable to fall asleep again. He listened to Akbar's small voice asking what he was getting in his lunch pail.

"Oh, you will be happy today, young Akbar," Sophia said seriously. "Funny, I thought I had cookies in this jar. Well, anyway, I obtained an apple yesterday and it is already waiting in your box for lunch. But no cheating. You must promise not to eat it in class while the teacher isn't looking."

"I would never," he protested, delighted with the treat. "I will save it. Perhaps I shall share it."

"That would be nice," his mother replied. "But don't give away more than a quarter. You need fruit to make you strong."

"As my father?"

Sophia hesitated. "Yes, as strong as your father. Now finish your breakfast and be off."

"Can I visit Grandfather after school?"

"Yes, and come home with him, too. I will be waiting for you men with a hearty supper."

Abou could hear the baby mewing like a kitten. He waited until he heard the gate latch fall, which meant that Akbar was gone, and the shuffle of feet that indicated Sophia was in the rear of the house preparing to feed the baby, before he rose and made his way to the latrine behind the house. He found a portion of the day's paper left by a neighbor. As Abou sat there, he read of the Israeli official response to the killing of their soldiers at the checkpoint. Words like "measured response" and "provocative acts" sprinkled the pages like dust. Down in the far corner of the last page was a short item about how the mother of one of the dead soldiers pleaded with the Jewish leadership to seek peace. Abou read the words over and over, wondering if this were the mother of his young trooper.

Abou sighed deeply, dreadfully tired of living amid such strife, killing, and reprisals. Suddenly, two things happened. He evacuated his bowels and his mind cleared as he muttered aloud, "This violence must stop! It doesn't matter who is right or wrong. It simply must stop!"

His spoken words shocked him. Although skeptical at times, never had he seriously questioned the rectitude of the Palestinian cause. He had mouthed appropriate words about the desirability of peace, but he realized that it was always a peace that better suited the Arabs than the Jews. Fifty-odd years of mayhem was enough. He thought again of the young Israeli soldier who had given him the headache tablet. He was probably gone from the earth forever, dead for no other reason than some intangible advantage in what seemed an endless struggle. Abou decided there should be no winners or losers. The hostility should just end.

After cleaning himself with his left hand, Abou marched back to the house determined to make his new thoughts known. When he entered the kitchen, he said, "This killing must stop, Sophia! We must stop killing the Jews and they must stop killing us."

Mixing dough with her strong fingers, she looked at him and said, "That would be nice, Papa. Have you been at the cookies? I thought I had more." When he looked away to cover his embarrassment, she asked, "Who is to tell both sides?"

"I shall," he replied, deciding to ignore the question about the sweets. Certainly this wasn't the time to explain about Cohen's sweet tooth. "Our lives are intolerable. Confrontation has led to nothing but death, poverty, and hatred. That young Israeli gave me medicine and is now dead."

"He also participated in your getting knocked about. If he is dead, I am sorry, but what he was doing was wrong. We were bothering nobody. Why force us off our bus and beat you on the head?"

"None of it is right," Abou replied. "This strife is absolute madness. I intend to tell anyone who will listen that violence must stop on both sides. We should simply give up fighting. If the Israelis don't, so be it."

Sophia shrugged and muttered, "You are elderly and most people will ignore what you say, so hopefully no harm will come to you."

Abou looked at his daughter in shock. "So, if you are old, you can speak the truth without fearing retaliation, but if you are young, you must be close-mouthed for self-preservation."

She kneaded the dough vigorously. "I do not want to hurt your feelings, Papa, but you know this is true. One must be careful about what one says. Only the aged or the demented can speak the truth, and it's even better if you are both old *and* demented."

Abou nodded slowly. "You are a wise young woman, Sophia. Sadly, I must admit you are right. But I, and people like me, should try to end this foolishness. I have known some peace in my lifetime, but your entire life has been enveloped in hatred and war."

"We know nothing else," she admitted. "And probably my children will know nothing else."

Abou laughed. "I will be prudent, but I want others to know that everyone doesn't approve of this never-ending struggle. I can only hope there is one old, demented Jew who thinks the same as I."

"We can only hope," Sophia replied with a smile. "You will be with the children this afternoon?"

"Oh, yes," he replied, watching her work the dough into a tough pile, then beat it down with vigor. "Have you decided about your husband?" he finally asked, unable to say Yasser's name.

She shook her head. "No, I have not decided. I thought I had last night, but when I awoke this morning, I had doubts. I keep thinking it would be best for me to welcome him back. The children and I have no future here otherwise, but . . . I just don't want him."

She smiled weakly as she rolled the dough balls into flat bread. "Life becomes so uncertain," she murmured. "When you are young, the dream seems so simple. Marry a wonderful man, have beautiful children, raise them, and then enjoy them when they are grown. But reality never seems to work out so well."

"This will all work out, Sophia," he assured her.

"You are a kind and thoughtful man, Papa," she replied.

Abou blushed. He was not used to such compliments. "I must hurry," he said in a low voice. "First thing, I must ask Marwan to lend me a book. I do not want to disappoint the children. If he won't lend it to me, I shall have to find pictures of animals somewhere."

Abou dressed and left the house hurriedly, rushing down the roadway, feeling the hot, gritty sand between his toes. The sun was already beginning its daily task of baking the buildings, as well as the residents, stealing water from pails and wells, distorting the air so that it appeared as waves of heat. Abou slowed. It was not prudent to hurry in such weather.

Marwan's office faced the street in front of his palatial home. Abou had been invited into the courtyard of the house once, years before, to enjoy mint tea in the shade of the fig and lemon trees. Marwan was sitting in the shade inside the doorway, fanning himself with a paper fan covered with Chinese characters. A large ceiling fan turned slowly, now and then striking a sluggish fly.

"Ah, Abou," Marwan greeted him. "Come for more information on how to leave our great country?"

"No, my friend, unless you already have information about how I can leave with my family."

"Not I," Marwan admitted. "I have sent an inquiry, but I must be prudent. It is the sort of inquiry which could pique officials' interest."

Abou smiled. "I have come concerning another matter. I, and others, have been telling the children each afternoon about life years ago as our parents and grandparents lived it. The bank has donated the property, and my old herder's tent is one of the exhibits. In any case, yesterday I somehow began telling them about strange animals around the world, and I made the sound a llama makes. Since the children had no idea what a llama was or what it looked like, I told them I would attempt to find a picture for them, and that is why I have come to you."

"Why me?" Marwan questioned.

Abou shrugged. "Perhaps your extensive library might have a picture of a llama? I didn't know where else to turn. I promised the children that I would try to bring it this afternoon."

Against the encroaching sun, Marwan moved his chair backward and shaded his eyes as he looked up at Abou. "I find it odd that anybody would think I had such a picture. I'm surprised that anyone has thoughts about my library."

"I just thought I would try you first."

"And if unsuccessful?" Marwan asked. He was no fool, Abou decided.

"There is a little library behind the jail. It hasn't much, but maybe it might have a picture book of animals."

"Is Hamas sponsoring this?"

Abou was somewhat taken aback. "Hamas? Oh, the whole children's program is under its auspices, I suppose, but the members seem far too busy to concern themselves with it. Yesterday there were a couple of their men there to help feed the children, and Hamid and myself to entertain with our tales, but Hamas seems too involved with its own political business to be concerned with us."

Marwan stared a long time at Abou, obviously trying to decide upon his response. Slowly he said, "I have heard something of what's going on. It's a worthwhile endeavor, to give the children something educational to do after school." Marwan looked steadily at Abou for a moment, and then continued, "Far too much of their time is spent in the streets selecting just the right rocks to hurl."

Abou relaxed somewhat. "I have often thought we must find a way to reduce the tension. I wish to find a way to say that to the children."

Marwan laughed. "I wouldn't if I were you, as long as Hamas is involved with the project."

"Perhaps," Abou replied, unwilling to give up this new mission so easily. "But someone should say such things."

"Granted," Marwan answered, rising from his chair. "Come, we will see if I have such a book."

They made their way through the courtyard and up a stairway. Marwan opened a door and Abou found himself in a room, an office by the looks of the computer (Abou had not known there *was* one in the village) on one desk and papers with open law books on a second, but what startled Abou most were the books. The walls were lined with them. Abou tried not to gawk, but he read the titles rapidly, afire with a desire to draw out the substance of this one or that.

"My wife loves to read," Marwan said.

"It is remarkable," Abou replied in awe. "I have not seen so many books since I was in New York and my friend took me to this huge library in the center of the city."

"And you? Do you own many books?"

Abou raised a hand. "No, I survive on periodicals. Yasser, my son-in-law, brought old magazines and newspapers home from his shop and I would read them, as would Sophia, but not to his knowledge. He doesn't approve of women reading, but he thought my reading harmless."

Marwan pulled a cord on the wall and gestured for Abou to sit. "Perhaps some tea?"

Abou hesitated. "I can't stay long. I must try to find the book with the picture of the llama, if you don't have one."

"I have such a picture. I will lend you the book to show to the children. But try to keep it clean, will you? It is a book my wife and I dote upon."

"I shall be very careful. I would not want to disappoint the children, and I shall be careful about what I promise in the future."

Marwan continued, "You know, I haven't met many people who just read whatever comes into their hands. My wife is like that."

Abou waved his hand in embarrassment. "Please, you make too much of it. It is only lately I'm getting some insight into why we humans behave as we do."

"You are?" Marwan replied. "How interesting. And these insights are coming from reading?"

Abou laughed. "You will think me an old fool, but I dream and matters somehow become very clear to me in my sleep. Sometimes I wonder if being asleep isn't the real world and this is unreality." He swept his hand around the library.

Marwan pursed his lips. "I have heard of people solving problems in their sleep. Are you one of those?"

Abou hesitated. "Last night, or more precisely this morning, but as a result of dreams I have been having, it came to me that there was never going to be any satisfactory resolution in fighting the Jews. That both sides should simply stop. Only then will we be able to talk of peace and stability."

Marwan bent forward and said, "With whom have you shared this truth?"

"Just my daughter and you," Abou replied.

"Don't say such things in public, Abou. Hamas controls Helar and it would be taken amiss if they heard you were saying such things."

"Perhaps I could seek the protection of the Islamic Jihad?" Abou suggested.

Marwan shook his head. "The Jihad, and for that matter Fatah, has little power in this area, and all three would oppose your idea in any case. The unilateral cessation of hostilities would be considered surrender by all three organizations, and by a vast majority of nonaligned Palestinians as well. These groups would laugh at your idealistic notions, and if it looked like anyone was taking you seriously, they would find a way to silence you."

Abou replied, "I've been a loyal follower all my life. They would eliminate me for suggesting there might be a better way?"

Marwan shrugged. "Abou, these people are masters of intrigue and guile and have been nursed on hatred and weaned on mistrust. They will not tolerate dissent."

"Perhaps you are right," Abou conceded. "I shall be careful."

Marwan rose. "Let me get you the book. My wife purchased it in Paris. Lovely plates of exotic animals throughout the world. If I remember correctly, it has a picture of a llama in it."

Exotic Animals was extraordinary. Never in his life had Abou held such an expensive book. The photographs were sharp with beautiful color, exquisite shots of beasts from every corner of the world. He would certainly show the children the llama, but he vowed to himself that he would display as many pictures as he could in the time he had this afternoon, telling the children tales of as many animals as there was time. The picture of the llama was awe inspiring, set against a backdrop of majestic mountains. "It is very beautiful," Abou whispered. "Could you give me something to wrap it in?" At the same time, he saw the price of the book inside the cover and gasped. It was more than his monthly pension check.

Marwan returned with a burlap shopping bag. "Perhaps it will inspire the children to get an education and travel the world."

At the Camel's Hump, Abou selected a table far from other customers. He ordered nothing, not wanting to take a chance of soiling the book. Carefully he began turning the pages and found a picture of a Laplander with a herd of reindeer. When he had casually mentioned reindeer, the children had not believed that deer could be domesticated, and Abou had assured them that the Laplanders used deer for work as Arabs used the irritable camel. The picture did not exactly prove his point, but at least the deer looked docile.

"What is it?" Hamid asked, approaching the out-of-the-way table. "Why are you sitting over here?

Abou smiled. "I have borrowed this book from Marwan and I wanted to look at it without soiling it."

Hamid looked at the pages as Abou turned them. "What is that one?"

"An orangutan."

"A strange-looking beast," Hamid remarked, putting his leather pouch on the table. "You put my effort to shame, Abou. I gathered some material on computers. I understand that there is enormous information that can be gotten from those machines, and we don't have one in Helar, but I thought the children should know about them. I am going to tell them about electronic mail around the world, too."

Abou decided he wouldn't correct Hamid about there being no computers in Helar. He thought it was just possible that Marwan would suffer if it were known he owned such a device, although Abou wasn't quite sure why. "I think I'd better listen too, Hamid. Computers are a mystery to me."

"I fear someday they will replace mail," Hamid said sadly, looking at his satchel. "There will be no more letters."

Abou put his hand on his friend's arm. "If that is true, it is many years away. And in a way, it will make communication even more exciting. Just think of all the words flashing back and forth."

Hamid nodded. "But the letter in hand means so much." He was sad for a moment, then he brightened. "I'm told e-mail can be printed."

"You are lucky to have such interest in writing," Abou remarked.

Hamid smiled sheepishly. "Most think I'm just slow."

"True," Abou agreed cheerfully. "But most of us didn't really understand what you were saying about communication. It is very important."

"Sometimes *I* think I'm slow."

Abou smiled. "You may be the wisest of us all. Absollah thinks only of his bank. Ammon has his business. Me? I don't know what I think about."

Hamid laughed. "You think about angels!"

The outside eating area had slowly filled with noonday customers. Ammon waved at them from the street and moved between the tables to join them.

"Hello. Why over here?"

"I was trying to protect a book Marwan lent me. I sat over here so that no coffee or tea would spill on it."

"A book! What sort of book?" Ammon sat down.

"A book of animal pictures," Abou replied. "I was foolish enough to promise the children that I would locate a picture of a llama for them to see."

"A llama? I have never seen a llama," Ammon replied. He reached for the book, but Abou intercepted him.

"You must be very careful," he warned.

Ammon leafed slowly through the pages. "I have never seen many of these animals."

"The world is certainly filled with strange creatures," Hamid responded cheerfully.

Ammon looked at him sharply, closed the book, and handed it back. Something seemed to have suddenly darkened his mood.

"Is Absollah coming?" Abou asked.

Ammon nodded his head. "He said he would join us," and, as if his words were revelatory, Absollah appeared at the table.

"I thought you had all decided to eat lunch somewhere else," he said as he sat. "You are out of the way over here."

Ammon replied, "It is Abou's book. He must keep it clean."

"A book?"

"For the children," Abou explained. "I promised to find them a picture of a llama."

"A llama?" Absollah repeated the last words. "How in the world did you find a picture of one?"

Abou smiled. "By chance. I had heard Marwan had a large library, so I asked him. I believe the book belonged to his wife, who reads a great deal."

Hamid and Ammon exchanged glances. "Subversive," Ammon said. "Women reading can only undermine our society."

Hamid looked at him with a sour expression. "All our people should be able to read." Abou said, "I thought I would talk to Khaled about offering the children some sort of tutoring. What do you think?"

"Splendid!" Absollah responded quickly. "Perhaps I can help with their mathematics, or some of my clerks for that matter, if they are not busy."

"I shall mention you to Khaled," Abou replied with a smile, enjoying the perfectly seasoned goat's curd and lamb they had ordered after Abou put the book safely away. "And you, Ammon? Can you come some afternoon and tell the children about barbering?"

"I doubt if they'd be interested," Ammon replied. "It is neither an exciting nor a lucrative profession."

"You seem to be doing all right," Absollah said. "Two barbers working for you. Not half bad."

"I have been lucky," Ammon replied, nibbling at his lunch. "My wife's management has had more to do with it than my skill."

"My, how strange a fellow you are, Ammon." Abou murmured. "I thought hair was your whole life."

"I have other interests," the barber replied but didn't amplify.

Absollah was the first to mention the Israeli intentions. "I cannot believe the Israelis are going to let pass the killing of their patrol."

"Problems in their cabinet have caused the delay is what my customers are saying," Ammon replied, seemingly relieved that the topic of conversation had shifted from him. "Ariel's coalition is falling apart. Labor is in one minute, out the next, or so I hear."

"Still, the Israelis never forgive or forget an attack. Something will happen. A tank strike. Commandos. Something." Absollah was nodding his head as he spoke. "Their retribution is always so severe. You sometimes wonder why our people do these things when the response is so draconian."

"Why indeed?" Abou replied, and lowered his voice. "I have decided that we should call for a cessation of fighting on both sides. This war will never end unless we stop, and hopefully they will also stop, too."

The three looked at Abou in amazement.

"You are not saying this aloud," Ammon whispered. "Are you?"

Before Abou could answer, Absollah whispered, "Such thoughts are dangerous, Abou. You could get us all killed. There is such a thing as guilt by association. People will remember we were your friends, and in our world it is much easier to kill someone you have doubts about than to examine their words and thoughts carefully."

Absollah's words were sobering. Even Hamid was nodding in agreement.

"I shall be careful. I don't want any of you hurt," Abou replied, "and I certainly don't want to create more violence."

"Absolutely not!" Absollah replied with a smile. "It would be very bad for business."

WHEN AMMON AND ABSOLLAH DEPARTED, Abou and Hamid walked toward the bank. Abou carried the book against his chest, protecting it from being jostled by the crowd.

"Ammon seemed a bit out of sorts," Hamid remarked.

"I think it is his wife," Abou replied. "She is a very determined woman who is only interested in making money."

They crossed the street to the bank and went to the back. Khaled's men were working in the building at the rear, and one man was raking the lot, picking up the debris from the previous day.

"Khaled said the site must be cleaned each day," the man told Abou.

"That is kind of him," Abou replied and deposited the animal book in his tent. He brought out a stool and sat in the afternoon sun.

The warm sun had almost lulled Abou to sleep. His eyes were closed when he heard his name spoken. He found Yasser and Khaled standing before him. The younger man was looking down at his shabby sandals.

"He wishes to speak to you, Abou Ben Adhem, but he thinks you will not listen." Khaled spoke in his deep, rumbling voice.

"Of course I will listen," Abou replied. "I have a cushion in the tent."

Khaled waved his hand. "I will leave you two."

"I would speak to you, if you have the time," Abou addressed Khaled. "Will you be here this afternoon?"

"Alas, no. One more big meeting today and then perhaps my men and I can devote more time to this project. But certainly, before I leave, I will come to talk to you."

As the Hamas leader walked away, Yasser shuffled his feet. Finally, he said, "I was wrong, father-in-law. I was ashamed of my poor business dealings and didn't want you to witness my failure. I thank you for providing a home for my wife and children."

Abou shrugged. "These things happen. It is the will of Allah," he said and thought at the same time that it was really the result of Yasser's unfortunate personality.

"Sophia and I have been talking," Yasser explained, and then hesitated. "We are unsure of the future."

Again Abou shrugged. "It is something you will have to work out with her."

Yasser nodded, a small smile flirting with the corner of his mouth. "You are too generous, Abou Ben Adhem. But first, before Sophia and I can make plans, I must find work. Khaled has said he will help me, as has our holy man, Ariis Malluk. And Khaled has promised me work within the Hamas organization. It wouldn't be much money, I suppose, but it would be a job, and I have missed my son." Abou noted there was no mention of the baby.

Abou nodded. "Akbar should be here soon."

"I know. I thought I would wait to see him." Yasser smiled his thin, humorless smile. "I will be working on the building in the rear and will come to see him when he arrives." With a salute, he turned and strolled past the tent to the building in the rear, where men were carrying building material and wheelbarrows of debris in and out of the building. As Abou watched, he saw Yasser take an empty canvas carting bucket on his back and enter the building.

"He needed work," Khaled said. He had come up behind Abou.

Abou looked the Hamas leader in the eyes, trying to divine Khaled's intent in sponsoring a reconciliation between him and Yasser. The black eyes showed nothing, no humor, no malice. "You wished to talk to me?"

"Oh, yes." Abou replied. "The suggestion was made that we might want to begin some sort of tutorial program for the children, help them with their reading and sums. Hamid and I would be happy to help. If you approve, and perhaps some of the men working for you could help, too."

Khaled beamed. "A truly splendid idea, Abou. I must say, finding you has been a boon for the movement. We will begin planning tomorrow. Helping the children with their studies is generous. Perhaps we could read them poetry—Al-Mutanabbi or my favorite, Abu'l-'Ala al-Ma'arri."

Somehow it surprised Abou that the Hamas leader cared for poetry.

Children began to appear at the edge of the property. Khaled took note, looking at his watch, and then saying, "The children's snacks will be set out, and today we have a treat for them. We were able to obtain Coca-Cola. No ice, of course, but the children like it anyway. Another infernal product of the devilish Americans, but toothsome. They seem to have no end of these exports that seduce our people, but, as I said, the children like it."

"Thank you," Abou replied. He, himself, preferred Pepsi Cola.

"Sadly, I need all my men today. Can you and Hamid manage alone?"

"Yes, we can manage. Hamid is going to explain computers, and I will hand out the cakes and Coke."

"You are a good man, Abou. You will be rewarded in heaven."

"I had hoped for something a little sooner."

Khaled looked at him sharply but said only, "I must be off. Tomorrow we will talk about your tutoring program. We shall return today before evening prayer."

He stalked off, his men following as if mysteriously signaled. Abou watched as the workmen emptied out of the building in the rear. Even Yasser went along, evidently forgetting his plan to meet Akbar. Abou decided that Yasser was more deeply involved in Hamas than he had let on.

Akbar appeared and ran to his grandfather, who picked up the boy and gave him a huge kiss, which Akbar wiped away immediately.

"I wish to see a llama," Akbar said when he was returned to earth. "You promised."

"And I am a man of my word."

"The children said there is no such animal, and the teacher wasn't sure."

"I shall show you such an animal, Grandson. It climbs the highest peaks of the Andes, faraway mountains in South America."

Soon the area was filled with children and Abou handed out cola after cola. The cakes disappeared like magic, and soon twenty or so were seated around Hamid. Akbar was sitting right in front of the mailman, his face serious as he listened as Hamid explained how they could chat with people in Iceland (Impossible!) or China (Unbelievable!) and information was whizzing around the world as they spoke (Absurd!). Several of the children looked up at the sky as if expecting to see the whizzing words.

"All the books you read in a year can be stored on one of these small disks and you can play them back whenever you want," Hamid explained, holding up a soiled CD he had procured somewhere.

"Why do people stay here where there are no CDs or Internets?" one of the little girls asked. There was sudden silence as the profundity of the question sunk in.

It was a question that Hamid had thought about. "They are like me. I came here from Cairo, a more populous area, but I liked it here, for it was quiet and everyone knew each other."

The children frowned as if they disagreed with Hamid's choice. Hamid ended his lesson with the suggestion they listen to Abou explain about the strange animals of the world.

Abou took his seat in front of the tent, and Hamid, Akbar on his lap, sat on the ground on the outer fringe of the group. His leather mail pouch lay beside him.

"I have found the picture of the llama," Abou began. "Remember, I said I had heard one in a zoo and it made a sound like this." Abou made the short trumpeting sound he had heard years before. The children laughed.

"This animal lives high in the mountains in South America," Abou said, refreshing their memories, and pulled out Marwan's book. Unwrapping it, he said, "Normally, I would pass this about and let all of you look at the pictures, but this book cost a great deal and was lent to us by Marwan, the attorney, so I shall turn the pages and show you the pictures, not only of the llama but of other strange animals. Is that satisfactory?"

There was a murmur of assent and the children edged closer. Abou suggested, "If you are big and can see well, perhaps you can sit in the back so the little ones can see."

Several of the bigger children moved, but one wearing glasses, which were held together by wire and tape, sat where he was.

"First the llama," Abou said, and opened the book to the place where the strange beast appeared. The children's necks craned, their eyes bugged, and several shook their heads in disbelief.

"It looks like a woolly camel," one boy said and the others agreed.

"I have read they are distant cousins," Abou said. "I will have to look that up and make sure I'm correct."

What they really wanted was to see the rest of the pictures in the book. Abou started from the beginning with the aardvark. Each picture caused great excitement and discussion. Just as he reached the two-toed sloth, the distinctive sounds of helicopter rotors filled the air and a shadow suddenly crossed the pages of the book.

All looked up, and Abou, seeing the outline of the gunships, stared for a moment in disbelief and then, in spite of his natural reserve, yelled at the children to seek cover as he staggered to his feet, dropping Marwan's book and grabbing a small child who was sitting close to him.

"Hurry! Under cover! Close to the buildings," Abou called and, carrying the child in one arm, waved his other children to the back of the bank.

The first rocket exploded in the area where the swings and climbing bars were assembled, sending small fragments of metal in all directions. Soon a fusillade of stones, glass, and metal bombarded the whole area. A child in front of Abou fell to the ground holding his head. Grasping tighter the little boy he was carrying, Abou bellowed again at the children to seek the security of the bank's wall. In terror, the children—those who weren't lying wounded on the ground—dashed to the rear of the bank. Hamid ran toward Abou with Akbar in his arms, his leather satchel wrapped around the little boy like primitive armor.

The children clustered near the bank's wall. A clerk opened the rear door and several of the youngsters crawled inside, but others huddled with their knees pulled up and their heads covered with their hands. Abou knelt, covering several children with his body.

The second rocket blasted the building that Hamas had been renovating in the rear of the lot. A fireball engulfed Abou's tent. Stone and shards of metal and glass tore into the children, who screamed in terror. Abou felt a sharp pain in his shoulder and another on his cheek, and he saw blood dripping from his face onto the children beneath him.

And just as suddenly the helicopters were gone. Nothing was left but the wailing of the smaller children and the moans of the wounded. Abou looked down at one small boy and saw he wasn't seriously hurt. Next to them, one of the girls who had stayed near the wall stared at him with huge black eyes. A great gouge of flesh had been torn from her upper arm. Abou hastily pulled up the hem of her chador and pressed the cloth into the wound, placing her hand on the compress to staunch the blood. He saw her thin legs exposed and vulnerable in the afternoon sun. "Press it hard," he whispered.

Staggering to his feet, he turned and looked at the scene. Several children were lying quite still near the play area, and in the center, just ten feet from where Abou stood, Hamid lay facedown, his arms around Akbar, the leather pouch over the boy's head. Neither moved, and Abou saw the great wound in Akbar's back. Abou staggered to the bodies, touching his grandson's throat for a pulse. There was nothing. Hamid's face was twisted in a grimace, his eyes open. Abou again felt for a pulse. Nothing. A pool of blood was widening beneath Hamid and Akbar. Abou suddenly collapsed next to the bodies, sitting in the debris-strewn dirt, holding Akbar's little hand.

People were running into the area, screaming and tearing at their hair in rage and despair. Two emergency vehicles appeared from nowhere, one an ambulance, the attendants running from the rear doors with medical bags and various emergency devices in hand.

Abou sat silently on the ground, holding Akbar's small hand, feeling its warmth seep away. He touched Hamid's shoulder gently, then bent forward and kissed Hamid's cheek, one last gesture before his friend disappeared into eternity.

Khaled and his men appeared, cursing and shaking their fists at the sky, firing their weapons into the air. The leader stood by the bank wall, his great barrel of a chest expanded, and his deep voice cut through the din.

"These barbarians!" he stormed. "They, who complain of the Holocaust, butcher our children and attack our village without provocation! The world will know of this. Israel will not escape the condemnation of the world for this cowardly attack!"

Abou slowly removed Hamid's arm from around Akbar, cradling the boy's body against his chest. How the little fellow would have detested such a public show of affection, Abou thought, as he felt the boy's hair against his face. A medical worker stopped next to them, checked Akbar and Hamid, and then, without a word, pressed the wound on Abou's cheek together and put a plaster on it.

"You must have this tended to," he said, looking at the old man's shoulder. He applied a compress and taped it. "It must be cleaned and sewn." Abou saw Yasser standing behind the medic, holding a stretcher, but he said nothing to Abou, staring at his dead son as if he were a stranger.

Abou nodded absently, still looking down at Hamid as he held Akbar. How would he ever be able to face Sophia's grief? Unsteadily, he rose, first on his knees, and then with great effort to his feet, still holding the small boy in his arms.

"Tomorrow we will have a state funeral!" Khaled bellowed. "All Palestine will know of this atrocity and people will come from distant places to honor these dead! The whole world will know what cowardly swine the Israelis are!"

As Abou started to walk away, carrying his grandson in his arms, he saw Marwan's book in the mud, the pages torn, the binding broken. He suddenly sobbed for his grandson, for his friend, for Marwan's book.

Khaled saw him. "Abou Ben Adhem, you are wounded! Let me help!"

Abou turned and looked at the Hamas chieftain. "No," he replied in a low voice, conserving what little strength he had left. "I must take Akbar to his mother."

Absollah appeared from nowhere and followed his friend at a respectful distance, ready to lend a hand if needed but somehow understanding that Abou must carry Akbar by himself.

The trek home seemed endless, but Abou, clutching the body of his grandson, placed one foot ahead of the other until he finally reached his courtyard. Sophia was waiting. Other women were already there wailing for the dead, but Sophia stood silently.

"You should have let others bring Akbar home, my father," she said in a soft voice, taking her son in her arms.

"I couldn't," Abou replied and suddenly sat on a bench in the courtyard. "I promised you I would bring him home."

"Thank you," she replied slowly, as if each word was painful. "We will take him inside and wash him in preparation for burial. Yasser's mother is coming, as is his sister. Others will be here."

Abou sat and watched his daughter carry the boy inside the house. The sun was gone and he sat in weary despair. Inside, the house lights came on and the anguish in the women's voices seeped into the courtyard. Abou found himself going over the events of the day again and again in his mind, as if something he might have done could have changed them. He had no control over the liquidation of the Israeli patrol, and he certainly had no control over the Israeli response. Little Akbar and Hamid had been caught up in these events like twigs in a roaring river, flung about aimlessly.

Sophia came and offered him a hot cup of tea. "I do not know what I will do without him."

Abou didn't know what to say.

"I scolded him this morning for not keeping his robe clean."

"He knew you loved him."

Sophia nodded slowly. "Yes, I suppose he did. I never said that to him, but I suppose he did. It is not something you often say to a male child." She didn't keen, but Abou saw in the dim light the tears on her cheek.

"It is the will of Allah," he murmured, hating the cliché even as he said it.

"It is the will of lunatics," she hissed, "killing innocents for no good reason!"

"Yes," Abou agreed. "That is true."

"I hate them all," Sophia cried out. "They have stolen Akbar's life from him. They are thieves."

At that moment, Khaled, with several of his men, entered the courtyard. The men all carried automatic weapons. "Abou, we have come to talk about tomorrow."

Abou rose with some difficulty. His bones ached. "This is my daughter, Sophia, the mother of Akbar."

"It is with great sorrow that we meet like this," Khaled said with a deep bow. Sophia simply looked at him. "What we came to say is that Hamas wishes to conduct the funeral tomorrow for those who died in this slaughter of innocents, and we will also see to the burial. Those who died are heroes of Palestine and should be recognized as such."

"My son is a hero?" Sophia asked. Her meaning was clear.

Holding up his hand, Khaled said, "He was just a little boy who had a right to live, but they took that from him and we feel partly responsible. We think it was our facility they wished to destroy."

Sophia agreed with a short nod.

"Who else died?" Abou asked.

Khaled focused on him. "Hamid, of course, and two other children. One boy lost an eye and another child an arm."

Sophia and Abou said nothing.

Khaled cleared his throat. "We will send an honor guard here at ten in the morning to bring Akbar's body to the square near the mosque and then to the cemetery."

Sophia and Abou remained silent.

"Yasser will lead the honor guard for Akbar. Again, we wish to express our deep sympathy."

Their heavy boots pounded on the stones of the street as Khaled and his men disappeared into the night.

"I would prefer burying him quietly," Sophia said with a sigh, "but Yasser would make a fuss if we rejected this honor."

"It makes no difference to Akbar," Abou replied wearily, sitting himself on the bench.

"And Hamid," Sophia. "Poor, gentle Hamid."

"He tried to save Akbar," Abou said quietly. "He grabbed him up and was trying to shield him with his mail pouch when they were both hit."

She sat beside him. After a time, she asked, "Why do you think the Israelis did this?"

"Retribution for their ambushed squad," Abou replied. "The Hebrew bible calls for a life for a life. And we do the same. It is never-ending."

"So it would seem," she replied and stood. "I must rejoin the women. Akbar is in his shroud. I must help sew it." She looked at her father in the dim light. "You should have your wounds tended."

LATER, WHEN THE STREETS HAD EMPTIED, Abou made his way into the village and went to the hospital, which was, in fact, little more than a clinic, with inadequate lighting and sanitary facilities, little or no medicine, and an exhausted staff. The halls were still filled with the wounded and Abou waited for treatment. The hopeless poverty of his world became clear to him as he looked at the moaning victims.

After treatment, Abou walked slowly up the lanes to his house, feeling a little dizzy. He stopped several times on the way to steady himself but finally made it back to the courtyard. There were voices from inside the house. He simply could not face people just then. Waiting at the bottom of the garden, he looked up at the sky and thought of Akbar and Hamid, the postman.

Later, when the house had quieted, after Yasser and his tribe had departed, Abou went inside and stood beside the small white form on the table. He touched the boy's shoulder under the shroud and wept. He could see Sophia sitting in the far corner of the kitchen among some neighborhood women, her back to him. She was hunched over, nursing the baby. The women around her were moaning in low voices.

The Twelfth Darkfall

ABOU MADE HIS WAY to his small room and lay on his pallet. His wounds were still painful but, surprisingly, he immediately fell into a profound sleep, so profound that he almost missed Cohen, who was standing in the far corner with his hands in his pockets, looking pensively at Abou's recumbent figure.

"I am terribly sorry, Abou," Cohen began, when he saw the old man had aroused himself sufficiently to visit. He crossed the room and sat on a stool near where Abou lay.

Abou blinked several times. He had suffered from dry eyes as of late and it took him a few moments to focus. "As I was being treated for my wounds, I found myself thinking it all seemed so . . . convenient."

Cohen leaned forward. "Convenient? A strange word."

Abou winced as he moved. "Three little children as well as my friend—all gone. I feel there must be a reason. Something. Explain human dissembling to me, Cohen. Tell me how and why we do these abominable things to each other. Are we just evil?"

"You think this attack was contrived?" Cohen looked intently at Abou.

"I don't know," Abou admitted, "but everyone in Hamas left except Hamid, me, and the children, and once the attack was over, they all appeared immediately."

Cohen rubbed his stubble in contemplation. "Do you really want to hear my prattle now, Abou?"

About nodded slowly. "If I don't understand this horrendous murder of innocents, I think I shall simply succumb."

Cohen scratched the stubble on his chin. "Well, the Israelis, like all humans, act in what they perceive as genetic self-interest. In other words, they are protecting their gene pool, their tribe, extended family, or nation, or whatever you want to call it."

"It's monstrous!" Abou's fury was boundless.

Cohen slowly nodded his head back and forth. "Wouldn't you do something similar to protect *your* kin?"

Abou stared at him without understanding.

Cohen shook his head. "You're unique, Abou. You *don't* really get it—the depth of certain motivations and the harm they can do."

"And what moves people to do good things—people like Marwan and his wife."

"And you," Cohen added. "Altruism. An intelligent concept. Actually the same motivation—genetic self-interest—but with a much broader vision. The Marwans of the world have no idea who they are related to—no children, no close relatives—so they help everyone. That's rather pragmatic, don't you think?"

"That's me?" Abou questioned. "A broad view?"

"Well, so to speak," Cohen agreed. "A very nice, broader view. You care about all people, not just those with blood ties. We sincerely wish more humans were like you."

"It is quite . . . impersonal," Abou managed.

"Oh, well, I guess you could look at it like that," Cohen agreed. "My colleagues and I see your view of life as a real step forward, but we've been wrong before. Actually it probably isn't a good time for us to be kicking our ideas around."

Abou held up his hand. "No, no, this has been helpful . . . I think."

Cohen looked at Abou closely. "Are you all right?"

Abou could only shake his head. "Akbar was so small, so defenseless, and I did nothing."

"Please Abou, don't distress yourself. You loved him and helped him. You did all any human could do."

Abou lay back on his pallet. "Hardly a recommendation as to my success as a grandfather, is it?"

"You have nothing to blame yourself for."

Abou was fatigued, but he persisted. "All this killing just to preserve some vague identity?"

"Generally. Selfish, short-sighted people who, as we have discussed, are still a bit primitive. You have to remember that the basic impulses—greed, theft, murder, rape—are still de rigueur throughout most of the world."

Cohen shrugged. "We all spent time today trying to think of some way to help you through this, Abou."

Abou looked searchingly at the angel. He did not want Cohen to see him cry.

The Thirteenth Day

ABOU WOKE A LITTLE AFTER SIX and listened for Sophia moving about. The house was silent. In the kitchen, Akbar's body still rested on the table, a white cloth wrapping it, no more. Abou wished more than anything else that the previous day had been a dream like Cohen's appearance. He did his ablutions quietly, pulling on a street gown and going outside for his morning prayer. He faced east, put his small rug on the ground, and went through the ritual carefully and slowly, in respect for Akbar and Hamid. Once finished, he rolled his rug, took a robe, for there was still a chill in the air, and made his way down the road to Marwan's. He knocked tentatively at the attorney's door.

It opened slowly and a sleepy-eyed servant girl looked out at him from behind the door.

"They are asleep," she said in a whisper. "They don't rise until eight."

"I know," Abou began. He touched the wound on his forehead. "I wanted to say something to your master before the day began."

"You are Abou Ben Adhem, are you not?" she asked. "It was your grandson who was killed yesterday?"

"Yes."

She nodded and said, "I will wake him. I am sure he will want to speak with you."

Abou wasn't sure why this was so, but he was grateful. The young woman had not admitted him to the house, so he stood in the street until she returned and opened the door.

Abou waited only a few minutes until Marwan filled the doorway. "Abou. I am so sorry."

Abou nodded. "I came to explain about the book. I wish to pay you for it."

"The what?"

"The picture book about animals. The children loved it, but when the rocket fire began, I dropped it and it was ruined. I am sorry."

Marwan studied him for a moment. "The children liked the pictures?"

"Yes, very much."

"My wife will be pleased. She said last night she should have children over to view her books."

"I am sorry it was destroyed."

"We will get another. You owe us nothing," Marwan replied. "It is we who mourn with you for Akbar."

"He loved the pictures," Abou said pointlessly.

"Yes, it is good to die with a pleasurable experience still in mind."

Abou thought this a strange comment. Instead of replying, he bowed slightly and began to turn away. "I must be back for the funeral."

Marwan watched as Abou started slowly up the street.

"Abou," Marwan called in a low voice. Abou turned and retraced his steps.

"Cairo," Marwan said. "My colleague tells me Cairo would be the best place to approach the Americans about returning to the United States. You, of course, can return, but your daughter and grandchildren . . ." He hesitated, realizing his error. "Your grandchild. They are another matter, but it is possible you will be allowed to take them with you. The staff in Cairo is the most understanding in the area, I am told."

Abou nodded and said, "Cairo? I have not discussed this with Sophia. I have no idea what she wishes to do now. Thank you," he added.

THE WOMEN HAD GATHERED again to help Sophia, and when Yasser appeared with several of his cohorts, they were ready to hand over the body. The men carried a wooden plank on which they secured the little corpse and then, with solemnity, shouldered their burden, as well as their weapons, and set off with Akbar on their shoulders. Yasser walked in the lead, behind him the trussed body carried by four men, with Abou, Sophia, and several of the relatives bringing up the rear. When the procession reached the market square, throngs had appeared and the small bodies of the two other children were being carried about, as well as Hamid's remains. There were three television trucks on the periphery, with cameras on their roofs, as well as several groups of men working their way through the crowd with interviewers and cameras at the ready. Abou took all this in with dismay. The revelry seemed so alien to the profound loss he felt. It was a circus with the weaving, chanting crowds showing anguished, tear-stained faces to the nearest camera. He turned to Sophia, who was standing close to Akbar's body, her hand resting gently on her son's chest. Shock and disgust showed in her eyes; next to her, a manic Yasser, tears streaming down his face, was howling and firing his gun at the sky as if noise would somehow bring his son back. His behavior, in sharp contrast to Sophia's calm sadness, was the norm for the crowd. Abou was sad that his grandson's funeral lacked dignity and solemnity.

The crowd surged and suddenly Akbar's corpse was disappearing toward the end of the marketplace. Sophia and Abou struggled to follow. Those with guns, like Yasser, were allowed free access, but the unarmed fought for advantage among themselves.

At the far edge of the square, a small stage, cobbled together, afforded Khaled and several others the advantage they needed, and speakers had been installed at the corners to insure their voices could be heard. Abou noted that there was a truck with a generator discreetly parked behind the platform. No power failure was going to disturb these festivities, for that was what the gathering had become in Abou's eyes, a celebration using dead children as the focal point.

The first speaker was a bigwig Hamas leader whom Abou had never heard of and whom he certainly never wanted to hear. The man emphasized over and over the atrocity that was committed, the Jewish plot to take over the Mideast, and how the jihad must continue until the last Israeli was thrown into the sea. Abou yawned, a reaction not lost on one of the Hamas warriors helping to hold Akbar's burial board aloft.

Khaled was next. His barrel chest expanded like a balloon and his deep voice boomed over the public address system. Abou listened for a minute or so, but his speech was more of the same, words to incite the converted, . . . but then Khaled was saying something new. "They knew where our day care center was. They destroyed it in revenge for their patrol, which disappeared just days ago, and they attacked children because children are our future and their deaths will cause the most pain." Abou nodded in agreement with this last statement, but Khaled's next words surprised him. "We have learned that they thought our renovation of the warehouse, which we intended for an after-school facility and eventually an infirmary, was a future headquarters for our movement. Their bungling spies misinformed them!"

Khaled's diatribe continued like shifting sand, slow-moving, inexorable, finishing only when every last grain of hatred was deposited in the minds of the audience, but Abou hardly listened. A great bellow came from the crowd and the TV cameras swept back and forth, catching the renewed anger and predacious nature of the crowd. More weapons were raised and fired, and shouts were heard from every corner demanding that the Israelis pay with their lives.

Somehow the crowd knew it was time to make its way to the cemetery. Like a giant lizard, it began to move slowly out of the bazaar, the head directed toward the town's burial ground, then the neck with the bodies carried overhead, and finally the great mass of people shouting and crying as the procession made its way through the town and up the hill to the cemetery.

Abou saw that graves had been dug in a new portion of the burial ground. Khaled again found a small stage that had been constructed near the grave site. He and Malluk, the putative imam, climbed to the stage and Khaled raised his arms.

"Hamas has obtained these plots as a holy memorial to those slain. Our heroes will be buried here with all the honor they deserve!" The crowd roared its approval, and then, with the bodies being carried forward below the stage, Malluk spoke in solemn tones, evoking the need for revenge for these brave martyrs. Hamid's long shroud looked strange next to the small bodies of the children. With a renewed feeling of sadness, Sophia and Abou watched Akbar lowered into one of the pits. Malluk said prayers over each grave. The last to be lowered was Hamid. Abou found himself crying for his friend, his grandson, his feelings of despair.

When the ceremony, if it could be called such, was finished, Sophia turned away and said, "Let us go. I will return to pray when this mob has gone."

"You go," Abou replied, clenching her hand. "Perhaps our cousins will see you home. I wish to speak to Khaled." An idea was growing that filled the emptiness within him, and, at the same time, he suddenly understood that the crowd's hysteria, the firing of guns, the forced tears, were all stratagems to cover a sense of immense desolation, just as Abou's rising anger was.

"What is there to understand?" Sophia asked. "These people have demeaned my son's death. I detest them."

Abou nodded. "I must find out the truth."

"As you will," she said indifferently and with the baby pressed to her chest she turned away, finding the arm of a distant cousin. Her position as a martyr's mother saved her from being jostled by the mob, which, for its own reasons, seemed loath to disperse.

Abou pushed his way toward Khaled, who was retreating with his retinue of gunmen. With difficulty, Abou finally reached the last of his guards.

"I wish to speak to Khaled," he said in a strong voice in order to be heard over the din.

"Impossible," the guard replied, shifting his AK-47.

"Nonsense," Abou replied, suddenly tired of all these theatrics. The idea that Khaled was in danger in this crowd was absurd, yet he was surrounded by armed guards as if the Israelis were about to pounce upon him.

"What did you say, old man?" the guard asked, stopping and confronting Abou. The movement caught Khaled's eye.

"Enough," he boomed. "He is a friend."

The guard looked at his leader as if for just a moment he questioned his judgment, but he did give way, and Abou made his way inside the circle.

"I wish to speak to you, Khaled. Privately."

"Ah, privately," Khaled repeated, his expression semiserious, as if he were entertaining a slightly impaired but loyal subject. "Well, yes, of course." Without introducing the guest speaker standing next to him, Khaled took Abou's arm and led him around to the back of the truck. The guards spread out at a respectful distance so that their leader had privacy. The guest opened the door of the truck's cab and sat down, lighting a long cigarette and gazing out at the milling mob of townspeople, who still seemed dissatisfied with the tepid nature of the rally and funeral.

"I am sorry about your grandson, Abou." Khaled's manner was unctuous.

Abou saw no reason to equivocate. "You knew beforehand, didn't you?"

"Knew what?" Khaled's face suddenly lost some of its assurance.

"You knew the attack was coming? That is why you absented yourself each day, so you and your men would be safe."

Khaled hesitated. Then, in a low, measured tone, he replied, "If I deny it, you will spread rumors that would be damaging, so I will be candid. Yes, I knew an attack was coming. Yes, your offer to start a day school got the council thinking about the possibilities of a propaganda coup. All we had to do was feed information about establishing a commando training facility to a local contact of *Shin Bet,* which would almost certainly guarantee an air strike. These Jews are so predictable. Truthfully, I am sorry it was Hamid and Akbar who were killed, but they died for the glory of the Palestinian movement."

Abou rocked back on his heels. "You don't deny this infamy?"

"No, not to you," Khaled replied evenly, "for I give you this information with a solemn warning, Abou. If one word of what I just said is divulged, we will kill you, your daughter, her baby, and every other member of your family we can find."

"And Yasser and his family, too, I suppose."

"No, that won't be necessary," Khaled answered, his eyes cold as stones. "He understands the reality of the situation."

"He knows! He knows you murdered his son?"

"He knows the Israelis murdered his son," Khaled replied. "It was a great tragedy."

Abou stood facing the Hamas chief, his mouth open, the ramifications of what he had been told flooding his mind. "I . . . I . . ." He attempted to reply, but no words came.

Khaled smiled his huge smile. "Have no doubt, Abou. I will do what I say if I hear one word of this from any source. Do you understand?"

Abou nodded, looking away, defeated by the enormity of the man's zeal. Khaled clapped him on the back. "We will reopen the day care. It was a wonderful idea, old friend, and we will be indebted to you for a long time. We were thinking of naming the center after the victims. What do you think?"

Abou could only shake his head, beyond understanding the monstrous act the organization had committed. It was so brazen, so outrageous, so hideous that it made some sort of mad sense. He turned away but stopped.

"Tell me one thing," he asked.

"Anything."

"Who is the Israeli agent in our midst?"

"Ah, yes," Khaled answered. "Let me suggest you be careful what you say when you get your beard trimmed, as well as your comments over your chatty little lunches, but . . . understand one thing clearly. We will not allow him to be denounced. Do you understand? He is a very useful conduit whom we have used for years and intend to use again. The Israelis think his information is valid. We, of course, supply him with accurate information from time to time to sustain his reputation, and he is such a valued link in our network that he must not be denounced."

"It's not possible!" Abou exclaimed.

Khaled pursed his lips. "It's devastating to learn you have been cuckolded by a friend."

"Ammon is a spy?" Abou gasped.

"That too."

"I . . . I don't know what you're saying."

Khaled shrugged. There was a malicious glint in his eye. "You were gone a long time, old friend. Something a wise man never does if he wants his wife to remain constant. Everyone knows women must be sheltered from themselves. Ammon's wife finally guessed and put an end to the affair. You were quite the talk of the town for a time, and of course Sophia's birth so soon after your return caused a spate of tongue-wagging." Khaled leaned back and looked down at Abou. He added, "So you see, I strongly suspect you really lost nothing yesterday. Akbar was probably no relation of yours."

Abou flushed. The anger rising within him was taking control of his whole being. With nothing else to say, he turned and marched out of the circle into the crowd, which was now moving slowly back into Helar, chanting slogans and firing weapons. He saw Absollah at the edge of the crowd but turned away. He wanted none of him, unsure how he would react to the banker's commiseration. When he felt the hand on his arm, he jumped and turned, finding Ammon at his side. "I am sorry, Abou. Akbar was a wonderful boy! But this is certainly a memorable funeral."

Abou looked at the barber carefully for some sign of remorse for his part in Akbar's death. He saw only innocence in his eyes. And suddenly his mind conjured up a vision of Salah standing by their sink, her warm eyes upon him. He shuddered at the vividness of the memory, as well as the thought of her in Ammon's arms, of him penetrating her body.

"I must hurry to join Sophia," Abou explained, hoping the excuse would rid him of his tormentor.

"I understand," Ammon replied. "When you are feeling better, you must rejoin us for lunch. It won't be the same without Hamid, but he would wish us to keep meeting, don't you think?"

"I'm sure he would," Abou agreed.

"Perhaps tomorrow or the day after."

"Perhaps," Abou answered. "I must stay with Sophia for a time."

"Of course. Goodbye, Abou. Allah be with you."

Abou rushed off, his heart pounding. Nothing would be gained by saying anything, and much could be lost, but Abou found the encounter extremely upsetting. For all those years he had known Ammon, he had no inkling of the full dimensions of the man and he hardly resembled the person he thought he'd known. Who else had a secret life? Yasser? Absollah? Abou suddenly wondered if you really knew anyone. You just encounter people now and then and this is what passes as friendship.

Sophia was sitting in the kitchen holding the baby, who gurgled and smiled at the tassel that Sophia was dangling in front of her. For a moment Abou's heart collapsed as he thought he saw Ammon's features in Sophia's face, but just as suddenly his heart inflated with love for this daughter of his. Flesh and blood meant nothing. "Playing with my beautiful granddaughter, are you?" he asked, trying to hide his distress beneath joviality.

"She loves the sunlight," Sophia replied. She had been crying. Her face was streaked, her eyes puffy.

Abou sat next to his daughter. In spite of her obvious distress, he took comfort in the bright cleanliness of the kitchen, the faint smell of baked bread, the pungent odor of strong soap. There was a half-filled plate of sesame cookies, which Akbar would have devoured upon his return from school. Without thinking, Abou took Sophia's hand and they sat like that for a few moments, the baby happily playing as the two adults contemplated the terrible past days. Finally, Sophia cleared her throat.

"Yasser divorced me today," she said in a low voice, pointing to a paper on the kitchen sink. "Akbar's death wasn't enough. He took time to set me aside."

Abou looked at her. He really wasn't surprised after what Khaled had said. Yasser had found a new home with Hamas, a new life.

"He has no interest in Leila," Sophia added, hugging the infant to her chest. "His cousin delivered a letter that said I can do anything I want with her."

Abou studied his daughter. She seemed to have aged ten years that very day.

She sighed and rose. "My life seems so hopeless. But I must put the baby down for her nap. Perhaps I will lie with her for a time before I prepare our food."

"You will feel better if you get some rest," Abou agreed, thinking a nap a wonderful idea. The day had been exhausting. Once Sophia pulled the curtain across her doorway, Abou rose slowly, his bones creaking as he made his way to his cubicle. Slowly he lowered himself to his pallet and pulled his robe around him. He was asleep in moments.

Cohen, wearing his original, grayish white suit, which looked far more wrinkled in the daylight, was walking back and forth in an agitated fashion, his hands clutched behind him, his head down, muttering, "Poltroonery! Poltroonery! Dastardly poltroonery."

Abou raised his head. "Cohen?" He really didn't want to chat with the angel at that moment.

"Ah, Abou, I'm glad you're asleep," the apparition replied. "Your taking this nap means we can talk now, not wait until evening." He sat on the small chair and leaned forward, his face only centimeters from Abou's.

"We have met in emergency session this very morning," Cohen began. "All of us. All leaves were canceled. Everyone was there. Frankly, we are outraged by Khaled's behavior. He, it seemed to us, has reached a new plateau in human malevolence. Even Gabe was incensed, and usually absolutely nothing ruffles his feathers," Cohen added then suddenly chuckled. "That's a good one. I'll have to remember that."

"Can I offer you tea and some sesame cookies?"

Cohen hesitated. "I feel bad about eating Akbar's cookies last night." He was torn. "But yes, I would welcome some."

He followed Abou into the kitchen, chatting as he walked, but once there, they saw the platter on the table was empty.

"I was sure there were more cookies," Abou said, looking about. "Let me put on the tea, and I shall search for them."

Looking at the empty plate, Cohen screwed up his face in anger. "That damn, greedy Yousef. Gabe called him back from R and R this morning to attend this meeting and I had to mention the cookies to him."

Abou turned to the pantry, then the cupboard, and finally into the space beneath the sink in his search for Sophia's missing cookies. Abou was sure she had hid them so Akbar would get his share. He stopped suddenly, aware he was thinking that Akbar was still alive.

They settled for tea and a bit of honey bread. "It is strange," Abou observed as he settled himself at the table, looking at the empty platter. "Most strange."

"It is nothing. I, of all individuals, should not resent sharing," Cohen replied, sipping his tea and nibbling at the bread with relish. "We have much to discuss today."

"We do?"

Cohen nodded. "My associates have decided that I should visit you from time to time without the customary call-up."

"It isn't necessary," Abou replied. "You have been very forthcoming and most generous with me. I'm sure you have other worthy people who need your help."

Cohen looked carefully at Abou. "I'm handling this badly, Abou. Look, I mentioned this emergency meeting this morning in which we decided that Hamas's latest dirty deed goes far beyond normal human malice, so I was asked if I wanted to be your paladin, so to speak. This is a new activity for us. We can't, of course, interfere directly in human affairs, but we feel we weren't . . . sufficiently diligent in this matter. The whole thing caught us by surprise, and we feel we should have somehow done more."

Abou remained indifferent, absorbed in his own grief.

"Anyway, we decided Khaled's gratuitous malevolence must be brought under control. His behavior goes far beyond wrongheaded actions for a cause. He enjoys hurting people and we certainly learned our lesson with his type these past fifty years. Once they get a little power, they're horrible."

"What can anyone do?" Abou asked, his sense of defeat manifest.

"For starters," Cohen began, "he'll get a surprise visit tonight. We had to find ways to be more aggressive with our message. We are sending Kemal, by far our most obnoxious angel."

"You have obnoxious angels?" Abou asked incredulously.

"Well, it's that good angel/bad angel sort of thing. Kemal's really a rather decent chap, but terribly nasty-looking and rather abrasive when he wants to be. A Don Rickles sort of angel, if you know what I mean. Actually we have had only one really rotten angel and we sent him packing years ago, but you probably know about him."

"Thank you for trying to help, Cohen," Abou answered. "I appreciate your concern, but I don't need a paladin, whatever that is."

"Ah, I see," Cohen replied, stroking his chin. "You have the usual harebrained concept of guardian angels. A completely false idea, mind you. Well, false until this morning, when we sort of decided that there were some special people who we would look after a little better than others. Really a revolutionary idea."

"Whose idea was it?" Abou asked.

"Well, mine," Cohen admitted. "But everyone embraced it, and I was asked if I would like to be your special angel, and, of course, I said yes."

"For my lifetime?" Abou was quite confused.

Cohen nodded. "Yeah, you know, I'll kind of be available on an around-the-clock sort of way. Like AA. I'll be on call, day or night. In addition, we are going to appear, even when unbidden. That is totally new! Yousef is in with Sophia at this very moment, consoling her and offering advice. She needs solace and reinforcement, just as you do. You both have commitments!"

Abou sighed. "What commitments? My grandson is dead, and he may not have been my grandson anyway, although that really doesn't matter. My daughter, who may not be my real daughter, is utterly defeated. One of my best friends slept with my wife, as you once implied, and then he betrayed us to the Israelis, if Khaled is to be believed. I have asked my attorney to look into taking our family to America, but that doesn't seem very promising, and Sophia doesn't seem to care, anyway.

Cohen nodded. "I'll admit it's a little bleak, old buddy." Cohen considered what he was going to say next. "About this Salah business. I would give her the benefit of the doubt, if I were you, and does it really make any difference? You love Sophia, don't you?"

Abou nodded his head. "You know I do. It doesn't matter what her bloodline is; she is my daughter. And I would do anything I could to help her, but she is a woman of her time and place. She is afraid of new things, and she fears for her daughter's future, as do I."

"All true," Cohen agreed, "but what binds you to Helar? Couldn't you find some other place?"

"I would if I could," Abou agreed, grinding his teeth. "If it were only me, I would set out and tell everyone who would listen about the treachery that transpired here. In spite of Khaled's threat, I would tell Akbar's tale, so in death his life would have some meaning. It is not only the Israelis who are to blame, although they do seem to love retribution." He thought for a moment. "All good Arabs should know how evil some of our people are. Yes, that is what I would do. Travel about telling little Akbar's story!"

"Then why not do it?" Cohen asked. "I think it's an absolutely fab idea. You could lay the whole matter out, and perhaps you could even convince some people to change. It's dangerous, of course, but look what Gandhi did for India. You might become a hero. Just remember to call on me and my colleagues for consultations whenever you feel you need us."

The fire inside Abou quickly subsided. "But there is Sophia. I can't leave without her, nor force her to go with me, and, as you say, it could be very dangerous for both her and the baby. Khaled will kill us all; he said so. And where would we go? Who would take me seriously in America? They aren't really interested. They just want the shooting and rock throwing to stop. Perhaps we could settle in Cairo for a time, explain about Akbar's murder there." His indecision was evident.

"Then try something else, Abou," Cohen snapped. "Take hold of yourself! Sophia only needs encouragement. You must talk to her. She may even wish to help in your crusade."

"Crusade?"

Cohen raised his hand defensively. "Perhaps not the best choice of words, but you know what I mean."

Abou studied Cohen for a moment or two, trying to decide. "Why are you doing all of this for me?"

Cohen replied, "Abou, I have told you you are unique. You love almost unconditionally, you are nonviolent, you abjure primitive emotions such as revenge, and as far as we can determine, you hate nobody, yet you and your family have been ravaged by these primal forces. You are what we are looking for in humans, and we intend to cherish people like you."

"You make me sound like a project."

"Exactly! You and people like you have become our projects. We will nurture you, guide you, and try to protect you as much as possible." The angel paused for a long moment and then added, "What we have decided to do is continue this experiment that you and I started. Every one of us will select a candidate who is similar to you, and each of these individuals will be given a full, coherent view of human development in a new ten-week course we are developing at this very moment. Something like what I attempted with you, but better organized, not so haphazard. We will give a certificate at the end of the program and urge the participants to go out and spread the word carefully. Within a year we hope there will be millions who understand where they are in their development and eschew violence and other distasteful human traits."

In spite of himself, Abou found himself listening. "Millions, you say. People who will be sympathetic to what I've said?"

"Well, we can't be assured of that exactly," Cohen cautioned, "but we do believe that when people with mature sensibilities hear how they got where they are, they will act in a more reasonable fashion. At least that is our hope."

"But you're not sure," Abou replied.

"Hey, with humans, who knows anything, but this is what we decided we should do," the angel replied. "At the same time, we feel you, Abou, as our first student, should try to spread the word very carefully to help others. As we work behind the scenes, you will meet more and more like-minded people. This is our plan. What do you think?"

Abou considered this. "It is far too dangerous for Sophia and the baby."

"Nonsense!" Cohen replied. "Put your stereotypes aside. She's tough. Act, man! You'll have allies very soon. Our program is starting tonight. In just ten days we will have our first graduating class."

"But Sophia . . . ?" Abou objected.

"Yousef is talking to her at this very minute," Cohen replied. "She will soon see how desperate her situation is. For the child's sake, she must do something."

"Yousef? My angel?" Abou was stunned.

Cohen's face fell like a slow-moving avalanche. He turned away.

"Oh, Cohen, I didn't mean . . . ," Abou began and then added, "I meant my original angel. You are my angel now. You are my friend."

Cohen peeked at him out of the corner of his eye. He wasn't exactly crying, but his distress was obvious. "Friend? You think of me truly as a friend?"

"Of course I do," Abou assured him. "Hasn't that become obvious? Do you think I could have gotten through the last two weeks without you?"

Cohen turned and pinched the bridge of his nose. "I need to compose myself. Angels never make friends."

Cohen finally turned back to Abou. "You must follow Sophia's lead. A solution must come from her. But if you could encourage her, well, that would really be something. Telling the world about this rapacity, this stupidity, this cupidity you two have witnessed and suffered from. Wonderful! It could be a turning point in human behavior, you know."

"I think I understand," Abou agreed, but Cohen was gone.

ABOU AWOKE WITH A START. His heart was pounding with excitement. He arose, oddly refreshed, and made his way into the kitchen, where he washed out the four teacups.

Sophia came from the bedroom, Leila on her hip, her hair loose about her face. The rest had done her worlds of good, Abou thought. Her face was relaxed, her skin aglow, and the lifelessness in her eyes was replaced with light. She placed the baby in the small sling by the door.

"I had an extraordinary dream, Papa," she said, her face showing deep concentration. "I do not want to forget a moment of it. A man came to me. He sat in the far corner where I couldn't see him too well, but I offered him tea and cookies, and I remember he seemed to enjoy them immensely."

"That goes without saying," Abou replied, glancing at the empty platter.

"Oh, no, that was in my dream," she replied, looked at the platter, and then asked, "Did I forget to bake more? Were they all eaten last night?"

"It was a terrible day. You must have forgotten them."

"Yes," she agreed. "Yes, that must have been what happened." She drew in her breath and continued. "In any case, this dream was very helpful to me. I suppose we really sort out our problems in our dreams, don't we?"

"I think so," Abou replied. "What did you decide?"

"Well, this strange man pointed out how impossible my position is in the village. I am a divorced woman with a female child. He said I must take responsibility for myself and my baby, and he is right. I can't depend upon Helar for help, and I cannot depend on you, or the generosity of the mosque, if I become indigent." She hesitated for a moment, and then added, "There are three things we decided I must do."

257

Abou sat at the table, delighted by this newborn determination.

"With such continual violence in the Strip, I should have taken Akbar and the baby from Helar long ago. He was such a dear boy and his father was only corrupting him with his complaints about unfair treatment, imagined slights by his customers, and the Israelis, who he somehow blamed for all his other woes. I was weak, but I am not going to be weak anymore. Nothing is going to happen to Leila."

"Three things," Abou reminded her.

"Ah, yes," she continued. There was fire in her eyes. "I must leave this village, I must find work, and I must learn a skill—foreign languages—certainly English and perhaps French. Oh, and I must learn to operate a personal computer. This is a great asset, the strange man said, for anyone looking for work."

"And where will you go?" Abou asked.

"Well, that is something I will have to think about. I want Leila to be educated, and of course I want a place where there is work for women. The strange man suggested Jakarta."

"Indonesia!" Abou exploded, suddenly panicked.

"Well, he admitted there is some trouble there right now, but that the attitude toward women is quite progressive and there is work to be had. Of course, the expense of getting there must be considered. He also said that Turkey is a possibility, as well as Egypt."

Somewhat calmed, Abou forced a smile. "Am I to be left behind to spend my remaining days encountering Yasser every time I go to the market?"

"But you have your friends," Sophia replied. She was making them tea without asking whether he wanted any. He hoped she wouldn't think of the honey bread and go looking for it. Cohen's sweet tooth was becoming a problem.

"Ah, yes, but Absollah is very busy with his bank, as is Ammon, who is involved in other matters," Abou replied. "And I would miss you and Leila terribly."

Sophia put the pot to steep and turned to look at her father. "I did not think you would ever call her by name."

"She is my granddaughter," he replied with dignity.

"Females are so unimportant in our world."

"She is a beautiful baby," he said lamely.

"And you would miss us?" Sophia asked. Standing by the stove in the sunlight, her hand on her hip, she examined her father critically.

"And you are willing to uproot yourself?" She hesitated and then added, "At your age?"

"I would be more than happy to uproot myself to be with you and Leila," he replied.

"I do not wish to be a burden any longer," Sophia replied.

Abou shrugged. "Sophia, you are not a burden! You will have your own money from this house, and you will find work wherever we go."

"I just don't want to be dependent, and I don't want to use you for my selfish purposes. There is nothing I can do to repay you for your help."

"Oh, yes there is," he corrected her. "You could teach me how to make those wonderful sesame cookies. I have developed a nighttime craving for them which is difficult to explain."

"You wish to learn to bake? That's women's work."

"I have read that the world is filled with males who cook, and in Europe and America men cook all the time. If you are to become so independent, it seems to me I have to learn some new ways, too. Making those cookies is just a small step, but it is something."

"New ways? You sound braver than I feel. Secretly I am very frightened of what I am proposing, while you, on the other hand, sound like you almost look forward to the adventure."

"Yes, it is very exciting!" Abou exclaimed, and then slowly added, "I would like us to visit Mecca first, and Cairo, of course, and perhaps Damascus. And certainly I would like you and Leila to see Istanbul. It is a modern city where there is work for women."

"Mecca! How I would love to go on a pilgrimage." She actually clapped her hands, and then impishly she asked, "Are you sure you wouldn't consider Jakarta?"

"How about America?" he asked with a slight smile.

"If these other places don't work out, who knows?"

"Exactly how I feel about Jakarta," Abou replied.

"How would you occupy yourself when I am working?" she asked tentatively.

He grinned at her. "I suspect I will be baking a great deal and I want very much to talk to people."

"Talk? About what?"

"About Akbar and how his life was sacrificed simply for revenge. I would be very careful selecting people to talk to, but I would tell how both political and religious factions conspire endlessly and cause needless pain and death. I will tell about emotion over reason, which spirals out of control with Jews killing Arabs and Arabs killing Jews. Even more importantly, people must understand that unrestrained violence could easily end all human life, that it must stop now before we all destroy each other."

Sophia looked at her father thoughtfully. "You would speak of Akbar's death?"

"Yes, the senselessness of it."

She was quiet. "That is a beautiful thought, that my son, and the others, could become the motivation for peace. I could help."

Abou took his daughter's hand. "We must be careful, Daughter, but I think, as time goes on, we will find more and more people responsive to our message, and each person we talk to will remember Akbar and Hamid. We will see to that."

She was excited and the baby, who had been snoozing in the sun, awoke and began to make impatient sounds. "Oh, would you hold her?" Abou accepted Leila on his lap, regarding her fondly. She, in turn, examined him critically, as if not sure he could meet her needs.

"Our life from now on will be dangerous," Sophia continued, pulling a pot from the cupboard.

"It will be," Abou admitted. "I intend to be cautious. I have learned there are a great many unreasonable people in the world, but there are many reasonable ones, also. Akbar's memory will inspire us."

Sophia crossed the room and kissed her father on the forehead, something she seldom did. "Would you like to make cookies now, Papa?"

He smiled at her fondly. "Yes, I would. Lots of them. I will always think of Akbar when I eat these cookies. He enjoyed them so." As does Cohen, he thought to himself.

"That's true, Papa," she replied, removing the jar of sesame seed from the shelf. She looked directly at her father's stomach. "But I'm beginning to suspect that Akbar had an elderly helper who consumed much more than he did."

Abou flushed. Much to his surprise, he was sure he heard Cohen chuckle in the distance.